THE BODY

IN THE

BOUDOIR

FAITH FAIRCHILD MYSTERIES BY KATHERINE HALL PAGE

THE BODY
IN THE
BOUDOIR

A FAITH FAIRCHILD MYSTERY

KATHERINE
HALL PAGE

wm

WILLIAM MORROW
An Imprint of HarperCollins*Publishers*

THE BODY IN THE BOUDOIR. Copyright © 2012 by Katherine Hall Page. All rights reserved. Printed in the United States of America. No part of this book may be used or reproduced in any manner whatsoever without written permission except in the case of brief quotations embodied in critical articles and reviews. For information address HarperCollins Publishers, 10 East 53rd Street, New York, NY 10022.

HarperCollins books may be purchased for educational, business, or sales promotional use. For information please write: Special Markets Department, HarperCollins Publishers, 10 East 53rd Street, New York, NY 10022.

FIRST EDITION

Designed by Diahann Sturge

Library of Congress Cataloging-in-Publication Data

Page, Katherine Hall.
  The body in the boudoir : a Faith Fairchild mystery / by Katherine Hall
  Page.—1st ed.
    p.   cm.
  ISBN 978-0-06-206548-3
  1. Fairchild, Faith Sibley (Fictitious character)—Fiction.   2. Women
  in the food industry—Fiction.   3.   Caterers and catering—Fiction.
  4. Massachusetts—Fiction.   5. Marriage—Fiction.   I. Title.
PS3566.A334B6475 2012
813'.54—dc22   2011025712

12 13 14 15 16   OV/RRD   10 9 8 7 6 5 4 3 2 1

To Roger Lathbury
Orchises Press
Dear Friend and Publisher Nonpareil

And when two lovers woo

They still say, I love you

—Herman Hupfeld, "As Time Goes By,"
from the show *Everybody's Welcome*

ACKNOWLEDGMENTS

Many thanks to my HarperCollins publicist, Danielle Bartlett; Dr. Robert DeMartino for medical expertise; car-savvy Michael Epstein and Scott Schwimer; photographer Jean Fogelberg; my agent, Faith Hamlin; my editor, Wendy Lee; and HarperCollins director of library marketing, Virginia Stanley. And thank you dear Helen Scovel Grey, Faith Greeley Scovel, and Rebecca Scovel Harris for sharing your family wedding memories and cake recipes.

THE BODY
IN THE
BOUDOIR

PROLOGUE

The airplane cabin was almost completely dark, with an occasional pinpoint of light indicating a reader. It was blessedly quiet, too. All she could hear was the steady hum of the engines, reassuring and slightly soporific. No wailing infants, not even the usual hacking coughs that punctuated a long flight. Faith Sibley Fairchild pulled the thin airline blanket up to her chin and considered putting on the sleep mask thoughtfully provided as well. She looked at her husband, Tom, who had been deep in the arms of Morpheus the moment the lights dimmed after consuming dinner—steak tips with "seasonal" vegetables—with relish. He'd consumed her portion, too. She'd opted for the sandwich she'd tucked in her carry-on bag—a ciabatta roll with a light film of olive oil, fresh mozzarella, prosciutto, basil, and tomato—washed down with the not bad little bottle of Chianti the steward offered. After all, they were on their way to Italy. Faith had offered to pack food for Tom as well, but he'd insisted that he wanted "the full flight experience" and liked eating from "those little trays." She sighed. Even after all these years with a wife for whom food was not simply a passion but a business, he still opted for Campbell's cream of mushroom soup over hers and Ritz crackers with peanut butter in times of stress.

He wasn't stressed now and she smiled as she moved closer to him. The earlier dubious food smells were gone, leaving one that she could identify as belonging to him and no one else in the world: a combination of Ivory soap, the slight citrus of his aftershave, and something ineffably Tom Fairchild. She kissed his cheek—nothing short of a sonic boom would wake him—and settled back against her seat. In the dark she could imagine that the two of them were alone. Alone enclosed in this silver cylinder speeding in an arc through the air, the ocean far below. He'd been the one to come up with the idea of a trip, a trip sans kids. A significant anniversary needed a significant marking, he'd said, and somehow it had all happened.

They'd been married in the first year of the last decade of the twentieth century. And now they were past the first decade of the twenty-first. Someone had once told her that as you got older time went faster and Faith did feel she had been propelled from one era—landline phones, snail mail, Cabbage Patch dolls—into the current one where kids had virtual toys and all ages communicated on Facebook "walls." Yet, mostly, she didn't feel any older herself. But she was—and so was her beloved. A few streaks had turned his reddish-brown hair to cinnamon toast. Without these visible markings on the people around her—their parents, their two children, friends—Faith could almost sense that time stood still. That she would wake up back in the New York apartment she'd lived in before she was married, making a mad dash to get to work, while wondering when, and if, her prince would come.

When he showed up, he was not what she had envisioned, but in the end it hadn't mattered. Not at all.

Getting there had been a journey—she realized she was thinking in travel metaphors, must be the altitude. From their whirlwind courtship to the wedding ceremony a few months later under a clear blue sky, facing Long Island Sound, the ride had often been a turbulent one and there were times when she had longed for a route map.

To start, there had been the geographical differences between the two of them. Growing up in a small town on Boston's South Shore, where not only did everybody know your name but you were related to a sizable number as well, was as foreign to Faith's own upbringing on Manhattan's Upper East Side as if an ocean, not a state or two, separated the couple. Then there was Tom's job. She could move, he couldn't, so she'd left the Big Apple for the bucolic orchards of Aleford, Massachusetts. The geographical, and the other differences—he loved board games, she didn't; L.L.Bean met all his sartorial needs, Barney's hers—were smoothed out by time, and love.

No, the updrafts and downdrafts in the path from her engagement to wedding weren't caused by Tom, or Faith herself, but others—some with intention, some by chance. She thought of Francesca—they'd be seeing her soon in Tuscany—and the turmoil the then young girl had involved Faith in all those years ago. Beautiful, and Faith knew from a recent photo that Francesca was, if anything, more beautiful now, but the secret she had harbored was not. Faith felt her eyes start to close and a host of people, people she hadn't thought about in a long while, began to flicker through her thoughts. Great-aunt Tammy—larger than life—and her husband, Faith's great-uncle Sky, always so well turned out—and tuned out? Mrs. Danforth, so loyal, but not to Faith. Her nana, clinging to the proprieties of yesteryear despite what might be crashing down around her.

Then there was Faith's sister, Hope, happy now, but so very troubled then.

And herself. Different hair. Definitely different clothes. And, she thought with a shudder, totally oblivious of the deadly threat that had been so close at hand. She wasn't a runaway bride, but almost a run-over one . . .

When she traveled by air, Faith always opted for a window seat, and she'd left the shade next to her open a crack, peering out into the darkness every once in a while. Now a faint light was beginning to appear at the horizon and she closed the shade. They wouldn't be landing for another two and a half hours; she could try to sleep until the flight attendants came by with cardboard Danish and something that looked like coffee. Despite what would be a strong need for caffeine, she'd wait for Italian coffee—espresso, cappuccino, caffe latte, *marocchino*. Italian food names sounded musical, operatic even. *Pomodoro,* porcini, osso buco, tortellini, *marmellata*—she was making herself hungry.

They were seated just behind a wing and the jet engines looked like small rockets, flashes of flame against the darkness. Flying wasn't as much fun as it used to be, what with removing shoes and the rest, but Faith still got a thrill at takeoff watching the world instantly miniaturize and then disappear altogether, hidden beneath that other world above the clouds. But she didn't want to venture higher—into outer space—although she would like to see the earth from there, the spectacular blue orb that we continued to threaten in so many ways. No, she wasn't about to suit up and head for the moon. She'd be afraid she might not be able to get back. Back to everyone and everything she treasured so intensely. Back to what had started with that wedding all those years ago. Their wedding.

It had been murder.

CHAPTER 1

"I lost a client!"

Faith Sibley stopped filling a container with trays of bite-size crab cakes and moved the phone from the crook of her neck to her hand, slightly alarmed by her younger sister's uncharacteristic lugubrious tone. This was "lost" as in gone forever, not "lost" as in a momentarily misplaced toddler in Bloomingdale's or a houseguest boarding the wrong subway train.

"I'm so sorry, Hope. Were you close?"

"I thought so, but then you never know, do you? Not until it's too late to do anything about it."

Noting that the tenor of the conversation had changed from emotional to philosophical, Faith replied in kind.

"That's so true—and sadly a reminder that we need to be more aware of other people's needs."

"I thought I was! But it wasn't enough."

Faith hadn't heard her sister express this much remorse since missing Apple's IPO at age eleven.

"When is the funeral?"

"Funeral?"

"Or are they having a memorial service?"

"Fay"—her sister had started using the nickname when they were in their teens and Faith had never found a nice way to tell her to stop. An attempt to call Hope "Hopey" only made it past her lips once before both of them were convulsed with laughter. "Fay, what are you talking about?"

"Your client's death. Again, I'm so sorry. How old was he, or she?"

"It was a he. He's forty-two, and although I'd like to kill him, he's very much alive. Alive and well with someone else, trailing his fat little account behind him."

Faith stuck the phone back under her neck and started transferring trays of phyllo cups filled with a wild mushroom mixture into the container. Her catering business, Have Faith, had a big wedding reception uptown—she looked at her watch—much too soon.

"Sweetie, I'm still sorry. Very sorry. But I have to go. We have a wedding at Riverside Church."

One of Hope's less endearing qualities was her single-mindedness. It was a quality that kept her successfully focused on climbing the rungs above her, but also meant that she often paid absolutely no attention to what her sister said.

"I called Phelps right away and he's as puzzled as I am."

Phelps Grant was her sister's current beau, and as far as Faith was concerned the jury was still out, but without ever stating the policy, the two sisters, a year apart, had made a practice of never interfering in each other's love life.

"What more could I have done? Besides making money for him in this disastrous economy, I got orchestra seats for *Phantom of the Opera* during the holidays for his family—roughly half the population of someplace like Pittsburgh—which cost me a pretty penny, plus when I took him to lunch, it always had to be Windows on the World. Anyway, he called just last week to thank me for the tickets and said he was looking forward to a long and happy relationship together. 'Long and happy relationship'—his exact words. And then today, a knife in the back!"

"I really have to—"

Hope had paused a nanosecond for breath but kept going.

"He, or rather his secretary, sent me a scarf from Hermès at Christmas, which I can't take back because I've already worn it twice. It's one I don't have, Flacons, you know, the dark background with the tiny perfume bottles, whimsical."

"Hope! I do know and I'm very happy you got something out of it and we'll talk about your loss later. I have to go. Call me at home. I'm planning to sleep until Monday, when we have an MLK Day breakfast to do, no jobs tomorrow."

"Another odd thing. He sent flowers, through the secretary again—and okay, no mums or maidenhair fern, such an odd name—with the kiss-off note and at the end of it said he hoped I would feel better soon. As if I'd been sick. I was sick when I read it, but not before, so what could—"

"Hanging up now. Toodles."

She could hear her sister sigh. Hope didn't like not knowing. She wasn't a control freak. She just liked, well, being in control.

"Bye, Fay. Have fun at your thing."

Faith had been able to benefit from the late 1980s "Money's No Object" when she started the business and although there had been an Icarus-like plunge in the economy during this second year, she had been doing well enough to move Have Faith to larger quarters despite the recession. Yet Faith's sister still regarded her big sis's livelihood as something between a quirk and a hobby. Not a real job. For a real job you wore a suit and carried a Bottega Veneta "When Your Own Initials Are Enough" briefcase.

During the holidays, Faith had catered a number of events where her sister had been a guest. Manhattan was like a small village in many respects, especially the circles in which the Sibley girls traveled. Hope had registered surprise each time at Faith's checked chef pants, admittedly altered to a nice fit, and crisp white jacket.

Faith closed the container and observed the swirl of activity around her. It had been a hectic couple of weeks combining the move with a busy holiday season. There had also been some personal turmoil that she firmly pushed to the back of her mind.

"Okay, guys, about ready?"

Howard, her bartender, gave her a thumbs-up. He was not an aspiring actor, poet, or anything other than a bartender, he'd told her during his interview. He liked the flexible hours and the changes of scene. An office job or anything else repetitive was not for him. More to the point, he enjoyed creating new concoctions. She'd hired him on the spot, as she had her assistant, Josie Wells. Josie came from Virginia and had brought with her her grandmother's recipes for cornbread, hoppin' John, red velvet cake, and the best fried chicken in the world (a vinegar/water soak and evaporated milk in the batter before a vigorous shake in seasoned flour). She'd also brought a wicked sense of humor and down-to-earth practicality. Her goal was to open her own restaurant, Josie's, someday, which she'd made clear at the start, and she was taking courses at the New School in everything from Opening Your Own Small Business to Culinary History.

It didn't take long to get to the church, and soon her staff had unloaded the van. Everything was running smoothly—and on time.

Standing not quite at attention along the back wall, Have Faith's waitstaff was all set, black pants, fitted white shirts, and thin black ties. The exception was Faith's newest hire, Francesca Rossi, a young Italian woman from Tuscany who worked at Josie's health club and had recently taken the place of one of Josie's ever-changing roommate population. When Josie reported that Francesca possessed an uncanny ability to create terrific meals from a seemingly empty fridge and olive oil, Faith was definitely intrigued, and Francesca was now juggling two jobs ably. She would be at the buffet serving and had asked to replace the generic black jacket with a velvet one that sported discreet white satin lapels. Her dark hair was pulled sleekly back in a low ponytail. Her oval face and pale skin were more Modigliani than Titian, but Francesca was definitely in a class with all their models.

Everything except the food had been set up earlier in the church's Ninth Floor Lounge—the name belying the space, which was Gothic, not cocktail. Faith loved the Riverside Church, the 1930 Chartres replica that John D. Rockefeller had built overlooking the Hudson. Over the summer, she'd catered two weddings in the large South Hall, but the Lounge's smaller space was prettier, she thought, even without the spectacular views through the stone arches of the river on one side and the city on the other. The late-afternoon ceremony in the church's Christ Chapel would be followed by drinks and passed hors d'oeuvres in the Lounge before dinner.

She was picturing the jeweled carpet of lights the guests would see during the evening as she looked down through the windows at the deepening shadows in the streets. Turning back around, she let her eyes feast on the room in front of her—a warm glow in contrast to the view even without a fire in the baronial fireplace carved into one wall.

When Faith had checked the space earlier to make sure that everything was in place, she had been stunned. The bride had opted for a party planner her mother, a well-known Manhattan hostess, used instead of the caterer's contacts. The Lounge's architectural details had been transformed with yards of pleated white tulle and masses of roses, and hydrangea with a faint celadon cast to it. The roses ranged from iceberg white to warm pink, with a few nodding toward apricot to warm up the pale stone pillars. They'd lucked out with the weather, warm for January and no snow. January was an iffy month for a wedding, but the couple had wanted to take advantage of the three-day weekend. She was a native New York, but he was from Massachusetts, which meant out-of-town guests. From what Faith had gathered, the groom's first introduction to his future in-laws was also one of his first trips to the Big Apple. It had been hard not to show her surprise.

New York City was not simply the city of her birth but the city she adored. She'd been to Paris, London, Madrid, Rome, even Boston—surely the groom had been to that city, and how could he possibly prefer paltry Boston Common to Central Park's acres? Yes, she'd enjoyed exploring all those other cities—she'd done Boston in a day—but whenever she'd stepped off the plane, or train, back home, she felt not a sense of relief but a sense of excitement. She could never live anywhere else.

Granted, her upbringing hadn't been that of a typical New Yorker, if such an animal existed. Her father was a man of the cloth, with a large congregation in a church that was also, like Riverside, a landmark, but on the east side of Manhattan. Jane Sibley, née Lennox, was descended from those canny Dutch who'd made real estate history with a few baubles and beads. The family had remained rooted in Manhattan ever since. Quickly deciding that the impoverished divinity school student she'd met through his sister, a fellow classmate at Barnard, was a similar once-in-a-lifetime chance, Jane had said yes, but . . . The "but" was the stipulation that he find a parish in the city—she didn't care where so long as she recognized the zip code—and they invest as soon as possible in their own place. Jane didn't know what sort of parsonage the future might hold, but she knew she wanted to be able to move the furniture around when she wished and paint the walls purple should the spirit move her.

By the time Faith was born, her mother was making a quiet name for herself as a real estate lawyer—"quiet" since the Lennoxes, especially Jane's mother, belonged to the school that believed mention in the press should be restricted to marriage and death. The Upper East Side bargain duplex Jane had pounced on as soon as Lawrence accepted the call to his current pulpit was as far from Mosses from an Old Manse as one could get while still sporting a turned-around collar.

Hope had followed almost a year to the day after Faith, and there the Sibleys stopped. Accommodating in all respects to the wife his secular side unabashedly worshipped, the Reverend Lawrence Sibley would not budge on the family tradition, established not long after Noah stepped on dry land, that called for Sibley girls to be named Faith, Hope, and Charity, in that order, subsequent female issues' names unspecified. The oldest male in each generation was Lawrence, followed by Hosea and Luke. Faith had questioned her father and various other Sibleys as to the origin of the male naming tradition. "Lawrence"? The other two, overtly biblical—yes—but where did her father's name, and all the Lawrences preceding him, come from? No one had ever provided a satisfactory answer. The conundrum was an indicator of the insatiably curious little girl she'd been—and still was. It was the type of question she used to mull over first in Sunday school and then in church to entertain herself during the boring parts.

Despite the spacious apartment—each girl had a room of her own—and location—steps away from the park, also Park and Madison—growing up as a preacher's kid, a PK, resembled growing up in a fishbowl, no matter how holy the water or attractive the tiny decorative castle. "Is she old enough for makeup?" "Do you think it's wise to let two young college girls go to Europe on their own?" Quite polite people who would never ordinarily make comments about others in public felt entitled by membership in the congregation not only to comment but also advise. "Faith, you seem to be having trouble finding your path, not like Hope. Did I hear she just got another promotion? How about teaching? You'd be so good with small children." Or worse, "My adorable nephew is in town. The one who just finished Harvard Law. I know you two would hit it off."

Smile, just smile. Think about converting to Buddhism and definitely repress the impulse to hit the speaker.

It was true that Faith took longer to "find her path" than Hope, but Hope had been reading the *Wall Street Journal* all her life, moving rapidly from *Pat the Bunny* to *The Little Engine That Could* and from there to the Dow Jones. After college, Faith had returned to the nest, where she had in fact spent most weekends, and embarked on several months of serious socializing, becoming a regular on the Hampton Jitney. By the end of August, her mother's unsubtle hints left on Faith's pillow—jobs circled in the newspaper, a copy of *What Color Is Your Parachute?*—were having the opposite effect intended. Faith felt even more lethargic and depressed about her future. She had no idea what she should do. There was no clear path that she could see. The last straw was when her dear father left a copy of Robert Frost's poems open to "The Road Not Taken" next to her place at dinner—she was eating at home for the first time in a week and they were having the usual, a variant of a nice piece of fish or a nice piece of chicken and a little salad. Jane Sibley still fit into her wedding dress and the one she'd worn when she came out.

Faith had been annoyed and embarrassed. "Two roads." Great. Yet, as the meal progressed and she listened to her mother talking about the real estate boom and Hope talking about the stock market boom and her father not talking much, but presumably thinking about some sort of celestial boom, she made a decision. She would take the road "less traveled by," and she wouldn't talk about it. Not yet.

The next day she enrolled in Peter Krump's New York Cooking School and talked her way into an unpaid apprenticeship at one of the city's top catering firms. Whether they were swayed by her interest or the fact that they thought she could use her influence to get them jobs didn't matter. She was in.

When she mentioned vaguely to her family that she was taking some career courses, they didn't seem to notice that she was coming home dead tired and with the occasional smudge of flour on her face. It was enough that their darling daughter was doing something.

Jane Sibley had always had a housekeeper who dropped off the evening meal or stayed to cook it. And Faith had always enjoyed being in the kitchen with these women, some happier to have her underfoot than others. Over the summer, and even more during the fall, Faith had realized that the one thing she liked to do—that could translate into a respectable career, that is—was cook. The brownie recipe with dried cherries she'd invented when she was thirteen had given way to other desserts and then meals, although her mother warned her not to get in the latest hire's way: "Good help is hard to find these days."

So Faith had decided to be the help, and after she finished her studies, went to her parents with her business plan, informing them that she was using some money her grandparents had set up for their granddaughters in a trust as capital. They were taken aback at first, advising that she work for another firm to start, but Faith had quickly realized that the jobs she'd been getting for the company where she apprenticed could just as easily be hers. And she was right. Have Faith became a success in a New York minute, people she knew—and didn't know—recognizing the cachet in having Faith Sibley not solely as a gorgeous guest but preparing gorgeous food. And here she was at Riverside, the caterer, about to serve two newlyweds their first married meal, which she hoped would launch them into a life of connubial and culinary bliss ever after.

She glanced around the Ninth Floor Lounge (surely they could have come up with a more inspired name?) once more, her eyes searching for missing place settings, an unfolded napkin. Across the river, New Jersey was disappearing into the dusk, and many floors below, the couple, according to her schedule, should be saying their I dos.

Faith had met someone in December and for a few moments, maybe for more than a few, had entertained the idea of plighting her troth forever and ever before he'd casually mentioned he would be out of town for the next year or so working on a book. She still wasn't sure whether she'd been dumped, and if she had it would have been a first as the dumpee. Not pleasant. She'd resolved never to get in that position again. Now, less than a month later, she'd realized much of her infatuation had been with his career as a journalist and the desire to have someone during the holidays, a time when it was always hard not to be a twosome, especially in New York, where romance was in the air, from the couples waltzing on the ice below Rockefeller Center's tree to the ones gazing in Cartier's sparkling windows. Richard had been Mr. Right in so many respects—smart, funny, good-looking, and above all, not now or ever a member of the clergy. Hope and Faith had made a pact to avoid that particular cut of fabric, not a difficult promise for a PK to make.

The elevator doors opened and the first guests stepped into the room, immediately heading for the views. Faith knew the bar would be next and nodded to Howard, who gave her a big smile. She went into the adjoining kitchen and sent out the first of the hors d'oeuvres as well as several trays of drinks: champagne-filled flutes, ice water with and without lemon or lime, white wine. The DJ started playing *Lohengrin* and the newlyweds stepped into the room amid great applause. Both were tall and seemed like people who would be spending their honeymoon on the ski slopes or somewhere else outdoorsy. The bride wore a pleated silk Mary McFadden gown that made her look classically elegant, an updated version of a Grecian caryatid. The couple paused, smiling somewhat shyly at being the center of so much attention, and then the groom swept his wife into his arms for the first dance. The party had begun.

An hour later Faith sent out the last tray of oysters. She'd prepared them raw, with a choice of mignonette sauce—that simple combination of wine vinegar, shallots, and freshly ground pepper with a bit of champagne added at the last minute—cocktail sauce, or au naturel, serving them in the bowl of a Chinese soup spoon rather than the shell. Neater and much easier to handle. The bride and groom didn't need an aphrodisiac—the adoring looks they were sending each other was evidence—but Faith liked to serve oysters at weddings for their symbolism and above all for their flavor. Besides, like caviar—which she'd offered with thin, crepe-like blinis or toasted brioche triangles—oysters marked an event as special.

"Has Francesca started serving?" she asked Josie as she came back into the small kitchen after circling the room pouring refills of champagne.

"Yes, and from the look of it, we'd better get ready to replenish the beef fast."

The groom had not been able to come to the city for the tasting, but the bride and her mother had selected a menu with him in mind. "He likes meat," his fiancée had said, so meat it was: roast pork loin stuffed with winter fruits, prime rib with a choice of horseradish sauce or au jus, and pecan-encrusted boneless chicken fillets. Faith had added *saucisson en brioche,* substituting a mild sausage for the traditional garlic one and offering several flavored mustards. It was such a nice presentation—the rich, buttery bread surrounding the rosy circle of meat. Despite its fins, they'd done a fish-shaped mold of salmon mousse with green mayonnaise, the color provided by dill, parsley, and chives pureed with the sauce. The bride thought they could sneak in one seafood dish. Roasted root vegetables, Josie's heavy-on-the-cream mashed potatoes, an assortment of breads and rolls, plus a salad with hearts of palm and grape tomatoes, rounded out the offerings.

Amanda, one of Faith's part-timers, came through the door.

"We need more potatoes and another brioche."

"You grab the potatoes and I'll bring the brioche. I want to cut a few slices here first," Faith said and did so quickly.

As she walked toward the buffet, set up in front of some of the Hudson River–side windows, the mother of the bride stopped her.

"Everything is delicious. Just perfect. Thank you so much— and although I won't be doing another wedding, I will be in touch for a luncheon I'm giving at my apartment here next month."

This was terrific news and Faith hoped it might mean a steady client—perhaps, in her dreams, a gig at one of their other homes someday! She'd heard the bride's family had apartments in Palm Beach and Paris as well as a house in the Hamptons.

"I'd be happy to—and I'm so glad you're pleased. Your daughter looks absolutely beautiful, radiant, everything a bride should be. And the groom, too."

Faith stopped herself from babbling on.

"I'll just take these to the buffet."

Crossing the room, she switched her thoughts from the celebratory scene in front of her to her earlier conversation with Hope. Her sister never discussed work with Faith. Granted, Phelps had been the first one she'd called about the account loss, which made sense—he was downtown on Wall Street in some line of work that mirrored Hope's—but she had then called Faith and her deep distress was evident. It must have been a major client. Faith might not know much about the intricacies of what Hope did high in her Citicorp office, but she did know that in her sister's chosen field, the wolves were always at the door and any weakness shown would be fully exploited. The reference to feeling better in the man's note accompanying the flowers was odd, but could simply mean he knew how much his account had meant.

"Sorry, here let me help you with that."

Preoccupied as she was, Faith had walked into the path of a buffet-bound guest. He took the tray from her. She took it back.

Smiling, she said, "I don't think you're on the payroll and I walked into you."

"Must be my lucky day."

As lines went, it lacked originality, but the slightly chagrined expression on his face indicated he knew that.

"Well, I have to put this out." Faith moved quickly toward the table.

"Funny. I was just coming for more." He followed her, and when she'd handed the brioche to Francesca, he didn't pick up a plate for a piece, but continued the conversation.

"I'm Tom, by the way," he said, putting out his hand.

"I'm Faith," she said, taking it. Warm, but not too warm. A strong grip, but not too strong. He held her hand only a few seconds too long.

"Faith as in Have Faith, the outfit that has provided me with the best meal I've ever had?"

He must be one of the New Englanders, Faith thought, disappointed that this handsome—tall, rusty-brown hair, deep brown eyes, yes, with those little flecks of gold—stranger wasn't local. Of course he could also have been on some weird diet or from out of the country, say London, subsisting on boiled veg and tough mutton.

"Yes, it's my company."

"Great name."

"We still get the occasional call from individuals looking for a different kind of provisioner—they think it's an escort service—but I wanted something that would let people know we were serious about food, but not too serious about life."

"Not at all?"

The conversation was beginning to resemble one of those

down-the-rabbit-hole ones, and Faith had a job to do, but it was hard to pull away.

"Of course serious about some things, just not in general. Oh dear, this isn't coming out right. Listen, lovely meeting you, but I have to get back to the kitchen and start putting out the desserts."

"My favorite course. Wedding cake, I assume. Anything chocolate?"

This guy's heart was definitely in the right place.

"I'll surprise you," she said, heading toward the kitchen.

"I certainly hope so."

Again, not the most original, but that smile and, yes, those eyes . . . Faith turned her steps firmly in the opposite direction.

The next time she left the kitchen, the party was winding down and the room had thinned out. Faith had sent some of her crew back with a load and the rest were clearing the dessert dishes now.

Faith was filling the platter of candied fruits and bite-size cookies on the buffet with more of the heart-shaped shortbread she'd made when she felt a tap on her shoulder.

"Would you like to dance? Somehow I have the feeling you're good at it."

Faith was a good dancer thanks to the white-gloved Knickerbocker Cotillion during childhood and less staid forays throughout her teens. The DJ had been playing oldies for some time now. Extremely old oldies. Cole Porter, and wait a minute, was it "Easy to Love"? It was. She hesitated.

"Come on. We'll dance over here by the window. No one will notice."

It was the Ella Fitzgerald version, Faith's favorite, and without consciously deciding, she found herself in the stranger's arms, their steps matching perfectly and not minding when he began singing along softly, " 'So easy to idolize all others above.' " Not minding at all.

She closed her eyes.

Another tap on her shoulder. Someone cutting in? For a moment she forgot where she was, and she didn't want any interference, not now. She was humming along with Ella—and Tom, nice Tom.

"Boss, I'm clearing the coffee. Howard's closing the bar, and the bride went to change into her going-away outfit. The party's over."

It was Josie and she was grinning.

Faith sprang away from Tom.

"We were just—"

"Dancing," he finished for her. "Your boss is a very good dancer."

"So I've heard," Josie said.

Flushed, Faith said, "I'll bring the urn and we can finish packing up. The church will take care of the tables and chairs—they're theirs, but we have to see to everything else."

"May I help?"

"Thank you, Tom. We're all set, and I'm sure you'll need to be on your way to the after party. I enjoyed meeting you." Faith backed away, bumping into the buffet.

"There isn't one. They're leaving right away for Vermont. They both have to be back at work on Wednesday, so only a short honeymoon."

Which, a few minutes later, explained the bride's going-away outfit—a shiny white Gore-Tex ski ensemble complete with tulle-trimmed faux fur earmuffs; the groom's outfit was black. She was carrying her bouquet, lifted it high, much like an Olympic torch, and tossed it, hitting one of the beams in the vaulted ceiling. The cluster of French lilacs, tea roses, and ivy bounced down not into one of the bridesmaids' outstretched hands, but Faith's—the hand that was reaching for the coffee urn. Startled, she threw it toward the laughing throng of unmarried women, where it appropriately reached the bride's unmarried sister.

"You're having some night, lady," Josie said, filling a tray with unused cups and saucers.

"Don't be silly, and we'd better get going."

"Yeah, wouldn't want to be up in this tower past midnight. You might turn into a pumpkin or something."

Faith ignored the reference and got busy. A half hour later they were done—standing in the Lounge, empty of all save the tables and chairs. Josie was headed to a party nearby and Howard offered to drive the van back to work.

"Why don't you grab a cab and go home?" he said to Faith. "There's not much we have to unload. Nothing left for the fridge. I'll take these linens down and head off."

Faith was tempted, but she was sort of like the captain of a ship and her place was on the bridge until docked.

Or not.

Tom stepped out of the elevator and said, "I could say that I wanted your card, but that wouldn't be true."

Faith moved away from Howard and Josie toward him.

He lowered his voice. "I'm only in town until tomorrow, or rather, today, and you're probably very tired, but if not, would you want to spend some time showing me around? I was here in my senior year in high school and once in college. Been to the top of the Empire State Building and out to the Statue of Liberty, but that's pretty much it."

Her staff had sharp ears.

"The poor man needs to be educated, Faith. It's your duty as a New Yorker," Howard said.

"Only been to our great city two times, huh, huh, huh!" Josie weighed in.

So much for privacy.

"Well, I guess—"

"Great! I'll get my coat."

"Reminds me a little of an Irish setter I had as a kid," Howard said once Tom was in the cloakroom. "Same eyes and always wanted to play, day or night."

Faith gave him a look.

"I'll take him to Michael's Pub for some jazz. Maybe Woody Allen will be on clarinet even though it's not a Monday. That's pretty quintessentially New York, right?"

"Faith, honey, you could take the man to the Port Authority Bus Terminal and he'd be happy. Now, get going," Josie said.

"Humor me. I've always wanted to do this. Could you pull over, please?" Tom, Faith had learned his last name was Fairchild, said, addressing her, then the cabdriver. She was startled. They were at Columbus Circle, the New York Coliseum looming on one side, the entrance to the park on the other. No significant landmarks unless you counted Gaetano Russo's seventy-foot monument with the Italian voyager atop the granite column. And they'd already detoured to see another notable site before heading straight down Broadway. Tom had requested a quick detour to Grant's Tomb after they left the church. He hadn't told a joke of any nature or even the mythical Lincoln anecdote about Grant's drinking: "If I knew what brand he used, I'd send every general a barrel." Instead Tom had seemed awed by the impressive structure and talked about Grant's genius—also his heartrending last days trying to hold off death in order to complete his autobiography, hoping that with Mark Twain as his publisher the book would make enough money to pay off his debts and support his family when he was gone, which it did.

Tom was pointing away from Columbus Circle, toward the line of horse-drawn carriages on Central Park South, short at this time of night.

"How about it?"

How about it? Faith thought. She had never set foot in one of the touristy rip-offs, but Tom was already paying the cabbie and she found herself choosing between a spirited-looking white horse drawing a black carriage and the reverse. Tom helped her into the first and after firmly rejecting the blanket that had covered God knows how many knees, Faith settled back against the admittedly comfortable arm of her escort and decided to relax and enjoy the ride.

The park was beautiful. Even more so as the carriage wended its slow way across town, past the lights of Tavern on the Green. The clip-clop of the horse's hooves was the only sound Faith could hear. She found herself resting her head on Tom's shoulder. The driver was blessedly silent, and miraculously, she could even see stars above despite the city's notorious light pollution.

"Thank you," Tom murmured, his lips lightly touching the top of her head. "I'm sure you must do this all the time, but it's something I've always associated with New York City and had to experience."

Faith sat up. She'd heard of a lot of things associated with the city: Broadway shows, skyscrapers, crime, egg creams, but never the horse and carriage. Well, why not? And why had she never succumbed before? The vehicle, with its echoes of a bygone, much slower city, was the perfect way to see the park.

The ride was over too soon and they stood facing the Plaza Hotel. Even Eloise had to have been in bed by now, Faith thought.

"Tired?" Tom asked. He had never taken his arm away.

"We could still go to Michael's. It's not far. Down on Fifty-fifth."

They arrived just before the last set. Woody wasn't there, but Tom declared himself very happy with the place, noting the "Ye Olde" décor as a nice contrast to the Gothic flavor of the wedding locale. Drinks arrived, and Faith led up to the question that had been nagging at her for the last few hours.

"I've heard all about the rafts, tree houses, and mischief you and your little buddies made in Norwell, which sounds more like it should have been a town on the Mississippi than the—what was it—North River? And you have an older sister and two younger brothers. The groom was your roommate at Brown and he met his bride your freshman year in a poli sci class. They're going into the Peace Corps and want to enter the Foreign Service. You played basketball in high school and came to the city with the Model UN club. In return, you've quizzed me about virtually everything except my grandmother's maiden name, and I'm sure that will come, but I still don't know what you do! How, Mr. Fairchild, do you earn your keep up there in Massachusetts?"

Tom looked surprised.

"I thought you knew. I was the co-officiant today, or rather, yesterday."

"Co-officiant? You mean . . . ?"

"Yup. Parson, cleric, sky pilot, possibly devil dodger. It hasn't been Mr. Fairchild for a while, it's Reverend."

Faith had ordered Irish coffee. She took a big swig.

"So, up there in New England, you have . . . ?"

"A church? Yes. As of last fall, First Parish, Aleford, Massachusetts."

Faith was familiar with the historic place. All that 1775 famous-time-and-year stuff. Before Tom continued she had already pictured the scene from countless calendars.

"The church is one of the oldest in the state. Your basic white clapboard, steeple, and very hard pews facing the green."

She was clutching the mug, trying hard to process what he was saying. How could this incredibly attractive, incredibly charming man be everything she had sworn to avoid?

She gave it one more try.

"But you're not wearing a collar."

He reached over and took her hand. "I was—robe, too—but I'm allowed to get out of my work clothes for parties, and other things, so I changed."

As the music started up with Ellington's "Take the A Train," in a spur-of-the-moment decision that she hoped she wouldn't re-gret, she said, "All those rafts. And I'll bet you're a sailor. Do you want to take a boat ride? There's a ferry you might like."

The Staten Island Ferry—a bargain, even though the fare was now fifty cents. The boat had barely left the Battery when Faith realized she was on the ride of her life. Between the two of them they were able to recall most of Edna St. Vincent Millay's poem "Recuerdo"—"We were very tired, we were very merry"—al-though they did not intend to go "back and forth all night" on the ferry as Millay and her lover had. They did see the sun come up over Staten Island on the return trip, though, a "bucketful of gold."

Tom kissed her then. It was a great kiss. Not too practiced, but just practiced enough.

"When can I see you again?" he asked.

"When do you want to see me?" Her head was spinning.

He kissed her again.

"Now."

CHAPTER 2

Tom Fairchild was an old-fashioned suitor. He sent flowers—a bridal nosegay the first time with a card saying "You can hold on to this one"; Millay's *A Few Figs from Thistles* with a bookmark at "Recuerdo"; even chocolates from Faith's favorite store in the city, L.A. Burdick (Josie confessed to spilling the cocoa beans on this one)—and he called.

His first call was from Penn Station just before boarding the train. She'd wanted to see him off at the station, but he'd insisted she go straight home to get some sleep. He'd conk out on the train, he said, so they'd parted on the sidewalk beneath the Brooklyn Bridge and her mind was crowded with all the things they didn't get to do, including walk across the bridge to Brooklyn Heights, the place where she had often fantasized about living in the future, when she was a grown-up with a family.

"I'm not saying good-bye, just wanted to tell you I had a great time. No, make that the best time I've ever had. Now close your eyes and dream of me," Tom said.

They had both been ravenous when they got off the ferry and she'd offered him a choice of a Chinatown or a diner breakfast.

The Empire Diner in nearby Chelsea was open twenty-four/seven and a great people-watching place, frequented by a colorful mix of actors, cops, musicians, gangsters, athletes, club hoppers, insomniacs, and young lovers. But when he opted for Chinatown, even closer, she was pleased. New England cuisine (what was with those boiled dinners?) left much to be desired, but she assumed they could do bacon and eggs. They couldn't do Chinese food. A friend had told her once about venturing into a Chinese restaurant in Cambridge and walking out when a bread basket, complete with foil butter pats, was brought to the table.

She'd taken Tom to a little hole-in-the-wall place, Hong Fat, on Mott Street and ordered steaming bowls of hot-and-sour soup to warm them up, followed by beef chow fun, extra smoky. He ate the flat, wide rice noodles with a fork, but the man had to have some flaws. Places were starting to open and they stopped for dim sum at HSF to fill in the cracks. Faith insisted Tom take some pork buns and spring rolls to eat on the train rather than suffer the cardboard sandwiches offered at exorbitant prices in the so-called dining car, a far cry from the kind of train travel pictured in her favorite movie, *North by Northwest*. Cary Grant and Eva Marie Saint had dined on brook trout, the table set with fine linen and cutlery. She'd made sure Tom had plenty of paper napkins and a plastic knife and fork, assuring him he would be the envy of all the other travelers. With a reluctance to leave him that both bothered and surprised her by its intensity, she'd grabbed an uptown bus. What was she thinking? He was absolutely, totally wrong for her.

Yet, when the phone had rung again late in the afternoon, waking her, she'd eagerly grabbed it before realizing Tom couldn't possibly be in Boston so soon. It was Hope.

"I think I may have overreacted."

"Un-huh," Faith said. Her eyelids were closing again.

"Who knows what's going on in the guy's life? Pressure from

someone. A family member or business associate forcing him to switch his account to their person."

"True, true."

"Are you okay? You sound funny. Funny peculiar, not ha-ha."

"Tired, very tired. Talk tomorrow?"

"I'll be at work, so call there." Hope didn't take holidays.

And Tom Fairchild did call that night. And the next, and the next . . .

"I have bad news, good news, and bad news," Josie said. They were freezing various cookie doughs and puff pastry for the Valentine's Day luncheons they were doing on and before the fourteenth. January was creeping out in a slothlike manner with only a few jobs on the books. Howard was in Belize with his friend Michael, snorkeling and coming up with ideas for all sorts of Caribbean-inspired drinks, according to the postcard he'd sent. Faith was going to have to put in an order for extra guavas, passion fruit, pineapples, and coconuts when he returned, but she drew the line at paper parasols, although she'd heard that tiki was making a kitschy comeback.

"Tell me in order," Faith said anxiously. "Nothing too bad, I hope."

"Let me get some coffee. You?"

"Okay." The news was coffee bad, not shot-of-brandy bad, she thought, relieved.

They sat at the counter with their steaming mugs.

"My grandmother passed. I got a call from one of my cousins this morning."

"Oh, Josie, I'm so sorry," Faith said, reaching to give her friend a hug.

Josie took out a packet of tissues and dabbed at her eyes.

"I knew this was coming. When I saw her at Christmas, she told me it was a final good-bye and that she was ready for the Lord. I teased her, 'Is the Lord ready for *you*,' and that got a laugh. I wish you could have met her. She was an amazing woman."

"I wish I had, too. Even though we only spoke on the phone a few times I could tell she was a very special person."

"I owe her my life. She's the one who insisted I finish high school and found the money for me to go to college. I was five when my parents died, and she's the only parent I had. My mother was her youngest and it was a lot for my grandmother to take me on at her age."

The tears started again.

"When is the funeral?" Faith asked. "You should probably leave today."

Josie nodded. "Wish you could come—and my cousin said the house was already filling up with food."

Faith wished she could, too. Aside from being there for her friend, she was picturing the platters of fried chicken, country ham, bowls of macaroni and cheese, collard greens, potato salad, succotash, deviled eggs, and sweets—banana pudding, pies, layer cakes. The Southern way of death was infinitely better than the triangles of bread sandwiching a millimeter of fillings like anchovy paste and perhaps a thimbleful of sherry that characterized Northern obsequies.

"My cousin also told me something else. It's the good news. Faith, she left me her house! And all her savings."

"I'm so glad for you," Faith said. If anyone deserved this, it was Josie. Her grandmother may have raised her, but Josie was devoted to the woman in turn, spending her vacation time in Richmond and calling every day. Faith had seen photographs of the turn-of-the-twentieth-century brick house that Mrs. Wells had purchased with her husband in the 1930s and lovingly restored.

"The location is perfect, between downtown and the historic

Fan District. And it has a wide front porch, a veranda in back, and a big garden. She loved her garden."

Faith got up to pour some more coffee, but Josie put her arm out and stopped her.

"She wanted me to use the house to open Josie's."

Faith sat back down. Richmond, Virginia, was not within commuting distance of Have Faith's kitchens, and in any case, Josie would be fully occupied. Faith had known this day would come, just not so soon. This was the "bad news" part, but it wasn't. She'd miss Josie like crazy, but it was a dream come true.

"I'll be there for the opening. We have to start thinking of the menu right away. You should be able to open by the summer and serve on both porches. Dig out those photos and let's start making lists."

It was Josie's turn to hug Faith. "I love you, boss," she said.

"I love you, too, but it's time to drop 'boss.' You're on your own now, missy."

"The estate won't be settled for a while. I'll be back after the funeral, and if you agree, I can train Francesca to take my place. She grew up cooking—she told me the women in her family are famous in her village for their culinary skills—and I know she'd be happy to quit her job at the health club. She's at the reception desk and gets all the complaints—so-and-so left sweat on the stationary bike seat, or is hogging the elliptical, or is, well, fill in the blank." Josie was beaming now.

"She does seem to know her way around a kitchen, and maybe we can add some of her family's Tuscan specialties. Let me think about it."

"And, boss, pardon me, Faith—you can figure out what she's hiding, our *bella donna*."

"Hiding? What do you mean?"

"Nothing sinister. Just a little puzzling. Last week I came back to the apartment unexpectedly—I'd forgotten an umbrella and

I've bought so many from those guys selling them on the street when it rains that I can set up my own business next downpour. Anyway, Francesca was sitting at the kitchen table writing a post-card. She had a stack of them next to her. When I came in, she quickly tucked the one she'd been writing into a manila envelope and when she did, she knocked the other cards to the floor. Of course I started to help her pick them up, but she told me it was no problem and not to bother. But, Faith, the odd thing was that before she scooped them up, I saw that they weren't postcards of New York City, but of London. No Empire State Building, World Trade Center, Saint Patrick's Cathedral, Statue of Liberty. Nada. Instead I spied the Tower of London and Trafalgar Square. And there were no stamps on the cards even though they were all addressed."

"Did you see any of the addresses?"

"The ones I saw were all addressed to Signora Rossi, presumably Francesca's mother, or maybe grandmother. And the big envelope she was stuffing them into was addressed to someone in London. The only thing I can come up with is that Francesca wants her family to think she is in England, not the United States. The question is, why?"

Always a silver lining, Faith thought happily. Nothing cheered her up like solving a mystery.

It was close to five o'clock on Valentine's Day when Faith turned the key of her apartment door. Both of today's luncheons had gone off well, but she could wait a year before seeing any heart-shaped food again after this week. All her clients had insisted on a traditional theme, not simply everything red, white, or pink, but hearts, flowers, and Cupid. Today the menu she'd suggested for the day itself had met with both women's approval—these were ladies' luncheons. It started with Kir Royale, and moved on to borscht with a piped sour cream heart, heart-shaped patty shells with lobster Newburg, endive spears with a pomegranate-seed-studded vinaigrette, finishing with *coeur de crème* in a raspberry coulis. Mädderlake supplied the centerpieces, using rococo white porcelain containers overflowing with roses straight from a Fragonard for one and for the other selecting a long, low glass heart shape filled to the brim with perfect red, deep purple, and rose anemones. Faith had scattered on the tables candy hearts with those mottos that always suggested to her that someone should be doing the Charleston—"I Go 4 U," "U Send Me, Kiddo"—and red-foil-wrapped chocolates as well.

She'd picked up her mail on the way to the elevator and was disappointed not to have a card from Tom. He'd been sending her a series of funny postcards, including one of an oversize bean pot. On the back, he'd written: "We do, too, have good eats in Boston!"

As usual, there was a card from her grandmother with a crisp ten-dollar bill tucked inside. It had started at a dollar when Faith was a child and it had bought a sundae at Rumplemeyer's. She still loved the place, and the ten might stretch to two sundaes. Tom and she could go to the Central Park Zoo first. She shook her head.

It wasn't that Tom hadn't sent a card. In a way she was relieved. No card might mean he was losing interest, didn't want a long-distance romance. She certainly didn't—or did she? Since she'd met the Reverend Thomas Fairchild, she'd gone back and forth on the relationship. Forget the whole church thing—although that was hard to do—he was a New Englander born and bred. Aside from the fact that he'd accepted the call to First Parish in Aleford and had to honor it for the foreseeable future, he'd never leave the Bay State for the Empire State. And she had no desire to live anywhere north of the Cloisters—and even that was too far from Midtown—no matter how great the baked beans were.

She'd avoided discussing any of this with either Josie or Hope. Out of voice, out of mind?

Hope was going out with Phelps. He'd snagged a table at the Sign of the Dove, in the Conservatory Dining Room, one of the most romantic spots in the city, especially in the summer when they opened the glass cupola that covered the ceiling. Phelps must be making many pretty pennies these days—they wouldn't be going Dutch on Valentine's Day. She'd have to make a concerted effort to get to know, and like, him better, Faith resolved. He was a fixture in her sister's life and there might be some bouquet tossing in the future, although with their schedules, the wedding might have to be on a federal holiday when the New York Stock Exchange was closed, forcing these two workaholics to leave their respective offices. Or not. People were getting married while skydiving; on Rollerbades; spelunking, dressed as Trekkies—why not in an office? Faith could see the notice in the *Times*: "The bride wore a white Armani pants suit, and instead of rice, the guests threw paper from the couple's shredders."

She was meeting Josie and Francesca for a girls' night out at Sylvia's Soul Food restaurant in Harlem. Comfort food: it was Wednesday, so that meant the meat loaf special, maybe some garlic mashed potatoes, green beans, and definitely peach cobbler. The secret to the meat loaf, Josie had learned, was barbecue sauce both in and on the meat. They were going for the food, but more because Sylvia Woods was Josie's inspiration. Herbert and Sylvia Woods started the successful restaurant in 1962 and it had been serving satisfied customers with food prepared with care—and in Sylvia's words, "Along with the seasonings, I stir in love"—ever since.

Josie would be leaving the city for good at the end of March; things were moving rapidly. She'd been going back and forth to Richmond to oversee renovations, and Faith had hired Francesca full-time. She was proving to be a great choice. Hardworking, delightful, she'd already added two dishes to their menu: *ribollita,* a Tuscan vegetable bread soup, Francesca's version heavy on fresh thyme, and a dessert—*torta della nonna,* grandmother's cake, a heavenly ricotta cheesecake concoction covered with almonds and a dusting of confectioners' sugar.

Josie hadn't reported any other "mysterious" incidents like the postcards, and the only thing Faith suspected was that the girl might be lying about her age. Her sophisticated appearance made her look in her midtwenties, but coming into work in a rush one day, her hair loose and no makeup, she didn't look a day over eighteen to Faith. She was in the States on a student visa, she'd told Faith, and put down that number and her passport number on her work application, filling in her age as twenty-two. Faith hadn't actually seen either the passport or the visa, she realized, not very professional on her part and now awkward to request. The health club would have checked everything out, though, she suddenly thought in relief. Maybe she and Josie were making too much of the postcard business. Maybe someone in her family collected stamps and wanted British ones. And maybe the moon was made of green cheese . . . or Parmesan.

She had time to shower before meeting the others at the restaurant. As she headed toward the bathroom, the intercom buzzed.

"Yes?"

"It's Tom. Happy Valentine's Day. I, well, I thought I'd bring you a card in person. You're in Four-A according to the mailbox I'm looking at."

"You're here? Downstairs?"

Of course he is, stupid, he's talking to you on the intercom! Faith chided herself as she pressed the button to release the lock on the front door.

She glanced quickly around the apartment. It was a studio— her goal was to be in a one-bedroom prewar building with a doorman, a gas cooktop, and an electric oven in the next year or two.

This had been a good choice, however. She'd been attracted by the windows that looked straight out to the park. The fact that she had to transform her sofa into her bed every night was a small price to pay. The shoe-box size also meant minimalist furnishings—two bookcases from IKEA, an ottoman that opened for storage, and a glass-topped Noguchi coffee table, plus a small chest of drawers from her aunt Chat, who'd recently moved out of the city. Everything was tidy, no dishes in the kitchenette's sink. She opened the door at his knock.

Tom Fairchild stepped in and held out a red envelope. As she reached for it, he pulled her into his arms.

"You're totally insane, do you know that?" she said after a while.

"Not totally. Maybe slightly."

"How long can you stay?"

"I have to leave tonight—or very early tomorrow morning."

"You're totally insane, do you—"

He cut off the rest of her sentence with a kiss.

She came up reluctantly for air. "Let me take your coat." His coat was a light raincoat, all anyone needed. So far 1990 had been the warmest year on record in New York history, but Faith had the feeling that this was a man who'd be wearing a sweater in a blizzard. The raincoat was a nod to the light drizzle that had been creating a dreamlike, but slightly damp, mist all day.

Tom sat down on the sofa. "I like your apartment. Compact. And great view. You said you'd be finished after some luncheons, so I can take you someplace great for dinner, right?"

Most of the "someplace great" places for a Valentine's dinner had been booked for weeks, but Faith knew a spot where she could always get in.

"There's a nice French bistro on the Upper East Side, Le Refuge. I could call them. My parents practically live there, so I'm sure they'll squeeze us in somehow. It's not the most happening place in town, but the food is good and you can have a conversation."

"Sounds perfect. A conversation is just what I had in mind."

Faith picked up the phone.

"They can seat us at nine. Is that going to be too late for you?" She'd covered the receiver with her hand. "What time is the train?"

"No train this time. I drove. Quicker, and I can leave when I want."

He *was* insane, she thought, and made the reservation. Driving all this way? Most of her friends didn't even own cars. Who needed one in the city?

"I saw a liquor store on the way here," Tom said. "How about I pick up something appropriately sparkling for the day?"

Orange juice and champagne were the two things always in Faith's fridge, but she wanted to shower and pull herself together. He could also swing by Zabar's, the ultimate food emporium, to pick up a few tidbits to go with the bubbly. In *The Seven-Year Itch* Marilyn Monroe dipped a potato chip into the bowl of her champagne glass, and salty things did go well with the wine, salty things like caviar, but they'd skip both the chips and the roe for now. Besides, her glasses were flutes—hard to get a chip in. She'd call over and put a slice of their chicken liver pâté, a heart-shaped Coeur du Berry fresh chèvre, and a baguette on her account. Proximity to Zabar's had been another deciding factor in picking this apartment.

He left and she called Josie, who was not at all surprised at the cause for the change in plans.

"I figured something was up when the dozen long-stemmed American Beauty roses didn't arrive this morning for you at work. See you tomorrow, late?"

Faith didn't answer the all-too-obvious question and just said good-bye.

By the time they had to leave for their reservation, the rain had stopped. Faith pointed out her parents' apartment from the cab window on the way across town.

"That's where I grew up."

"We should drop by and wish them a happy Valentine's Day on the way back," Tom suggested.

"Whoa, cowboy," she said. "First of all, they go to sleep following, and sometimes during, the ten o'clock news and would be certain there was a major calamity if I appeared after that hour. Also, don't you think meeting my parents is rushing things a bit?"

"I understand about disturbing them, but as to the rest, no, I don't think so at all."

At Le Refuge, Faith was greeted with delight and they were ushered into the pretty back room furnished with Country French antiques. She decided to save room for an entrée and dessert, but suggested Tom try the gratinéed oysters over blanched leeks. When it arrived, smelling heavenly, he urged her to take a bite and she recalled the test a friend advised when judging a possible mate. "Ask to try what he ordered, and if he says, 'If you wanted it, why didn't you order it yourself?' skip coffee and cross him off your list."

Tom proved to be a champion sharer, offering more bites of the stuffed lamb loin he'd ordered. In return, she gave him some of the salmon from her plate—the red wine and shallot sauce a departure from Hollandaise. By the time dessert arrived—poached pears with vanilla and praline ice cream, and a Valentine's special, a heart-shaped, oversize profiterole with plenty of dark chocolate sauce—they had placed both dishes in the center of the table.

"Coffee here—or I can make some at my place. You'll need it for the drive back," Faith said.

"Definitely your place."

Out on the sidewalk it felt more like May than February and

they walked up 82nd Street to Fifth Avenue and somehow kept going across the park instead of hailing a cab. He'd taken her hand as soon as they'd left the restaurant and she thought that this was what people meant when they said their hands fit perfectly together.

Oh, Faith, she thought—not for the first time that evening. What was happening to her?

Back at the apartment, where he already seemed quite at home, Tom loosened his tie and watched as she ground the beans and made coffee in a French press.

"You're the real deal. You've probably never had instant in your life, and that's all I know how to make."

She shuddered slightly. The thought . . .

He took his coffee the same way she did—strong and black. She offered to make more. He refused. The room was very quiet. So quiet she could hear cars outside on Central Park West, a siren in the distance.

"I don't want to leave you, Faith," he said, taking her in his arms.

"I don't want you to go either, but it's a long drive." She stroked his hair, such nice hair.

"I mean I don't want to leave you ever. The French call it *coup de foudre*—love at first sight. I never believed in it until I saw you at Phil's wedding. I literally felt as if lightning *had* struck. You said when I got here tonight that I was insane and I think I am a little bit—blissfully mad. I can't stop thinking about you. Well, what I'm trying to say . . ."

He kissed her, a long, hard kiss that left her breathless. She felt herself giving in to a passion she had never felt before for anyone. She was falling, tumbling, the room was spinning—and she didn't want it to stop.

"Here," Tom said. "This is for you."

He took a small box from his inside jacket pocket.

"Go ahead. Open it."

She sat up and took off the lid. It wasn't wrapped. Inside there was a watch.

"Try it on. I hope it fits—and I hope you like it; it's an old one."

The watch was an elegant gold Longines on a mesh bracelet.

"Oh, Tom, it's beautiful. You shouldn't have . . ."

"Yes, I should have, now put it on. It's wound."

Faith turned the watch over, examining the craftsmanship, and then as she realized there was something more, much more, she brought it closer to her eyes, reading the words engraved on the back.

WILL YOU MARRY ME?

"I think I'm engaged," Faith whispered. Tom was sound asleep.

After lying awake for what seemed like hours, she'd called her sister, who, like the city, never slept.

"What do you mean you think you are? How can you not be sure? And why are you whispering?"

"I have company. Is Phelps there?"

"Nope. He wanted to put in some time at the office after dinner, but back up. It's the guy from Massachusetts, right? I mean there and the being-engaged stuff."

After meeting him last month, Faith had given Hope a few brief facts, omitting the most important entry in Tom's CV.

"Yes to both."

"Okay, has he passed the food test?"

It was Hope's friend who had created it.

"With flying colors."

"Good. But, sweetie, isn't this all a little sudden?"

Faith looked over at Tom. Light from the window streaked across his face. *Coup de foudre,* he'd said. This wasn't first sight for her, but second or third or whatever sight—one she had started to realize that she never wanted to lose.

"It's hard to explain. I know it sounds like I'm rushing into this, but I'm pretty sure he's the one."

"Then what you have to ask yourself is whether you can imagine being with him every day for the rest of your life and its corollary, not being able to imagine being with anyone else."

There it was. The thought that had been keeping her up, tossing in the wee hours, despite her physical fatigue from the full workday. The thought that she'd phrased in any number of ways ever since he'd given her the watch. Yes, she could imagine being with Tom forever, and no, she didn't want anyone else. All the other men in her life paled in comparison, receding into distant memory as she looked at the face she wanted on the pillow next to her now and always.

"I'm taking your inability to answer coherently as a yes, et cetera."

Hope should have gone into law, Faith thought fleetingly before the matter at hand crowded everything else out.

"Now this is very important, Fay. Has he actually proposed?"

"Yes, on the back of a watch."

"What!"

"It's a very nice one. Vintage Longines. Gold. He had 'Will you marry me?' engraved on the back," Faith said defensively.

"And you said yes? Otherwise quite a pain to get off, although I suppose he could save it for another prospect."

Hope was nothing if not practical.

"I said yes, but."

"Yes, but what?"

"But I'd have to come spend some time in Aleford. That's where he lives. It's not far from Boston, though."

The moment she'd seen the words and heard Tom say them

aloud, she knew she was betrothed to him—knew she had probably loved him from the start as well—but she just couldn't take
the plunge without testing the water.

"Can't he move here? What does he do anyway? You never
said. You're talking about giving up a thriving business, although
you could start it up again someplace else, but, Fay, are you sure?
Leave New York!"

An impediment, but this wasn't the biggie. Faith took a deep
breath.

"I don't know how to say this, but, Hope, he's a minister."

"Like Dad! And Grandpa? You mean he has a church in this
Aleford place? You'd better be crazy about him, because you have
definitely gone crazy. I thought we had an agreement."

"I know. Believe me, I've thought of nothing else since we
met. How was I to know he'd come into town to perform the
ceremony? He'd changed his clothes before the reception."

"Definitely not fair. Call me when he leaves. We have to talk."
Hope lived on the Upper West Side, too, but in a considerably
larger apartment across from Lincoln Center with not only a full
retinue on the ground floor at the door but an indoor pool on the
top floor with a killer view of the city.

When push came to shove, there was no one like a sister, Faith
thought a few hours later, after seeing Tom off, reluctantly on both
their parts, and he'd come back once for what was supposed to be
a quick kiss and wasn't.

She made coffee, something she seemed to be doing with
greater frequency lately, and put out what was left of the cheese
and pâté. Hope was always hungry, the result of an extremely ir-
regular eating schedule. She was touched that her sister was going
in to work late—it was already six A.M.—in order to stop by.

The two had always been close. Faith couldn't remember life
without Hope, and they made a nice pair, although Jane had never
dressed them at all alike. Faith was a blue-eyed blonde, her thick

hair curved below her chin. Hope's chestnut hair was shorter and she'd inherited the Sibley deep green eyes. Tall and slender, they still shared clothes.

She buzzed her up, and an hour later, they were still not talked out. Hope had devoured the leftovers and the croissants she'd picked up on the way. Faith wasn't hungry, but sipped at her coffee as the torrent of words came spilling out—all the reasons why she was head over heels and all the reasons why the whole thing was, to use Tom's word, "insane." Blissfully so.

"To be continued," Hope said. "I have a client coming into town for a breakfast meeting at the Mark, and I have to get going." At the door, she gave her sister a big hug. "So this is what it looks like."

"What?" Faith asked, hugging her back.

"True love."

"Poppy wants to give you a shower, and it has to be before we go away."

Emma Morris was sitting at Faith's desk at work with the chair facing out, toward the kitchen. The counter was lined with trays of cooling divinity fudge, another of Josie's specialties and destined to be packed into small gold boxes as favors for an anniversary party. The significance of the name had taken on new meaning for Faith, as had pretty much everything else in her life these days. She was engaged. She was getting married. The "but"—the contingency that was her trip to Aleford—had fallen by the wayside. No time, and no inclination now. The universe was whirling madly as her emotions plunged from euphoria to fear and trembling. And here was Emma announcing that her mother wanted to give Faith a shower. A bridal shower!

Emma and Faith had been at Dalton together, but lost touch during college. Last December Emma had turned to Faith for help. She was being blackmailed, and the deadly journey the two took together had forged something more than mere friendship. They'd initially reconnected at a party she was catering, Faith recalled, looking over at Emma—startlingly beautiful, like a Pre-Raphaelite-era Rossetti painting, even in a plain gray Eileen Fisher outfit. She also recalled the look of fear on Emma's face that evening as she'd dashed into the host's kitchen, where Faith had been busy with coconut shrimp, and paused to greet her former classmate politely—Emma was very polite—before asking desperately whether there was a back way out of the apartment. Two parties: one in December, one in January; two life-changing events. Faith had had no idea catering would prove so perilous, so delirious.

And now it was March and Emma's mother, Poppy, wanted to give Faith a shower.

Poppy Morris was a legend. During the sixties she'd invented radical chic, throwing dinner parties where Bobby Seale might be seated next to Brooke Astor and across from Henry Kissinger, with Jane Fonda to his left. Far left. It was Poppy who'd first put the iconic photograph of Che on a T-shirt, pairing it with Ralph Lauren pants. She marched her way through the seventies and ever onward, while maintaining close ties to whoever sat in the Oval Office, sending Ronnie jelly beans, banning broccoli when George and Barbara dined chez Morris. Power was Power.

Never a white wine yuppie, Poppy stuck with martinis. She preferred poker to bridge and wasn't a lady who lunched. Her husband, Jason, seemed content to sit and watch the show, with a cast of characters that had changed with each decade. At the moment Poppy was devoting herself to Emma, having coming very close to losing her, and had typically decided that what her daughter needed now was to embark on a round-the-world voyage with Poppy, stopping not in Paris or Rome but in Morocco, Istanbul, and "a divine little place" Poppy had discovered while trekking in Nepal.

"She doesn't have to do this and anyway it's too soon," Faith said.

The wedding wasn't until June. Many months away, she kept telling herself. Many, many.

Emma was nibbling on a piece of fudge Josie had handed her.

"Yum. I wish I could make things like this. No, I don't really. Anyway, Faith, you know Poppy. She's not going to take no for an answer. Check your calendar. She wants to do it the last Sunday of the month. Late afternoon. It will be fun. She has some sort of idea she read about that she says will liven things up. I don't know what it is, but we have to have at least twenty-four people."

Poppy's idea of fun usually was, but Faith couldn't imagine what kind of shower this might be.

"You're a bride. Brides have showers given for them. Relax," Josie said. She'd greeted Faith's news with delight and proclaimed herself the first to know, although Howard was saying the same thing. So far as Faith could tell, these claims were based on the way Tom had looked at her across the tray of *saucisson en brioche* she'd been carrying at that wedding or, Howard's contribution, the way Tom had held her when they'd danced together.

"You're supposed to give me a list," Emma said. "And it's not a Jack and Jill shower. She doesn't like those. Only women."

"She should be a wedding planner. How often does she do this?"

"Oh, this is the first. My ex's sister gave me one"—Emma's divorce had possibly been the quickest, and most dramatic, in New York state history—"not Poppy and certainly not Lucy."

Lucy was Emma's older sister, and there were adult women who still shuddered at the name when they cast their memories back to the merciless bullying they'd endured as teens at Lucy's hands. She'd had an uncanny ability to ferret out one's weak spots, which Faith believed was not due to a curse from an evil witch at birth but because Lucy was an evil witch herself at birth. She had a sudden thought.

"We won't have to have Lucy, will we?"

"No, Poppy's rather off her now after, well, all that business."

Lucy had blamed Emma herself for almost becoming one of Manhattan's last 1989 murder statistics and, what was worse, casting off a "one of us" mate for what Lucy viewed as merely an odd peccadillo or two. Others, particularly the police, thought not.

"And of course you can't cater it yourself. She's going to make her popovers and the cook will do the rest."

Poppy had learned to make popovers as a bride—"One did those kinds of things in the fifties before dear Betty wrote her book"—and there was no mystique about them. They were delicious (see recipe, page 241). She'd taught Emma and Faith during a sleepover at the Morris's Upper East Side town house when they were in elementary school. She'd taught them how to make s'mores on another occasion, and there Poppy's culinary expertise had ground to a halt.

"So I'll tell her you're beside yourself with joy or whatever else you want me to say and will give her a list soon?"

"Look at her. She's overflowing with joy," Josie said. "Me, too."

Faith smiled obediently—after all, it was dear of Poppy to want to do this. Francesca was smiling, too, although her smile was the puzzled, What Are These People All About? kind.

"Won't your house already have one, a *doccia*? Why is Emma's mama giving you a shower?"

Faith was seated in a large club chair in what Poppy called her Garden Room, a sizable solarium on the top floor of the house. She may have burned a bra or two, but when it came to interior decorating, Poppy was a traditionalist, strictly Sister Parish and Mario Buatta. The living room, dining room, and library on the main floor were straight from the set of *Brideshead Revisited*. Here the Colefax and Fowler chintzes were less formal—flowered trellises, some exotic birds with bright plumage—but the food had been set out on a Hepplewhite sideboard. The fabled popovers had been filled with a creamy mixture of asparagus and ham, a nice change from chicken. There was a green salad with pears, walnuts, and Gorgonzola. A basket of plain popovers, piping hot, was constantly replenished, as was the butter and an assortment of jams ranging from savory to sweet set out in Poppy's Royal Crown Derby next to them. They were drinking a fruity champagne punch (see recipe, page 244), and whether it was the alcohol or the occasion that was producing the merriment, Faith couldn't say. She could say that she was enjoying herself very much, however.

The list had easily risen to twenty-four and then some. Besides Faith, Hope, Jane Sibley and her mother, Eleanor Lennox, Aunt Chat—Charity Sibley—several other relatives, Josie, Francesca, and Amanda from work, Poppy, Emma, and Dalton and college friends, Tom's family was represented. Faith had already received a phone call from Tom's parents welcoming her into the family and a note from Tom's mother accompanying a cameo brooch that had belonged to Tom's great-great-grandmother and was passed on to the first Fairchild bride in each generation. Faith mentioned the shower when she wrote back thanking her and also asking for the address of Tom's sister, Betsey, as well as that of any others Marian Fairchild thought should be included. Tom's two younger brothers, Robert and Craig, were single, Craig in his first year at the University of Massachusetts. Betsey, the oldest, had married Dennis Parker, her college sweetheart, immediately after graduation. Dennis was a periodontist. They had a year-old son, Scotty, whom Tom adored, as well as had proudly baptized, and lived in Hingham, the town next to Norwell.

Marian had been very sorry, but she and Tom's father, Dick, would be attending a relative's fiftieth birthday party that day.

Having colonized the South Shore early in the twentieth century, arriving from Ireland by way of Boston's West End, various
Fairchild branches had established Fairchild's Market, Fairchild's
Realty, and later, Fairchild's Ford. Faith understood from Tom
that the birthday relative was from the car dealership branch. Fairchild's Realty was Tom's father. Betsey had accepted and asked to
bring a guest, "an old family friend."

Faith looked over at her future sister-in-law, sitting ramrod
straight on a footstool despite Emma's urging that there was plenty
of room on one of the couches. Like Tom, Betsey was tall and
had an athletic build. It had already come up in conversation that
she'd be running the Boston Marathon again this year. She was a
brunette, like her brother, but whether she hadn't been graced by
nature with the red glints he had or whether she had obliterated
them, Faith couldn't tell. Her thick hair was pulled severely back
from her face and anchored at the nape of her neck with a sturdy-
looking tortoiseshell clip. So far, attempts at conversation had been
heavy going and at first Faith had wondered why Betsey had bothered to come—like her brother, she drove, and it was a long drive.

It soon became clear that the purpose was to display the
woman who should be the guest of honor at a shower for her future sister-in-law. The "old friend of the family" was a ravishing
young sylphlike blonde named Sydney Jerome with the biggest,
deepest blue eyes Faith had ever seen. Like Betsey, she was wearing a Talbots wool ensemble more suited to their mothers' generation, the kind of jacket dress that "could go anywhere" in New
England—the Friday-afternoon concert at the Boston Symphony,
the local Friends of the Library annual tea, and of course lunch at
the Chilton Club. The boxy jacket and pleated skirt were, however, unsuccessful at masking the attributes underneath, a killer
body crying out for something clingy.

Faith had heard all about Sydney from Tom. The Jeromes lived
next door to the Fairchilds, and Sydney had been part of the tree

house, raft-building gang from the start. A regular on Fairchild family ski trips and their touch football game every Sunday after church, Sydney was also part of the garage band the gang had morphed into during their adolescence. Oh yes, Faith had heard all about Sydney, starting that first evening at Michael's Pub. The only thing she hadn't heard was that "Sydney" was a girl. She looked over at her again. Quite a girl.

Just as Tom had omitted mentioning the reason he was in town that day, he'd omitted mentioning this piece of information. Faith would have to get used to it. It seemed to go along with the job, minds concentrating on higher-level subjects rather than life's more mundane details? Her own father was notorious for this sort of thing, and conversations with him were often like a sort of parlor game—Twenty Questions or Animal/Vegetable/Mineral. Over the years Faith and Hope had noticed their mother's aptitude at deciphering her husband's derailed trains of thought and Faith assumed that with time she'd also develop the skill. At the moment Sydney's presence, somewhat of a shock at first, was now striking her as funny—and raising an important question. What was behind it all? Betsey's desire to have the family chum remain in the fold? Whose idea had it been to bring Sydney to the shower, Betsey's or the "dear family friend's"?

Poppy clapped her hands.

"Time for prezzies. You all got the invitation with the explanation, but it's time to tell Faith." She looked terribly pleased with herself.

"It's a Round-the-Clock shower. Everyone was assigned a time and had to bring something appropriate, and I hope amusing, for each hour. Let's see, we'll start with one A.M., shall we?"

Pure Poppy. And it was a fun idea—or so Faith hoped. If it worked, it would be something to suggest to clients. She felt a sudden stab. Clients. She wasn't taking on any more, aside from small jobs, and everything would stop in mid-May. She'd had to return the deposits and smooth some ruffled feathers for the weddings she'd had scheduled for June. The brides had, fortunately, been understanding, swept up in bridal sisterhood, and were relieved that all the plans, and quality, would remain the same with the firm Faith was recommending.

Faith had had many a middle-of-the-night thought about what giving up the business meant. The business that she alone had created; it was a part of her now. She fully intended to start it again in Massachusetts and Tom had been adamant that she should, but at times the idea was overwhelming. And what did they eat up there? Baked beans, Indian pudding, those boiled dinners . . .

She caught Hope's eye. Her sister was having a good time catching up with various friends. Hope nodded to her as Faith took a large box from Josie, the one o'clock guest, and prepared to open it. Faith interpreted the nod as Hope's way of saying that everything was going to be fine. It wasn't that her sister was a mind reader, although often they were able to communicate quite nicely without words.

Faith nodded back. She was at her shower. It would all work out. Wouldn't it? The it being what? She tried to articulate the "what"—the wedding, the move, the marriage? No, not the marriage. She was sure about that.

"This is what I thought I'd like to have on in the early hours of the morning," Josie said as Faith removed a beautiful—and very sheer—peignoir and gown from the tissue paper. "Or off!" someone called, and the room burst into laughter. Faith darted a quick look at the Massachusetts contingent. The tight-lipped smiles they'd worn throughout remained frozen in place.

The other early morning gift givers had had much the same idea as Josie, with the exception of Poppy, who'd presented Faith with a set of Pratesi sheets so silken the thread count rivaled the national debt. Hope's 7:00 A.M. gift was a stainless steel French-press coffeemaker from Germany that kept the liquid hot, and an order for a year's supply of freshly roasted beans from Zabar's. Emma handed her a small box from Cartier, saying, "I know I'm supposed to be noon, but I knew you'd love this after seeing the watch Tom gave you." Faith did love Emma's gift, so Emma—a Longines vintage mantel clock similar in style to the watch.

Poppy handed Faith a card. "It's from your uncle Schuyler. He came up here earlier to deliver it himself, said he knew his wife was coming and it was all girls, but he wanted to 'shower' you himself—the dirty old man!" Everyone laughed. He was a favorite with Poppy and she had shooed him away with reluctance. The man was such fun.

"His gift is under the table, and don't bother to unwrap it. It will be a bore to pack it up again. He said to tell you it was a Waterford punch bowl and cups so you could get your parishioners to unwind."

Faith was delighted. At the gift, typical of him, and his notion of a roomful of tipsy parishioners. Her middle name was Schuyler in honor of him. He was her grandmother's baby brother. Uncle Sky was either a little dotty or wonderfully eccentric, depending on the speaker. In any case, he'd been in great demand on the Manhattan party circuit even when he was a mere stripling at Princeton.

And so it went, a giddy journey through the bride's day that even Betsey's extremely practical Tupperware offering, which she presumed Faith would use at 2:00 P.M. for some reason, could not dampen. Sydney's 6:00 P.M. oven mitts and matching dish towels decorated with the logos of Boston's beloved teams—the Red Sox, Bruins, Celtics, and Patriots—brought shrieks from the group. "Remember when we went to the Harvard-Yale game," one of Faith's college roommates reminisced, "and you asked why all the men in the striped shirts kept dropping their hankies on the field!"

Having watched the proceedings with a slightly bewildered expression, Francesca handed Faith a large box.

"It's for the antipasti, made near my home. I had the dinner-time."

Faith gave her a hug. The large ceramic platter was beautiful, and she could picture the way an assortment of antipasti—olives, prosciutto, mortadella, roasted red peppers, artichokes, eggplant caponata, Pecorino cheese—would look, mingling their colors and shapes with the pottery's traditional swirling Tuscan design.

Jane Sibley's was the last gift—midnight—and she presented her daughter with what she proclaimed essential for a long and happy marriage: an Itty Bitty book light. She also gave her a lovely royal blue velvet robe with her new initials on one quilted satin cuff.

"No backing out now, Faith," someone said, and someone else put another brimming cup of punch in her hand.

"Not a chance—and thank you all so much. Especially Poppy!" Faith raised her cup—among a vast number of other items, Poppy collected antique sterling christening cups to use on occasions like this.

"To Poppy," Faith said and drank deeply as the others echoed her words. She was filled with gratitude. In one afternoon, Poppy had accomplished what Faith had been trying to do for herself in vain since Tom's proposal: she had made her feel like a bride. A happy, blushing bride!

The popovers and other food had been replaced by fruit salad—Poppy had declared that she wasn't going to have her cook bother to bake a cake that the women wouldn't want their fellow guests seeing them eat more than a bite of, no matter how yummy. But she had set plates of François Payard chocolates and his mini pastries around the room, where presumably those who wished could indulge discreetly.

Faith went over and sat down next to her grandmother. She was suddenly feeling very tired. Being a bride was hard work. She'd already spent hours with her mother and grandmother drawing up lists. Lists of guests, possible menus, even gifts, which had started to arrive before the announcement had been made officially—major to-do lists. And then there was her dress. They had an appointment at Bergdorf's bridal salon for Wednesday afternoon, the only time Hope could make it, and she'd insisted she had to be there so Faith wouldn't end up wearing what looked like a slip or dressed like Little Bo Beep.

Her grandmother stroked her head. Faith hadn't realized she'd laid it on Nana's shoulder.

"You feel a bit warm, child. Are you feeling all right?"

Faith wasn't feeling all right. She was feeling extremely ill. And if she didn't make it to the adjoining powder room, she was going to be ill all over Poppy's Aubusson carpet. She clapped a hand over her mouth and stood up, swaying slightly.

The voices in the room mounted to a crescendo of sound, sentences bouncing out at her—"Too much to drink?" "You don't think she's, well, you know?" "Cold feet?" "She looks like she's got a fever—that bug that's been going around?"

As Hope steered her through the door just in time, Faith heard her great-aunt Tammy's voice above the rest.

"The bride's been poisoned."

CHAPTER 3

Great-aunt Tammy, a voluptuous, big-hair brunette from Louisiana, had been coyly admitting to being thirty-five for the ten years she'd been married to Faith's great-uncle Schuyler Wayfort, known to all as Sky. He'd been twenty-six years her senior when they met.

Her dramatic pronouncement at the shower produced instant silence in the room until her sister-in-law said, "Don't be absurd, Tamora"—Eleanor Wayfort Lennox never employed nicknames—"my granddaughter is merely indisposed."

Since the sounds of Faith's indisposition were penetrating the door, everyone hurriedly resumed talking again. Her mother got up to join Hope. Meanwhile, Poppy Morris had followed Faith immediately, always levelheaded in a crisis—red wine spilled on Princess Di's snowy white Versace; no Coca-Cola, only Pepsi, in the kitchen for Joan Crawford (hangers not a problem, Poppy *never* had wire ones). She returned a few seconds later to call 911 and her private physician, in that order. Poppy knew her number by heart "just in case," as she had memorized those of certain lawyers over the years for the same reason. The next thing she did was usher everyone down to the living room.

The doctor arrived before the EMTs.

"Her pulse is more rapid than normal, but she's not running a fever. Yet it's clear that her system is experiencing a shock and I'd like to admit her if the vomiting doesn't stop soon. She'll need an IV to prevent dehydration."

Faith shook her head violently and managed to say, "No hospital."

"Does she have any food allergies?" Dr. Ginsburg asked.

"None that I know of, and I should know. I'm her mother," Jane Sibley said.

At this point the EMTs stepped into the Garden Room with what seemed like enough equipment for a four-alarm fire. Poppy's powder room was the size of a master bath, but it was getting crowded. Hope and Jane moved out. Poppy stayed.

Faith was sitting on the floor, leaning against the commode she had been hugging. Her throat felt as if someone had taken sandpaper to it.

"I'm fine," she croaked, wishing everyone would leave so she could take a nap on the floor. The tile felt cool to her touch and she closed her eyes in preparation. Maybe when she opened them the room would be empty and, just as in the movies, it would all have been a horrible dream.

One of the EMTs was conferring with the doctor while the other was asking what the victim had eaten recently. Poppy listed the menu.

"We all ate from the same buffet, though, and served ourselves. It's been cleared away, but everything was in a large bowl or basket or on a platter."

The Payard chocolates and pastries were still in mouthwatering view.

"What about these?" He picked up a plate.

"Faith hadn't eaten any dessert yet. She was opening her presents," Poppy said.

"And they're from *Payard*," she added, popping a truffle in her mouth to settle the subject.

Dr. Ginsburg came out to speak to Jane Sibley. "My best guess is food poisoning of some sort, but quite puzzling as you all ingested the same substances. She wasn't on any medication, was she? The punch was alcoholic, so there could have been an interaction there."

Hope answered the question. "My sister is as healthy as a horse. All she takes is a multivitamin in the morning."

"Nothing for anxiety, depression?"

"She's getting married! This was a bridal shower. Of course not!" Hope exclaimed.

One of the EMTs—he was wearing a wedding band—looked slightly amused at Hope's declaration. "No jitters? It's been known to happen."

Hope didn't answer him.

In the end, Faith was moved to one of the Morrises' guest rooms, her mother by her side and Dr. Ginsburg on call should the symptoms worsen rather than abate as they were doing now. Emma had given the guests the favors Poppy had bought—pear-shaped kitchen timers nestled in small wooden boxes with clear covers that said THE PERFECT PAIR on the front—and sent everyone politely away, as only she could.

Faith woke up at eight o'clock, startled to find herself in an unfamiliar bed with her mother at her side reading the latest issue of *Architectural Digest*. It was dark out. The events of the afternoon came flooding back and she sat up abruptly. Too abruptly. She sank back onto Poppy's eiderdown European squares.

"How are you feeling?" Jane took her daughter's hand. Tom's engagement ring, a simple diamond solitaire from Tiffany they'd

picked out along with their wedding bands on another of his flying visits, sparkled even in the dim light from the bedside lamp.

"Better. What on earth do you suppose was wrong with me?
I've never been sick like that before."

Her mother shook her head. "Poppy had the cook write down
everything that went into the food and punch, no matter how
small the amount, and showed it to Dr. Ginsburg. No exotic ingredients of any kind. The doctor said she'd come by to check on
you when you woke up."

"I don't think she needs to do that. I just want to go home."

"You can, if you're sure you feel up to leaving here, but you're
staying at your home on this side of the city."

Faith felt like a child again, and it felt lovely.

Later that night, tucked into her own bed in her childhood
room, which had been transformed from Laura Ashley posies
growing up to a more sophisticated Brunschwig & Fils stripe in
her teens, Faith could once more scarcely keep her eyes open.
All her childhood favorites were still in the bookcase and she'd
selected Louisa May Alcott's *Rose in Bloom,* recalling that through
her title character Alcott had a lot to say about love and marriage.
She gave up after rereading the first page three times and let herself
fall asleep. Her mother had been in several times to "make sure
you don't need anything, dear," but Faith wasn't fooled by the excuse and felt very safe indeed.

Which was a good thing, because the words she couldn't get
out of her mind were the ones her great-aunt had uttered, "The
bride's been poisoned!"

Tammy Wayfort was sitting in her boudoir at her dressing table,
gazing at herself in a large ornate mirror. Her "boudoir"—she
loved the way the word sounded, stretching out the first syllable

and inflecting it with more than a hint of her Southern upbringing in the Delta.

With the abrupt end to darlin' Faith's shower—and really, didn't her sister-in-law know she didn't mean "poisoned" like from arsenic, but from some food that went down wrong!—Tammy had decided to come back to the house on Long Island rather than stay at the Carlyle as she often did when she was in the city. This house, The Cliff, located on the North Shore's Gold Coast, had been built by Sky's grandfather on a bluff overlooking the sea. The mansion had its own private beach, tennis courts, pool, stables, croquet green, and acres of landscaped gardens. The house was one of the reasons she'd married Sky, and as soon as they returned from their honeymoon in France, she'd claimed this bedroom as her own retreat and started dialing decorators. The result was a place where Madame de Pompadour would have been at home, especially as much of the furniture was authentic Louis XV, or so the antiques dealers had sworn. Swathed in ruby-hued Scalamandré silks, the boudoir could easily have found a home as a period room in any museum. Tammy's closets were another matter— twentieth century, from the fitted rows for her designer shoes to the custom racks for her couture clothes.

Her bath was a sybaritic mix of old, as in the Baths of Caracalla, and new, as in a shower with built-in tanning panels. A door opened at the other end into Sky's equally opulent suite, Prussian blue dominating the walls and draperies, baroque rather than rococo. Tammy smiled to herself thinking of the chilled bottle of Möet in her marble sunken tub's Swarovski crystal champagne holder, which awaited her husband's arrival along with the Rigaud Cypres votive candles—the same kind Jacqueline Bouvier Kennedy had taken with her to the White House. Tammy loved all these manufacturers' names, although calling them manufacturers sounded like they were churning out tires or something. When she looked at her possessions, she liked to say to herself, "There's one of my Judith Lieber minaudières," although she limited it to "one of my Judith Liebers" when she said it out loud, not altogether sure of her French or whatever language "minaudière" was.

It was quite dark out now. Time to put on her face.

She pulled her dressing gown's marabou trim down, exposing the cleavage that had irresistibly drawn Sky's eye years ago at a formal dinner each was attending in Louisville during the derby. It still drew his eye, but she gave the neckline an extra tug. It never hurt to direct a man's attention to what you wanted him to see—and away from what you didn't.

The deep amethyst gown was long and she had similar ones, some even more be-feathered, in every color of the rainbow, with satin mules to match. She lined her lips carefully and reached for more mascara, waterproof mascara. With plenty of bubbles and the soft candlelight, it was possible to slip into the bath without revealing the depredations of age. Not that she was old.

A soft knock and the door to the hall opened. She turned, expecting to see her husband. Her cosmetic smile turned into a single red slash. It was Mrs. Danforth, the housekeeper, who had been with Sky since Hector was a pup. The one immutable presence in her husband's life was walking purposefully into the room. Tammy had made a joke about whether the housekeeper would be coming with them on the honeymoon and another about the nuptial bed not being for three before she learned to keep her mouth shut on the topic. Sky's devotion to Mrs. Danforth, and vice versa, was not a laughing matter.

"Master Schuyler called to say he has been detained and will arrive within the hour."

Tammy knew for a fact that the woman had been born and raised in Hoboken, New Jersey, but to hear Danny, as Sky called her—and only he was allowed—you'd have thought the Danforths had been in service to Queen Victoria herself. The new Mrs. Wayfort's initial attempts at friendship had been firmly rebuffed, and as she was wont to say, "You don't have to tell me twice." The two women didn't have a truce; they didn't have anything.

Tammy had grown up with plenty of help and had even more later on as an adult. She'd never encountered anyone like Mrs. Danforth. (And whatever had happened to Mr. Danforth? Or was the "Mrs." an assumed convention? Tammy had watched *Masterpiece Theater*. Once, or maybe twice.) There was no way the two women would ever sit over coffee or something stronger in the kitchen the way she had with housekeepers in the Delta, and laugh about the guests who'd come to dinner the night before or gossip about family members. Various Walfort kin trekked out to the house for yearly vacations. It was Sky's house. He'd inherited it from his father, but his sisters all thought of it as theirs, an attitude he encouraged. He was the youngest, and the only boy. Handsome now, and even more so as a young man, Sky had been the apple of his mother's and sisters' eyes. Tammy shook her head, watching in the mirror as her hair ever so slightly moved, one strand dropping seductively over one of her eyes. It was her turn now, had been since they'd tied the knot. Not that she didn't appreciate family. Family was what counted.

The Walforts, a corruption of the original Dutch "Walvoort," had arrived with Hudson on the *Half Moon* and had never strayed far from Nieuw Amsterdam except to move farther and farther uptown. Thrifty and entrepreneurial, always a good combination, one generation had provided for the next and then some. Not that Tammy hadn't brought her fair share to the marriage, her third. The first—Bobby Ray Benson—didn't really count, the result of a particularly pie-eyed weekend at Ole Miss visiting a cousin who was a Tri Delt. Daddy had had the whole thing annulled before Bobby Ray, or Tammy herself, had sobered up enough to decide whether tying the knot had been as good an idea as it had seemed at the time. Bobby Ray married one of the Hayes girls and

Tammy had been at the wedding, necking a little with her ex at the party the night before just to be friendly, for old times' sake.

Tammy's next husband had been a perfect choice. They'd been to dancing school together and he was her mother's sister-in-law's third cousin, close enough to know what you were getting, but not so close as to break the law. She truly loved Wade and she truly loved their life together. He ran the family business and ran it well. By the time of their tenth anniversary, they had a big house and staff in Louisiana plus a nice vacation house on the inland waterway in Florida. Wade did love his boats. The only fly in the ointment was the good Lord's decision not to bless them with children, but there were plenty of nieces and nephews to spoil. Tammy was a firm believer in the Almighty's mysterious ways, and she had not given up hope until Wade's heart gave out on the eighth hole at the country club. It had been hotter than blazes that day and Tammy had always blamed the weather, not Wade's girth. It was a wonder they didn't all die from the heat that August. After the funeral, Aunt Susie's tomato aspic melted into a pool of juice before she could get it into the house from her car.

Wade had been as good a provider in death as he had in life, maybe better, given the size of the life insurance policy, and she liked the independence it gave her. She took her time before settling down with Sky. He was a Yankee, after all, but it had worked out. He'd been married before, too. She would never have married a man who didn't have the habit.

Tammy had never been one to dwell on the past, except for the South's glory days. She and her siblings had all learned early that in case of fire, they were to grab the sword Great-great-grandfather had carried at the Battle of Baton Rouge and the drawer containing the silver flatware his wife had buried with her own sweet hands in the family cemetery to protect it from the Union troops.

Therefore, she was a little fuzzy about Sky's past exes. She knew he'd lost one, or maybe it was two, to disease and then there were two more to divorce, but he'd never had any children, which was probably sad at the time, but a good thing now. She had no desire to be a stepmother and an even greater loathing for the idea of grandparenthood.

She liked his nieces and nephews, in small doses, though. She especially liked Faith Sibley, who knew a Judith Lieber when she saw it and didn't have to ask where Tammy had gotten the cute little bejeweled bag, or worse, not comment at all. Funny that Faith should set up her own business, but girls seemed to do that nowadays. Even down home. Her sister had written that her daughter, Tammy's niece, was starting a business, Magnolia Managers, with her best friend. From what Tammy could deduce from her sister's description, the girls would do everything from organize your closets to find you a house with plenty of them. Well, this wasn't a bad way for a girl to kill time before someone put a ring on her finger, Tammy had told her sister, adding that she wondered if they would get enough business to cover gas for their cars, since all the Southern women Tammy knew had the managing part of life down pat.

She was thrilled to pieces that Faith was getting married at The Cliff. It would be like having a daughter without those terrible teen years. Besides, Tammy loved to throw a party.

The door opened again and a familiar voice said, "Is my baby doll ready for some sugar?"

Her mouth curved up. Her man was home.

One of the lawyers in Hope's firm was handling the sale of Have Faith's catering equipment. Faith had been fortunate to get a good offer from a company already established in Westchester that wanted to take a stab at the city. They would take over her lease and were not interested in her name, which she was holding on to for the future. She'd toyed with the idea of putting some of her pots, pans, and the like in storage, but she felt she had to leave almost everything behind—or nothing. And that decision had been made. After she signed some papers at the office, she and Hope were meeting Jane Lennox Sibley and Eleanor Wayfort Lennox—Mom and Nana—at the bridal salon at Bergdorf's. Its Art Deco décor was an elegant and unique backdrop for their equally elegant, unique gowns.

Now they were waiting for the lawyer to get back from lunch. The phone on Hope's desk buzzed and she quickly picked up the receiver.

"We'll be right there."

She got up from behind her desk. "Take your coat and we'll go straight from his office. It's a few floors down."

Hope didn't have a corner office—yet—but she had a great view of the East River and enough space for a couch, which often served as her bed, Faith knew. They passed Hope's secretary on the way out. She was a recent hire and looked like the "after" in one of those old movies when Miss Pendergast or whoever loosens her hair and takes off her glasses. The sisters were alone in the elevator.

"Nice-looking secretary, Hope. Good typist?"

"We say 'keyboard' now. As in computers. And yes, she's a whiz. Why?"

"No reason. Just, well, you have noticed that she's spectacularly good-looking."

"Not really," Hope said as the doors opened. "I guess she is. Her aunt went to Pelham."

That explained everything. An affiliation with Hope's alma mater would have gotten a crash-test dummy a job.

It didn't take long to sign the papers and they were soon walking across 57th Street on their way over to Fifth Avenue. Faith spied a hot-dog stand with the familiar blue and yellow Sabrett's umbrella.

"Want one? My treat."

"Sure."

The sisters shared an affection for New York street food—roasted chestnuts; warm, oversize pretzels; and especially these hot dogs, with everything on them.

"Do they have Sabrett's in Boston?" Faith asked.

Hope had been to the city on a number of business trips and had lived in Cambridge while getting her MBA.

"Nope. Fenway Franks, as in the home of the Red Sox, and they eat them with pickle relish, not sauerkraut and onions. Not on the street—in the stadium. I've never seen any food carts outdoors except for ice-cream trucks in the summer."

It was as Faith feared. She'd evidently have to watch a baseball game.

"Here, have a Tic Tac. Somehow I don't think the picture of the bride wolfing down a frankfurter before picking out her wedding gown is what Nana has in mind, and you know how good her sense of smell is."

Faith took two. The time, some years ago, when she and Hope had come in from the beach after a bonfire at The Cliff and their grandmother had smelled the beer on their breaths the moment they'd come through the door was still fresh in her mind.

The two older women were waiting on the seventh floor with Mrs. Lennox's longtime saleswoman, Irene, and another saleswoman from the bridal salon. Their perfumes mingled deliciously—Arpège, Shalimar, and Bergdorf Goodman Number Nine, the inspiration for the catchy, but less classy, hit song "Love Potion Number Nine."

"We've just been discussing a wrap," said her grandmother, who was wearing gloves and a hat, without which she would no more leave her apartment than streak nude down Park Avenue. "June at The Cliff is usually dry and warm, but not too warm. Yet it might be a good idea to have something made up that you could throw on if you get cold. Of course if the weather is really dreadful, pouring rain, the whole thing will have to be indoors. Good thing Sky had the ballroom repainted last year."

Faith dearly loved her grandmother—and her father's mother, too, who had died when Faith was only ten. And she adored Aunt Chat, and the list went on and on. But her favorite relative was Uncle Sky. And his house, the Wayfort family's house, was her favorite house in the world. She'd learned to swim, play tennis, and ride at The Cliff, although Sky hadn't kept horses for some years now. She'd always hoped to be married there, picturing her wedding ceremony in the front garden, the sea as a backdrop, the reception under a tent behind the house, with all sorts of good things to eat. She and her cousins had played endless games of dress up as children, raiding the trunks in the attic. Her mother had a picture of her daughter as a very young bride, in a small frame next to her bed. She was wearing a flapper ancestress's chemise with a frilly crinoline pulled low on her brow for a veil. Faith looked about the salon at the gowns. She was about to play dress up again. For keeps.

An hour later she thanked the wedding gods for granting her a grandmother, mother, and sister with not only good taste but taste she shared. Before she tried anything on, the group had quickly decided that the Lady Di dress designed by the Emanuels with its puffy sleeves and twenty-five-foot train was not for Faith. No train at all and a simple, short tulle veil.

"It can be windy in front of The Cliff," her grandmother reminded Faith. "We don't want you blown over the side, off to sea."

No billowing veil. No leg-o'-mutton sleeves, definitely no bustle, unaccountably a current bridal trend, and Faith further narrowed things down by saying she wanted a white dress. "Not ivory, ecru, or cream. White."

Hope laughed. "You don't have to prove anything to anyone, Fay. It's not as if you're preggers—you're not, are you?"

"Faith wants to be an old-fashioned bride, don't you, dear? And that's enough out of you, Hope." This last was said with a smile, but Hope got her mother's message, although when Jane wasn't looking Hope stuck her tongue out at her sister just for good measure.

Faith was having fun. Yet, fun as it was trying on all these gorgeous dresses, she didn't want to look further, but wanted to make a decision today. Not to get it over with, just to move on to the million and one other things she had to do, knowing one big item was crossed off. She sighed.

"Are you feeling all right, darling?" her mother asked anxiously. She'd wanted to postpone the outing despite Faith's assurance that Sunday's episode had not left any ill effects.

"Fine. Better than fine. It's just that picking out your wedding dress is a big decision."

"You could always wear my dress," her grandmother offered. "But you've seen it. Long sleeves, heavy satin, and ivory at that. We were married in December, just before your grandfather was called up. It does have lovely lace trim at the neck from *my* mother's dress, though."

"And mine," her mother said, "wasn't a dress at all. We got married in June, too, but I had the idea that I wanted to be different and wore a raw silk evening gown that wasn't really a bridal gown at all and no veil, just some flowers in my hair."

"Oh, you hippie," Faith teased her. "I'm surprised you didn't gather daisies from the meadow at The Cliff and get married barefoot."

Irene from Bergdorf's gently cleared her throat.

"If I might suggest?"

"Of course," Mrs. Lennox said. "You always have such good ideas."

"The third dress Miss Sibley tried on, the fitted one with the full skirt and the off-the-shoulder cap sleeves, fit beautifully and it would be possible to take the lace from Mrs. Lennox's dress and have it appliquéd on the bodice."

Hope clapped her hands. "Perfect! And that will take care of the something old and the something borrowed things all at once."

Faith had loved the dress, but it *had* seemed a bit plain. Irene's solution was perfect.

"Now all we have to do is find clothes for the rest of the wedding party," she said. "Tom's college roommate is going to be his best man, and since we met at his wedding, it's extremely appropriate, and Tom's brothers will be ushers, but I don't know what to do about bridesmaids. Hope, naturally, is my maid of honor . . ."

"Honored," said Hope, bowing slightly. She hadn't been in such a good mood since before her big client walked out on her.

Faith continued, "I don't know how or how many bridesmaids to choose." She was blessed with a large number of close female friends and relatives. And then there was the problem of Betsey. Shouldn't she be included? I mean, Faith hastily told herself, of course I want her to be included, and then just as hastily admitted that she didn't. Not Betsey and definitely not Sydney.

"Children," suggested her mother. "Like the British, and so sweet at an outdoor wedding. Your cousins have plenty from which to choose." She made it sound a bit as if they were having litters. "A few of them scattering rose petals will look charming."

"I love it," Faith said. She had a hunch that children would be much easier to handle than her future sister-in-law.

Hope had to dash back to work. Faith walked with her mother and grandmother to the nearby Plaza Hotel, where they were having tea in the Palm Court, but declined their offer to join them. She, too, needed to get back to work, and she also wanted to be by herself for a minute to think. There was a coffee shop she liked near the catering kitchen. It was the real kind, not a chain or something with a cute name and a menu of ever more bizarre flavors—she'd recently walked out of a place whose special of the day was a peanut butter–Marshmallow Fluff mocha. She just wanted to sit at the counter with a thick white mug of steaming black coffee that was fresh, since Demetrious, one of the brothers who owned the coffee shop, and also made a great BLT, tossed any coffee that had been sitting for more than fifteen minutes. A popular spot, the brew rarely made it past five.

A little time. That was all. A transition. From the Bergdorf's world to her Amsterdam Avenue workplace reality. She wasn't having second thoughts about the dress. It would be beautiful with her great-grandmother's lace. And Nana thought she might have another piece tucked away, enough to make a Juliet cap for Faith's veil.

No, it wasn't the dress. Everything was going smoothly so far in the bridal department, unless you counted the shower. Was that what was nagging at her? The whole thing was so inexplicable. She didn't have food allergies. And no one else had gotten sick. With her customary thoroughness, Hope had called all the guests to be sure.

Betsey and Sydney were driving back to Massachusetts the next morning, so Faith had called Tom on Sunday night to tell him how great the shower had been, how great it was meeting his sister and his friend (and she did not say a word about the he turning out to be a she), and just before hanging up she briefly mentioned her "upset stomach." His sister would be sure to tell him, and Faith wanted her version to be the first. He was concerned, but not alarmed. Lord knows what Betsey would say.

At the coffee shop she was greeted warmly and had a mug of coffee in her hand as soon as she sat down. She looked at the stack of blue-and-white paper cups next to the coffeepots. They were decorated with Greek keys and amphorae. WE ARE HAPPY TO SERVE

YOU was emblazoned on the side. One more disappearing New York City icon; she was always relieved to see them displayed anyplace. Demetrious *was* Greek—or his parents were—and it was to appeal to the many Greek coffee shop owners that the "Anthora," as the paper cup was dubbed, was produced in the 1960s.

"Something to eat?" Demetrious asked. "A sandwich? Or I have some nice apple-cinnamon muffins. I can put one on the grill."

Faith was tempted, but she had to watch herself or the dress wouldn't fit in June. Demetrious made his own muffins and slathered them with plenty of fresh butter before toasting, so the halves turned golden brown. That's what made them so devastating, and so good.

The restaurant was filled with people enjoying a late-afternoon snack before going back out into the cold. Faith returned to her thoughts. Not second thoughts, no. She wanted to marry Tom Fairchild. Maybe it was just that she wanted to *be* married to him, not marry him. She wanted to have taken the leap, not have this long running start to the jump. She'd attended, been in, and catered more weddings than she could count and had never realized how many decisions a bride had to make, how much she had to consider. But elopement was out of the question. And not just because you didn't get as many gifts. No, she wanted to stand in front of her family and friends, saying, "I do," as a public statement of her commitment to Tom forever and ever.

Hope had been pushing her to do a prenup, but not pushing hard. She knew her sister. Faith had told her, with a smile, that it was out of the question. What she was about to embark on was for keeps, not about keeping.

The place was filling up, but there were still spaces at the counter. She wanted to sit a little longer, reveling in the luxury of being in a spot where she didn't have to talk, listen, or do. Her back was to the tables, and hearing chairs moving across the floor, she was aware that people had sat down at the empty table just behind her. There was a swirl of conversation. She heard a man ask for coffee, then as she began to tune back into her own thoughts, she realized that the other voice was Francesca's. She swiveled partway on the stool to greet her. Francesca's back was toward Faith, but there was no mistaking her glossy dark hair and the fawn-colored Searle shearling coat that she said she had found in a thrift store, brand-new, still with the tags. As Faith was about to reach out to tap her on the shoulder, she heard Francesca's words more clearly, as well as her tone of voice. Have Faith's newest employee was angry, extremely angry.

"You know what I'm paying you for! Here's half the money, and you'll get the rest when I get what I want. *Presto!*" she said.

Faith quickly turned away and motioned to Demetrious.

"You changed your mind about the muffin," he said. "I knew you would. Good for a cold day like today."

She nodded. There was no way she could leave the shop without going past Francesca, and she couldn't sit at the counter drinking more coffee. She'd already had two cups. Whatever was going on, and whoever the man was, one thing was clear. It wasn't a meeting Faith felt comfortable barging in on. She stole another look at the couple. Francesca was leaning across the table, saying something more. Faith could only overhear a few of the words—"no one," "know," and then a longer string, "back here Monday."

The man was older than Francesca. Midthirties, maybe a bit more. He looked like a fellow countryman, dark hair and eyes. He was wearing a heavy black wool overcoat. He hadn't unbuttoned it yet or taken off the muffler wound around his neck. The waitress put down two cups of coffee in front of them and the man started to order something else, reaching to remove his scarf.

"You have time to eat?" Francesca asked sarcastically. She leaned back in her chair again and Faith could hear everything now.

The man mumbled something and reached out to take the check.

Francesca was already on her feet and moving toward the door. Faith hunched over the counter. The girl hadn't seen her and Faith wanted to keep it that way.

"*Ciao*. Don't forget what I said—or you know what will happen."

The man threw some money on the table and followed her.

Demetrious put Faith's muffin down in front of her. It would be a shame to waste it, she told herself, taking a bite. Heavenly. And the scene that had just unfolded had successfully driven all other thoughts from her mind except for one. What was Francesca Rossi up to and how was she, Faith, going to find out?

Faith let herself in, contemplating the time in the not too distant future when she wouldn't be coming to work, her work. She was surprised to see that Francesca was there, although she was supposed to be. Somehow the scene Faith had just witnessed in the coffee shop had placed the girl far away from ordinary routines.

March had come in like a lion and was staying like one, one with an extremely heavy pelt. It had been cold and rainy. No sign of any lambs. Come the end of the month, though, Josie would be gone for good. Josie's wouldn't open until the second week in May, and then on a limited schedule, but her time with Faith would be over. Josie had asked to meet to go over the jobs for April and May, still feeling responsible for what her absence might mean.

Francesca had the large booking file open.

"Josie will be here soon. She just called. I've been making a list of some dishes we can add to some of these menus. The dinner April sixth. *Asparagi* will be in season, yes? We can use it in risottos and tortas, but it is so good by itself. I like to make a little butter-and-egg-yolk sauce for it with ground walnuts and orange peel like they have in Venezia. It's a change from *limone*."

"Sounds delicious. And I want to make that Campari granita you mentioned. We can serve it as a dessert or between courses as a palate cleanser."

The girl was flushed, and as Faith took what she knew was a list prepared in advance, she felt the girl's hand. It was still cold. She hadn't been wearing gloves.

"Did you just get here?" Faith asked.

"Oh no, I've been here awhile going over the, how do you say it, possibilities?"

"Yes, 'possibilities.' That's exactly how we say it."

Francesca's English had flowed effortlessly in the restaurant, as well as other times, Faith recalled. Now she was suddenly searching for words? Josie was right. The girl was a mystery.

Josie rushed in. "Sorry I'm late, but I stopped to pick up the latest pictures. I want you to see the kitchen, and the main dining room is almost done, but first, did you get your dress? Tell all."

Faith described it, and the entire experience—omitting the scene in the coffee shop, however.

"No tacky bridal stuff here," Josie said. "My cousin's wedding last fall. All of us bridesmaids in apricot chiffon bustiers with turquoise satin ballerina skirts. Kind of a Howard Johnson thang. Do not want to even go there. I'm sure everything you Sibley ladies decide will be fine."

"I've seen Nana's wedding photo, and I'm so glad the saleswoman thought of using the lace. Hope saw some shoes at Bonwit's, Valentino, pale gold lace, that would match. I don't know, though. I'll be outside, so maybe something more practical."

The three discussed alternatives and Francesca suddenly blurted out, "My *nonna,* my grandmother, made her dress from parachute silk. She got it . . . from someone. The war, you know."

Faith nodded. "It must have been beautiful. American soldiers brought the parachutes home for their sweethearts or the brides in their families. The air force used a hundred percent silk, not nylon, in those days. Did your grandmother save it?"

"I don't know," Francesca said quickly. "Can we see your photos now, Josie?"

While they were exclaiming over the amazing changes Josie had accomplished in such a short time—the large front parlor, now the dining room, retained the charm of its origins without being a period piece. Josie had painted the walls soft lemon, like a lemon square, and hung summer-squash yellow valences over the windows to let in plenty of light and make the room feel larger. The kitchen was state of the art, yet she had kept her grandmother's wood cookstove, where each night she could set out her desserts within easy reach. Faith knew she was making all the appropriate noises, as was Francesca, but Faith's mind was back on what she had just overheard in the coffee shop, not whether Josie should use another yellow tone in the restroom or go for a different hue.

"When I get what I want," the girl had said just a little while ago. Which could mean any number of things. Francesca was on a student visa—she was attending classes part-time at the City University of New York—and the visa would run out at the end of August. Did she want to stay longer? Was she trying to get a green card under the table? What else could Francesca want? Faith looked up at the girl, who was perusing Josie's photos with an appearance of intense interest. Where were *her* thoughts?

Drugs. That had been the first unbidden idea Faith had had as she left the coffee shop. Francesca had never appeared to be using, but a functioning addict was sadly all too common. Or she could be selling them, the man her supplier? Faith was tempted to grab the girl's shoulder, look her in the eye, and demand the truth. Then again, she could return to the coffee shop at the same time on Monday, sit in the last booth, out of sight but able to see the door, and watch. "Back here Monday." She'd take the words at face value—and then what?

It didn't take long to go over the jobs. Francesca said good-bye and was off, seemingly her usual affectionate self—always a kiss on both cheeks and a friendly "*Ciao, bellas!*" to Faith and Josie.

"I'm off, too, but I don't want to go," Josie said.

"Aren't you meeting your friends from the New School? I thought you wanted to go."

"Tonight, yes, but I don't want to go to Virginia! I must have been nuts to think I could take on a restaurant pretty much by myself. And leave New York! I love it here and I love working with you."

Change a few words and this was the refrain Faith had been singing, too.

"Josie's is going to be a big success. You *love* Richmond. It's your home. If all this had happened last fall, I could have added that you could come back anytime, but . . ." She looked pointedly around the room, already envisioning someone else presiding over her domain. "But," she finished, "I'll be far away in the land of the bean and the cod."

Josie made a face. "Oh, Faith, what the hell are we doing?"

Tom had been down to the city several times. He'd met Faith's family and had been heartily approved. There was just a tad too much relief on her parents' faces, Faith noted—were they *so* anxious to marry her off, or was it concern about some of her earlier objects of affection? In any case, Tom Fairchild was the answer to a whole lot of Sibley prayers. She'd continued to show him the city, her city, taking him to the last remaining Automat at Third Avenue and 42nd Street, all the while explaining that it wasn't a "real" one, taking tokens instead of coins. But the dolphin-headed beverage dispensers were still evident, maybe not as brightly polished, and the macaroni and cheese was still her favorite version of the dish, ambience being everything. The same for the chicken pot pie. They went to a few shows, more museums, and walked and walked and walked. Weekends were out, Sunday requiring Tom's presence in the pulpit, and they'd been out for her as well with Have Faith's last hurrahs. Yet as March drew to a close, there was no postponing the inevitable. It was time for Faith to go north.

To Aleford.

CHAPTER 4

A woman noted for her calm, Marian Fairchild was a nervous wreck. It was an odd sensation. The crisis was not medical or financial. And really, it wasn't a crisis. How could meeting your future daughter-in-law be called a crisis? When said woman was arriving in a few hours for dinner and an overnight at your house and said woman was a professional chef and sophisticated New Yorker, that's how.

Tom had always been the most reliable of her children, the least likely to present her with any surprises. Craig, the youngest, was having a rocky start at college and Robert, the next in line, frankly puzzled her these days. Handsome, a good job, why didn't he seem happy? She was picking up a kind of sadness in him, a distancing that rang an alarm bell since he'd always been the one who was closest to his parents. And Betsey! A new mother, married to her longtime beau, why was she so angry all the time? Marian did have to admit that this wasn't a big change in her eldest. Betsey had emerged from the womb complaining vociferously and had never stopped.

But Tom. Even tempered, steady. When he'd come home from

Brown his junior year to tell them about his decision to enter the ministry, she had actually been a bit in awe of him. To be so sure about one's life—in awe, and perhaps a little jealous. It wasn't that Marian didn't like her life. She loved her husband as much as the day she had married him, more, and she'd never regretted skipping her senior year in college to do so. Nor did she regret moving to his people in Norwell, away from hers in Connecticut. And the children. Motherhood, like old age, was not for sissies, but she'd coped very well with it, starting with those dreadful bouts of morning sickness, through years of skinned knees and the occasional broken arm—the Fairchild kids lived outdoors even in the coldest weather—and on through the turbulent teens, although Tom and Robert had both been eyes in the storm. No regrets, but she did sometimes wonder about roads not taken.

Tom! When he'd called Monday morning after that weekend in New York City, she'd expected to hear details about his college roommate Phil's wedding, not details about the fantastic woman who had catered the event. And then less than a month later he announced he'd proposed to this Faith Sibley and she'd accepted! Marian had tried to explain her reaction—"It's so fast, and we don't know her" to Dick, who annoyed her by saying it was time Tom got married, otherwise his parishioners would be trying to pair him off with every eligible female in Aleford if they hadn't already started, and they'd get to know the girl plenty in the years to come. He reminded her that Tom had always known what he wanted and had gone for it, whether it be the state basketball finals or God.

Marian had been upset that she wasn't able to attend the shower, although Dick's brother's fiftieth birthday in a private room at the Union Oyster House had been lovely—especially since that was where Dick had proposed to *her* and the place where they went to celebrate anniversaries and their own birthdays. It was, in fact, the only place in Boston where Dick would eat, and at his brother's party he was able to enjoy the same dishes he ordered every time—Wellfleet oysters on the half shell, a bowl of clam chowder, broiled scrod with a baked potato, and Boston cream pie for dessert. There had been other selections possible at the party—scallops wrapped in bacon, Yankee pot roast, even lobster scampi—but Dick Fairchild knew what he liked and stuck with it. Marian had the scampi and it was a little too garlicky.

Returning on Monday, Betsey had called her mother, reporting first of all that the baby had weathered their separation well and then launching into a description of the house where the shower had been held ("A little over the top for my taste"), the gifts ("Not very practical. I got much better ones"), and finally Faith herself ("Pretty, I suppose, but very New York. Not an outfit we'd choose, very tight black skirt, hard to sit in, I'd have thought, and turquoise blouse, very sheer over a camisole, but that could have been her underwear"). Sydney had called as well and reported much the same, in less detail, but was sure Marian would like Miss Sibley. She'd said this last in a slightly doubtful tone and Marian hung up wondering whether the comment referred to Miss Sibley as a bride for Tom or Miss Sibley recovering from her mysterious illness at the gathering. Betsey had told her about it, but had no opinion as to the cause, tossing out a few hints, however—"heavy-drinking crowd," "binge dieting"—which served to propel Marian's imagination into overdrive.

And why did both Sydney and Betsey refer to the girl so often as "Miss Sibley" rather than Faith? Was she that intimidating?

Marian had been up since dawn, her usual time, but today had spent the hours preparing for the visit. That sounded rather like one from a royal—"the visit." No time for that second cup of coffee and a leisurely perusal of the Boston Globe. What would this girl—Tom's fiancée!—make of the Fairchilds' house? It was one of the oldest houses in Norwell, and the original clapboard dwelling had been added to and pushed up by successive generations, creating an architectural hodgepodge. The Fairchilds' décor was a hodgepodge, too, family pieces, some Ethan Allen—purchased when they'd gotten married—and the recent addition of a La-Z-Boy in the small den where Dick watched games on TV. The overstuffed armchair he adored had collapsed during the Super Bowl and he'd come home the following Saturday with what Marian was sure Faith would think was a decorating nightmare; it was what Marian herself thought. Perhaps she could throw something over it to disguise the Naugahyde; one of Great-great-grandmother's paisley shawls?

And the food. Marian was a good, plain cook. Better than that, according to her family. For tonight, though, she'd turned to Julia, a member of Marian's kitchen trinity that also included Irma and Fannie. Marian had made *The French Chef*'s boeuf bourguignon for dinner parties before, and she'd made it a day ahead to enhance the flavors. Served with egg noodles, it was the main course. March wasn't a good month for fresh vegetables, and she was sure her freezer friend the Jolly Green Giant wouldn't do tonight. Deciding to forego a green vegetable entirely, she'd made her butternut squash soup as a first course, supplemented with a loaf of French bread. The bread was from Stop & Shop, but Marian wasn't about to try her hand at the real thing, which took up twenty-one pages in *Mastering the Art of French Cooking*. If she didn't have bread, the men in her family would ask where it was, and that could be embarrassing, as in "Where is the bread, Mom? We *always* have bread at dinner." She'd have to remember to get some unsalted butter for the table, although from the sound of her, Miss Sibley didn't do fats. She probably didn't do carbs either. Dessert had been a challenge, and she'd gone with apple pie in the end. She knew she made a good crust—lard was the only way to get a truly flaky one—and she still had apples in the cellar. Cheese.

She made a note to add a big wedge of sharp cheddar to her list. Otherwise she'd hear, "Where's the cheese, Mom?" She should have done something like Julia's soufflé Grand Marnier, but one of the boys was bound to come stomping through the door at the critical moment, and in any case, the timing defeated her.

She looked at the clock. Barely an hour to shower and change. Tom had said they'd get here between four and five. She had called everyone, reminding them that dinner would be at seven o'clock sharp, but to come as early as possible for drinks. She eyed the decanter of sherry she had filled. It was a good dry sherry. Faith probably only drank martinis or Manhattans. Marian couldn't remember at the moment what Manhattans were. Rye? They might have a bottle, but what else went into the drink? Tom said he'd bring wine for dinner, so that was a relief. She'd picked up some Brie, not very imaginative, but she didn't think it was a WisPride with Triscuits occasion, Dick's cocktail hour favorites. She did get two kinds of Pepperidge Farm Goldfish for him to nibble on. She wanted him to be in the best possible mood, although he'd left the house this morning beaming at the thought of meeting his son's bride-to-be and Marian knew that unless Faith Sibley declared she was an ax murderess, Dick would engulf her in a bear hug and start the toasts. And even if she did wield an ax, he'd probably just get her to replenish the woodpile. His son was getting married and Dick Fairchild was tickled pink, his words.

Marian went down her mental checklist. There wasn't anything more she could do. The guest room was all set. Tom's room was always ready for him. And no, she hadn't been modern enough to put them together. Her son was a man of the cloth, after all, and this girl had better get used to keeping up appearances, although she should be, given her background. But she didn't sound like any preacher's kid Marian had known.

Tom was an early riser. Marian would be able to have some

time alone with him. He'd been so busy in Aleford, plus running down to New York, that they hadn't seen him for weeks. Faith would sleep in. They did that in New York, Marian had heard. Brunch, not breakfast. She hadn't felt comfortable asking him about Faith's illness at the shower. It was odd, though. Quite a mystery. Betsey had said Faith was the only one who got ill, although the food was "very rich." Surely it couldn't be . . . they had only met in January! Yes, a mystery.

Shower. A long, hot, steaming shower. That's what she needed.

Oh dear, she'd have to tell Robert and Craig not to shower in the morning. The hot water was sure to give out.

It had been a beautiful train ride and Faith had found herself looking out the window as Connecticut and then Rhode Island sped by, thinking that Tom had gazed at these very scenes on his way back after they'd first met. She was feeling very sappy. She supposed she should be feeling nervous, too. She was about to meet his entire family and there certainly seemed to be quite a number of them. She'd met Betsey, so that was over, and his parents had sounded lovely on the phone. Warm and welcoming. He'd described his brothers in detail—Robert, serious and "just one of the best people I've ever known"; Craig, the baby, funny, a born athlete (as all the Fairchilds seemed to be, Faith thought with a twinge of dismay), and a tad irresponsible. She was looking forward to her time in Norwell. What she wasn't looking forward to was Aleford. This was what had made her reluctant about coming north. She knew herself well. If Tom had been in any other profession, she'd have been on this train weeks ago. No, she knew that once she stepped into the parsonage, it would be all too real. She wasn't backing out; she just wasn't ready to back in.

Tom's description of the house, facing Aleford's green, had

been sketchy at best. Faith was prepared for extremely quaint and extremely uncomfortable. She'd be cold and the kitchen wouldn't have enough counter space.

The plan was to spend tonight in Norwell with his parents and then drive up to Aleford, which was west of Boston, tomorrow. She'd spend the night chastely with parishioners who lived next door—no need to shock the congregation so early in the game— and she'd take the train back to the city late Sunday afternoon.

Her stop was next. South Station. She'd been fortunate to get a spot in one of Amtrak's quiet cars, and the whole trip had been a bit like being in a cocoon. She got her suitcase and rolled it toward the door, looking out the window at the platform as the train slowed, shuddered, and came to a halt. The door opened, and before the conductor could help her off with her bag, Tom was there. They were in each other's arms. They were together again and Faith suddenly didn't care what color the linoleum was in the parsonage kitchen.

"Where's Scotty?" Marian asked her daughter. Betsey and her husband, Dennis, had been the last to arrive for dinner.

"Where's Sydney?" Betsey said. "She's never late."

"It's just family tonight, dear," Marian said.

"Sydney *is* family, or should be." Betsey lowered her voice slightly at the end of the sentence, but not by much.

Her mother ignored her and repeated her question.

"I got a sitter. We had to wait for her. That's what held us up."

"Oh, I'm sorry," Faith said. "I was looking forward to meeting Scotty."

Betsey raised her eyebrows. "Really? I didn't get the impression at the shower that you liked children much."

Faith was determined to avoid the trap. She had no idea what remark she, or someone else, might have made that Betsey could blow up to an aversion to offspring, but she knew what was going on now.

"My sister isn't married yet, but our older cousins have provided us with plenty of little ones to cuddle, including my godchild, Diana, who is going to be in the wedding."

Before Betsey had brought her breath of cold air, they'd been discussing wedding plans. Marian Fairchild was in a happy daze not attributable to the second glass of sherry she'd imbibed. *Of course* Tom had fallen in love with Faith. She was in love with her herself and had been almost from the moment Faith arrived. The first thing she'd said when Marian was showing her the guest room was, "Now let's get the 'what shall I call you' thing out of the way. 'Mrs. Fairchild' is fine for now and we can move to 'Marian' perhaps at a later date. I already have a mother, so would prefer not to call you anything that involves that. Besides, 'Mother Fairchild' sounds like one of those Lydia Pinkham patent medicines— 'Mother Fairchild's Improving Tonic.' "

Since Faith had already remarked on the delicious smells coming from the kitchen—"Could it be boeuf bourguignon?"—the house's décor—"I love this sideboard. Is it Shaker?"—and the house itself—"You have to tell me all about it. Which part was added when"—it took Marian only a few seconds to declare that they should move straight to first names and she was sure her husband would feel the same way.

"We'll see Scotty tomorrow, sis," Tom said. "You're coming by in the morning before we leave, right? Mom's making pumpkin pancakes. Now, what can I get you? Sherry—or maybe Dad will break out some of his Chivas for you. Dennis, there's a Sam Adams in the fridge with your name on it."

"So your godchild is going to be the flower girl?" Betsey tended to stick like Krazy Glue once she'd introduced a topic.

"Not as such. We were just talking about this. Four of my cousins' children will be my attendants, strewing rose petals, or we hope they will. I was at a wedding last summer where the kids got carried away and pelted people with them."

"No adults in the wedding party?"

Tom shoved a tumbler of scotch and soda into his sister's hand and threw an arm around her.

I am definitely marrying the right guy, Faith thought, watching him with Betsey. He was smoothing feathers that Faith had the feeling were perennially ruffled, feathers he'd smoothed before. Betsey's husband had made a beeline for the fridge and was off in a corner talking about the Celtics with Robert, who worked for a sports equipment manufacturer.

Faith was tempted to answer Betsey by saying that she and Tom were definitely adults, but that would be too self-indulgent. Betsey was a very easy target. Faith counted herself lucky. She'd known she'd like the rest of Tom's family and she was right. So one thorn in the side wasn't too bad. And it was a thorn she'd known would be there after meeting her sister-in-law at Poppy's. Faith was an expert at snap judgments.

She'd selected her wardrobe for much of the weekend with Betsey's and Sydney's outfits at the shower in mind, not that she was about to appear as their clone, but she'd ditched black pants and skirts, her wardrobe staples. Tonight she was wearing a soft blue wool Calvin Klein dress with a full skirt and a cowl neck. She'd pinned the cameo on and was glad she had. Not only Marian but Dick noticed—"Wish you could have met my mother. She'd be so pleased the cameo has a new home. Tom was the first grandchild and they were very close."

Faith took a slight breath and answered Betsey, "No adults as in bridesmaids and groomsmen. Hope will be my maid of honor, and I think Tom has told you that Phil will be his best man with his brothers and brother-in-law as ushers."

"I'd have thought you wouldn't have a problem finding brides-maids. There were so many women at your shower." Betsey wasn't giving up.

Faith did start to bristle at this; it was getting to be a bit much.

"That was exactly the problem. I have so many good friends and female relatives that I didn't want to choose."

So there.

"Dinner is served. *Bon appétit!*" Marian called gaily. It was apparent that she for one was having a ball.

Aleford, Massachusetts, looked exactly the way Faith had pictured it. Or rather the way it had been pictured in countless books and on calendars. Kodacolor blue sky, white puffy clouds, historic buildings, but since it was still March, any daffodils or other flora foolhardy enough to emerge had been flattened by the most recent nor'easter. It was New England with a vengeance.

The day had already been a full one and it was barely two o'clock. Marian's pumpkin pancakes with maple syrup from a nearby friend's trees were so good that Faith ate three. She was adding them to her list of recipes for brunch, maybe putting pecans in the batter with a few sprinkled on top.

Like dinner the night before, breakfast with the Fairchilds consisted of much talk and much laughter. The brothers, in particular, kept things going, teasing one another and their parents. Betsey did bring Scotty over and the baby was adorable. Faith had hoped to see a softer side of Scotty's mom, but the baby produced even more rigidity in the woman as she described his schedule and the long list of "don'ts" in his future. No TV, no electronic-type games, no junk food, no fast food, limited play dates, assigned chores, etc. Faith had brought a selection of board books and a plastic one that could go in the tub as gifts. Scotty seemed quite contented, but his mother explained that he needed to learn to be careful, so they had gone straight to picture books and if a page got torn, the book was taken away. Her brothers hooted at this, Tom included, and she blushed, but defended herself by saying they would all see how well Scotty turned out.

"I think he's pretty great just the way he is," Tom said, tossing the delighted infant in the air. Faith felt herself getting sappy again. Tom was going to be a great dad.

"So, Bets, would Mom's pancakes fall into the category of 'junk food'—all this sugar—or what?" Craig said. "And what happens when he gets old enough to find out about your Mallomar habit?"

Marian had told them to stop bothering their sister and pushed them out the door for a game of touch football. Faith had declined. She hadn't brought any play clothes. "Next time we'll get you," Craig said, and she'd been afraid he was right.

After helping Marian clean up and making sure she hadn't left anything in the guest room, Faith had gone outside to watch them, feeling slightly as if she was watching those old movies of the Kennedys at Hyannisport. They even *sounded* like the Kennedys.

Sydney Jerome had come out of the house next door and was roped into the game. She was beautiful to watch. A graceful athlete. But, Faith told herself, if he'd wanted her, he could have had her. Or had he? She narrowed her eyes and tried to read Tom's expression as he threw a pass to Sydney. No, no indication of passion, as in lust. Just passion as in winning the game.

Uncle Will, Dick's oldest brother, arrived. The Fairchild's Market brother. News of Faith's visit had spread among the clan and she had met Fairchild's Ford and his wife the night before when they'd arrived for dessert.

He joined the group at the sidelines and, after greeting them, addressed Faith alone: "So you're the bride! Quite the little drinker, I hear. We should get along fine, missy! Although I guess I can hold my liquor better!"

Faith had seen a sporting event go into freeze frame only on television, but she swore later when she told Hope about it that the Fairchild family touch football game did exactly that. And then collapsed back into motion as Faith said, "I'm sure you can, as I start dancing on tabletops after two glasses of champagne. I'm afraid someone's given you a mistaken idea as to my capacity."

Faith saw Marian spin around to say something to Betsey, who had been behind her watching the game while holding Scotty, but her daughter had vanished.

Uncle Will had looked puzzled at the lack of response to his joke, so had started laughing himself, which got everybody going and the moment passed. For some of them.

On the way to Aleford, Tom had given Faith a quick tour of Norwell. It had been very sweet. Seeing where he went to school and worked summer jobs, and hearing about the town's history— it had been a major shipbuilding center during the eighteenth and early nineteenth centuries. Tom felt about Norwell, and the surrounding South Shore area, the way she felt about Manhattan. At least they both liked water, she told herself.

They'd stopped the car at the church, another First Parish, and walked across to the cemetery, where John Cheever, a favorite author for both of them, was buried.

"When he received the National Medal for Literature, he said in his acceptance speech, 'A page of good prose remains invincible.' I've always remembered that. It applies to sermons, maybe even more," Tom said.

Faith gave his hand a squeeze.

They'd driven up to Aleford after that. The parsonage was everything Faith had imagined—and more. Its previous tenant had been a longtime widower and apparently subsisted on food from the casserole brigade, those handmaidens of the Lord whose offerings took the form of tuna noodles in Pyrex. And Tom confessed that he generally grabbed a bite at the Minuteman Café, or heated up some soup. He'd never turned the oven on. The *batterie de cuisine* consisted of several dented aluminum saucepans, a small cast-iron frying pan, and a turkey roaster big enough for the entire Plantation at Plimoth. The stove was electric and the limited counter space was covered in the kind of 1950s Formica with squiggles that was unaccountably becoming fashionable again.

The rest of the house had possibilities, but the walls hadn't been painted since some war, perhaps Civil, and had dulled to musty beige. The windows were covered with heavy lined muslin drapes that obscured the light. The ceilings were low, typical of the period. But the dining room had beautiful wainscoting that Faith knew she could bring back to life, as well as a large harvest table, chairs, and sideboard that were original to the house, Tom told her.

Upstairs, the master bedroom ran the length of the house, with windows overlooking the front yard. There were two other good-size bedrooms and a small one that, judging from the animal alphabet frieze on the walls, must at one time have been a nursery. A half bath downstairs and the two upstairs needed attention, but nothing major. There was a large linen closet and an attic with drop-down stairs that Faith decided to leave for another time. You never knew what might turn up in these New England attics. It could be old chests of drawers with boxes of "string too short to be saved" or it could be something darker . . .

It was a daunting experience going from room to room and imagining living there, but they were sipping champagne, which helped enormously. There had been a bottle of Korbel on the kitchen table, cooling in a bucket that looked as if it was normally used in the garden. It was the first thing they had seen when they came in through the back door—apparently no one in New England ever used the front; in Norwell the Fairchilds' was blocked by lilacs in the summer and snow the rest of the year. There was a note of welcome and congratulations with the bubbly from the Millers, the next-door parishioners.

"You're going to love Sam and Pix," Tom said. "And they have three kids: Mark, Samantha, and Danny. Mark's in ninth grade and they go down in age from there. Their back door is always open, and you're to go over whenever you're ready to go to sleep tonight."

"I don't think I've ever met anyone named Pix," Faith said, wondering if it was some kind of old New England familial shorthand the way girls were called "sister" in the South. As for the sleeping next door, she had no problem with that. No need to start tongues wagging.

"It's a nickname, and I know her real one, but I can't remember it. Some kind of plant. Ivy? Anyway, no one calls her anything but Pix. We're having breakfast there and then they'll walk over to church with you. I have to leave a little earlier." He said this last with a slightly apologetic air.

"Trust me, I'm used to the routine. The whole 'no clean collars, last-minute checks for egg in the corner of your mouth, same color socks on both feet' thing. It all takes time."

She had been examining the closet in the big bedroom. Possibly it could hold one season's clothes. Tom put his arms around her and said, "Did I mention that I bought a new mattress for the bed?"

"I believe you did. And I believe you mentioned that the bed itself came from your parents?"

"To be more precise, a cousin of Dad's, and can you imagine, she was going to get rid of this perfectly good one when she got a new one from Paine's instead of putting it in her attic or basement, where it could get some use someday? Someday possibly in the next century. Dad almost had a fit."

"But here it is still in the twentieth and it's a very nice bed. Looks quite comfy."

"Only one way to find out."

Neither Tom nor Faith felt like going out to dinner. Tom had made a fire in the fireplace, which drew nicely. He was quite the Boy Scout, Faith realized, and was handy as well. It would be useful having a husband who could not only hang a picture but also apparently put up drywall, do wiring, and lay shingles. Her skills in these departments were limited to knowing which numbers to dial.

"I'll make dinner," she said. "You must have *some* food in the fridge and the pantry."

Tom looked doubtful. "Well . . ."

"Come on, let's go look. You'd be surprised what I can make out of nothing."

"No, I wouldn't be surprised at all. Anyway, there's always Country Pizza. Harry makes a great one with everything but the kitchen sink on it."

"I'm sure it's yummy," Faith said in a voice that indicated the opposite. She was as snobbish about her pizza as she was about other food and had still not gotten over her shock at being served a slice with pineapple and ham on it at a friend's apartment. She believed in fusion cuisine, but Italo-Hawaiian was some kind of oxymoron.

Tom's larder was almost as bare as Old Mother Hubbard's.

Faith stood with the refrigerator door open and took a head of cauliflower from the vegetable bin.

"What were you going to make from this?"

"I can't remember, but it seemed like a good idea at the time. I decided I needed more veggies. That's why there are all these bell peppers, too."

He had a large wedge of what he called "rat cheese" and there was a gallon of whole milk on the shelf, only partly drunk. Faith realized that Tom was what her aunt Chat referred to as a "big, hungry boy." The kind who went through gallons of milk regularly. Faith got her calcium from yogurt and made a mental note to add milk to every future shopping list. She looked in the pantry and found a box of elbow macaroni that hadn't been opened.

"We'll have mac and cheese with the cauliflower and the red bell peppers in the sauce. I've done it lots of times and it's delicious, very creamy. It might lack a little oomph, since the only spices I see are your salt and pepper shakers, but I'll use plenty of cheese so it will get brown and crunchy on top." (See recipe, page 239.)

After eating, they dozed off in each other's arms in front of the fire—the result of the food, drink, warmth from the hearth, and—for Tom anyway—mild fatigue from the earlier vigorous game of football.

"Oh no." Faith jumped up much later. "It's almost one o'clock! Whatever will the Millers think?"

"Not to worry. Pix said anytime. They're very easy people."

Faith was grabbing her coat and the small bag she'd packed in her suitcase with her overnight things. She'd come back to change for church in the morning. She couldn't take everything over now.

Not the impression she'd hoped to make. They'd be asleep, and she hoped soundly. She recalled with dismay that Sam was on the vestry.

She gave Tom a quick kiss. "See you in the morning, darling."

"Here, take this. I'll show you where you can get through the hedge to their backyard." He handed her a flashlight and took one from a number on the shelf in the hall closet for himself. She had a fleeting thought about the possible reasons for so many flash-lights—power failures?—and followed him out. The night air was freezing, and when he held back the Canadian hemlock branches, she sprinted to the Millers' kitchen door. It was unlocked and she crept in quietly.

The barking began the moment she took a step inside and she was pinned against the door frame by a large animal that she judged was friendly since it was trying to lick her face. Faith froze. The noise was deafening. Besides the Millers, she was sure all Aleford could hear it. Except this time it wasn't the British who were coming, just one lone New Yorker.

An overhead light snapped on and a tall woman wearing a man's flannel bathrobe strode into the room.

"Dogs! Be quiet! Down, Dusty! Stop it right now! I'm so sorry!"

The barks became whimpers then ceased. The light had revealed three large golden retrievers.

Faith put out her hand. "I'm Faith Sibley." She was sure this was *not* a situation Miss Manners covered.

Her hostess shook it heartily. "Of course you are, dear, and I'm Pix. Pix Miller. These bad children are Dusty, Arthur, and Henry—Miller, of course. My other children and my husband are sound asleep upstairs. It takes more than the dogs barking to wake them. I was afraid Tom, whom we all adore—we're so lucky to have him here—might not have gotten the hint. Go back to the parsonage. Everyone knows you're staying here, so you don't need to, and just in case, I left the light on in the guest room until eleven and the shade is down." The words came tumbling out matter-of-factly.

Faith didn't know what to say or do.

"Go on now," Pix said. "A nice surprise for your fiancé. Breakfast is at eight, but come over earlier if you want."

One of the dogs—Arthur?—was nuzzling Faith's knee. She picked up the case she'd dropped and prepared to retrace her steps.

"Everyone is delighted that Tom is getting married. Well, possibly one or two mothers harbored hopes for their daughters, but nothing serious. We're going to be friends, as well as neighbors. I can always tell with people."

"Me, too," Faith said.

It was a pancake weekend. Pix had made blueberry ones with berries she'd picked in Maine and frozen last summer.

"These are the last," she told Faith as they sat over more coffee after Tom left. "We have a cottage on Sanpere Island, in Penobscot Bay. It's wonderful there. You'll have to come."

Faith did not wish to mention that her idea of an island vacation was Aruba. Pix Miller had indeed in a very short time become a dear friend, a bit like one of her beloved dogs in human form—affectionate, loyal, and obviously intelligent. You had only to look into their eyes.

Faith liked the rest of the family, too, and appreciated the way they all carried on in what was obviously their normal Sunday-morning fashion, complaints about someone hogging the sports section; a plea from Samantha, the tween daughter, for help in locating the scrunchie she just *had* to wear; and mild bickering over whose turn it was to clear the table. And since it was April 1, there were a series of benign tricks, besides greeting each family member as they came into the kitchen with "Rabbit, Rabbit." Tom explained that this did not mean the Miller family was any more eccentric than any other New England family—which Faith was beginning to think might be more than a bit—but saying "Rabbit, Rabbit" on the first day of the month meant you and the recipient of your greeting would have good luck for the duration. A conversation ensued as to the origin of the custom, which no one knew. They had just done it. Always.

"And," Sam added, "if you forget, you can say it to yourself backward before you go to sleep, 'Tibbar, Tibbar.'"

This was greeted with some skepticism on his children's part, but Pix said it was true. Her mother had told her the same thing. That seemed to settle everything.

An hour later Faith was sitting between Pix and Sam, waiting for the service to begin. Faith had never been inside one of these picturesque white-steepled eighteenth-century churches, but the interior of First Parish was as she had imagined. Its simplicity was beautiful, not austere, and the strong morning light flooded the sanctuary through the tall windows. The altar was graced with spring flowers. She turned to look behind her. The pews were filling up and she felt pleased on Tom's account.

Sam Miller turned, too. "Tom draws people from many of the surrounding communities, but I think we may have a few more worshippers today because of you," he said.

Pix nodded. "Millicent is here and she's not even a member of the church. You'll meet her at coffee hour. Millicent Revere McKinley, keeper of the Revere family flame, and the person who knows everything that's going on in Aleford even before it happens."

Faith moved slightly, trying to find a comfortable spot on what were rather thinly padded pew cushions. Nice crimson damask, though. Coffee hour! She had forgotten about that ritual.

And soon she forgot about everything except listening to the Reverend Thomas Preston Fairchild.

Aptly the Psalm for the day was seventy-eight, the one about the Lord furnishing a table in the wilderness, and Tom took the notion of providing for a hungry people in body and soul as his sermon topic. This was a Tom she had never heard or seen before, the pastor challenging his flock to praise God not only with their lips but with their lives, dedicating their actions to Him in whose service lay perfect freedom. By the time they came to the last hymn, "The Voice of God Is Calling," Faith was filled with pride—and a little bit of trepidation.

Coffee hour brought her down to earth as she walked into the room filled with that familiar smell of the fresh brew mixed with the floor polish that seemed to be used in every parish hall she'd ever been in. Someone must have cornered the market shortly after Moses descended from the Mount.

"Faith, I'd like you meet Cindy Shephard. She's one of our most active youth group members."

The girl was standing slightly too close to Tom, and Faith had the feeling that the youth group was not the only place where Cindy was active. She was dressed appropriately for church, but managed to convey an air of sexuality that definitely wasn't.

"I'm looking forward to getting to know everyone in the group," Faith said.

Cindy answered, still with her gaze on Tom, "Great. We'll have to have a party. Celebrate the wedding." Her tone was nonchalant bordering on indifferent.

"Cindy's a great little organizer," Tom said.

I'll bet she is, Faith thought.

A small, energetic-looking woman with Mamie Eisenhower bangs—when you've found your style stick to it—came bustling over.

"I'm Millicent Revere McKinley. Run along, Cindy, I want to have a word with Miss Sibley."

Faith was impressed. The woman knew her name. Although she shouldn't be surprised. If Pix was correct, Millicent probably knew Tom was going to propose before he did.

"Once you're settled, I'll give you a tour of the town. You're so fortunate. This is a very historic place, as you know. But most people's knowledge stops after the battle on the green."

It was clear she was putting Faith in this group.

"I'll be able to acquaint you with what happened afterward, right up to the present," she said.

"That sounds wonderful. Thank you so much. I'm looking forward to learning all I can about Aleford."

Pix came over.

"I hate to drag you away, but I know you have a train to catch and you need to pick up your things from the house."

Millicent nodded approvingly and Faith almost burst out laughing at the twinkle in Pix's eye.

"Sam is getting Tom."

They got their coats and walked through the burial ground that separated the parsonage from the church. On a sunny day like this, it was a cheerful place unless one stopped to read the epitaphs on the headstones—the "Remember me as you pass by / As you are now so once was I / As I am now so you must be / Prepare for death and follow me" kind with the angel-winged skulls and weeping willows to match.

All too soon Faith was on the train, looking out the window and seeing only one figure in her mind. And only this man, this dear man, could make her move to Millicent Revere McKinley's bailiwick.

It wasn't going to be easy.

At her apartment the red light on the answering machine was blinking and Faith ran to check her messages without bothering to take off her coat. It wouldn't be Tom, because she was supposed to call him as soon as she got home, but maybe he'd called anyway. She wanted to hear his voice.

The first message from her uncle Sky. She smiled as she listened. Part of what would make getting married at The Cliff so special was the chance to spend time with him, and this was why he was calling.

"Hate these things. Call me back. Need to get you out here to do some planning. Cut down any trees you don't like. See if any of the rocks on the beach need to be rearranged. Bring your mother, but not my bossy sister. She'll take over. Oh, I know what you're thinking, not your sweet nana. Iron hand in the velvet glove, Faith." There was a pause. Faith imagined him in the library, probably with some sort of libation close at hand. "Call me. Good-bye, my dear. Such a lark. The wedding and all."

She *did* need to get out to Long Island, and perhaps her mother could get away next week. They should really spend the night and do the tasting. It was odd to be in the position of hiring a caterer rather than being the caterer.

The next message was from Hope.

"Fay! I need your help! This time I've lost a client I was in the process of signing. It was a done deal! Her secretary called, and what's weird is that she said the same thing about hoping I felt better. Phelps can't figure it out either. Call me. Immediately. Oh, and hope you had a good time up there."

Hope made it sound as if Faith had embarked on a trip to the Pole. She'd call her, just as soon as she'd spoken to Tom. If Phelps didn't know what was going on, Faith didn't see what she could contribute. And the loss of two accounts didn't strike her as extreme. Except there was that business about feeling better.

There was one more message. Francesca's voice.

"If it's all right, I'll come later tomorrow afternoon. We don't have anything until the luncheon on Wednesday, so it should be okay? *Ciao!*"

Monday. Faith knew exactly where Francesca was going to be. She'd be there, too.

Chapter 5

Faith didn't have a plan. Or to be more precise, she didn't have a plan past sitting in the last booth in the coffee shop and waiting to see whether Francesca would come in. The booth had a good view of the door, but was in the shadows, so anyone entering the restaurant would have to be looking straight at it to see its occupant. She'd arrived earlier than she had last week, well after the lunch rush and forty-five minutes before the time Francesca had appeared. Faith had immediately ordered a Greek omelet and settled back with coffee to read the newspaper, which could also serve as a screen if Francesca came back this way to use the restroom.

The omelet arrived—golden brown and oozing with feta. The chef used the traditional spinach and tomato mixture, but added a few sautéed onions, black olives, and a pinch of oregano. Some places added bacon, but Faith and Demetrious were purists. Although this recipe had no doubt been created in some long-ago Greek diner in Queens, since a more typical Greek breakfast consisted of yogurt and honey with some fruit, and maybe a slice of *psomi,* their crusty bread.

As Faith mopped up the last bits of egg with her wheat toast, she thought about what she would do if Francesca saw her, as well as what she would do if she saw Francesca. The first was easier. One of the life lessons Faith had stumbled on early was to use as few words as possible when called on to explain, or fib. Embellishing with details, however cleverly concocted, was not only unnecessary but usually unbelievable. It was how she could always tell when someone was fabricating. If you don't want to go out with someone, or do something, say no thank you. Don't add that you have to help an aged relative catalog a stamp collection or go visit a friend in the hospital. Invariably that will lead to more questions, "What kind of stamps—just American?" and "Which hospital? What's wrong?" until you've dug yourself in so deep, there's no way to get out except by capitulating. If Francesca spotted her, she'd say hello, period. It *was* a place Faith frequented, although Francesca might not know that.

The trickier part was finding out what the woman was up to and who her companion was. Again, the direct approach might be best. Faith had paid her bill as soon as the food arrived in case she needed to leave quickly. Once Francesca was seated, Faith could walk up to the table, ostensibly on her way out, and pause to greet her employee. Be obnoxious and sit down. Ask Demetrious for more coffee.

Francesca walked in the door at three o'clock sharp. She gave a look around and sat at the same table as before. She didn't see Faith. When the waitress approached she ordered something and soon a cup of coffee appeared. She kept her coat on. It didn't seem as if she planned to stay long. Five minutes later, the man walked in and sat down. He passed her an envelope, waving away the waitress. He was apparently not planning to linger either. Francesca passed *him* some cash—Faith saw Ben Franklin's face—and it was barely in his hand before he was out the door. Running. Francesca stood up, knocking over her chair as she ripped her envelope open, glanced at the contents, and dropped them both on the floor as she took off after him. Faith followed just as swiftly, but without yelling whatever Francesca was shouting at the top of her voice. Faith made out the word "*bastardo*," but that was all.

She took a second to retrieve what Francesca had dropped. All that had been in the envelope was a blank sheet of paper. Whatever the transaction's goal had been, this wasn't it and it was obviously why the girl had exploded. Outside on the sidewalk, Faith saw that Francesca was gaining on her quarry, who was heading for an uptown bus that had just pulled over at the end of the block. "Francesca!" Faith shouted and the girl turned her head, still sprinting toward the man, who had now boarded the bus. It was hard to read the look on her face. Anger, dismay, and yes, fear.

"Francesca! Stop! What's going on? I want to help," Faith called to her again.

This time Francesca didn't look back and made a final dash toward the bus before the doors closed. It pulled away from the curb. Faith looked frantically around for a cab. They were all headed downtown, and soon the bus was lumbering out of sight. There was no way she could catch up with it. She went back inside and paid Demetrious for Francesca's coffee, reassuring him that everything was all right.

Even if it wasn't.

Faith didn't expect Francesca to be at work, but she hoped that she would call, although the hope was a slight one. She left a message on the phone at Francesca's apartment, choosing her words carefully. One of the roommates might hear it first.

"Francesca. Hi, it's Faith. Could you give me a call when you get this? I want to finalize Wednesday's menu. In any case, see you tomorrow morning."

She debated calling Josie to enlist her aid in figuring this all out, but Josie was not only far away but swamped with everything opening a restaurant entails. And most important, Faith didn't want to upset her. If Francesca *was* involved in something shady, Josie would feel responsible for having vouched for her both to Have Faith and to her former roommates.

When the phone finally did ring, it wasn't Francesca, but the police—Sergeant Grady from the NYPD's 24th Precinct. After establishing who Faith was and that Miss Francesca Rossi was in the catering company's employ, he told Faith that the young woman had asked them to call her and he would personally appreciate it if she could come to the station and help them straighten things out. Miss Rossi was not under arrest at the moment, nor was the man who was the object of her rage, so extreme on the bus that the driver had called for the police to remove them both.

"We'd have let them both go, but she's insisting we charge him with theft. That's all we've been able to get out of her. She's boiling mad one minute and crying her eyes out the next. All Mr. Rinaldi has given us is his name and address. We've asked him to wait while we clear this up."

Faith told him she'd be there as soon as possible and headed for the precinct, which was on West 100th Street.

It looked like a school from the outside, a school with a great many police cars parked in front and a fire station next door. Inside she was directed to a large waiting room filled with an array of New York's population—some looked homeless, some looked as if they had several. Francesca was sitting on a chair in one corner, her hair escaping from the clip she'd pulled it back with and her arms folded across her chest. It wasn't hard to read the body language. She wasn't crying now, but she did look "boiling mad." The man from the restaurant was at the other end of the room, trying to appear as though he had no business being there and mostly succeeding.

"Faith!" Francesca jumped up and threw her arms around her employer.

Faith gave her a swift hug back and said, "What's going on? Who is that man?"

Francesca took a deep breath. "He's a cheater. He took my money. I want the *carabinieri* to put him in jail!"

"What were you giving him money for?"

"To do something for me."

The girl was obviously well trained in Faith's own nonembellishment tactics.

"Look, Francesca, you've just been ejected from a city bus for causing a disturbance. I saw you give him an envelope today and one last week."

Francesca interrupted. "I wondered why you were there!"

Faith pressed on. "Either tell me or don't, but I can't continue to employ you without knowing what this is all about. And the police obviously can't arrest someone just because you want them to."

Francesca considered this.

"Okay. He's a private detective. Only now I'm not so sure he really is. I hired him to find someone. Someone who lived in my village. I made a promise to find this person. Salvatore was supposed to give me an address, a phone number, all the information today. Instead, nothing!" Francesca shook her fist at the man. "And he won't give me my money back."

"How much did you pay him?"

"Five hundred dollars. Half in the beginning, half just now."

"How did you come to hire him, and did you both sign a contract?"

She shook her head. "No contract, and he had a card up in the *lavanderia,* the what do you call it?"

"Laundromat." Francesca's English had been flowing smoothly before this more obscure word stopped her cold.

"I thought I could trust him because he had an Italian name."

Faith was suddenly reminded how young the girl was, although people much older had been known to use similar dubious criteria for all sorts of decisions, even choosing a mate. As that thought crossed her mind, she was pierced with a sudden longing for Tom. If not beside her in the flesh, at least at the other end of a very long phone line.

"Do you still have the card?"

Francesca fished her wallet out of the large bag she carried, an expensive-looking leather one that she had brought with her from home, she'd said.

SALVATORE A. RINALDI, PRIVATE DETECTIVE SERVICES was written in elegant script above a phone number and an address in Brooklyn. ALL INQUIRIES CONFIDENTIAL it said and across the bottom some of his services were listed, including MISSING PERSONS.

Faith went over to the desk and asked the officer there if she could speak to Sergeant Grady. He appeared almost at once.

Faith introduced herself.

"From what I understand, Miss Rossi, who has been in my employ for some months and whom I value and trust, hired Mr. Rinaldi to locate an individual from her town in Italy who is now living here. She paid him a substantial amount. All he gave her in return was an envelope containing a blank sheet of paper. I witnessed the exchange. I'm sure Mr. Rinaldi"—Faith raised her voice so the man who was listening intently wouldn't miss a word—"wants to avoid a lawsuit for false representation. Miss Rossi will most definitely be pursuing one. If he returns the money and agrees to no further contact with her, I believe Miss Rossi will be content to leave him alone in turn."

With the man's address and phone number, Faith realized that they could go after him easily. The police had it as well.

"Mr. Rinaldi?" Sergeant Grady said.

"I just want to get out of here. She's crazy!"

"How much money are we talking about here?"

Francesca held up five fingers and pushed her hand in Mr. Rinaldi's direction. "Five hundred dollars!"

The officer raised his eyebrows. "Got it on you?"

"He must have half, because Francesca just gave him that. I saw the whole thing. We'd be happy to accompany him to the nearest ATM for the rest," Faith said.

"I got it. I got it," snarled Rinaldi. Until Faith spoke up he'd looked as if he was going to deny the whole thing. His body language was saying he was out of there, but instead he pulled out a wallet with a wad of cash that sparked definite interest in the sergeant's eyes, and peeled off five hundred dollars. Francesca reached for the money and stuck it deep in her bag.

"You're free to go, Miss Rossi, and please remember in the future that New York is a quiet little town. No more yelling on the bus."

Francesca dropped her head and whispered, "I will." She was looking very pretty.

The officer smiled. "And thank your boss here."

All three started for the door.

"Mr. Rinaldi," Sergeant Grady said. "Could you give me a minute? There are a few more questions I'd like to ask about your agency. Who knows, maybe you can give me some pointers to pass on to the detective squad here?"

Salvatore Rinaldi didn't look happy. Maybe he wasn't good at sharing.

Out on the sidewalk, Faith said, "Let's walk for a while. It's not cold, and you can tell me the roughly several hundred things you didn't tell me inside. Who you're looking for, to start—and why."

Another of Faith's learned life lessons was to be in a public place if you were going to have an uncomfortable, or possibly explosive, conversation with someone. And you choose the place. After they'd started walking, Faith changed her mind and hailed a cab.

"Come on," she said to Francesca. "Let's head down to Santa Fe.

They make a mean margarita and I'm betting you haven't eaten today."

"Santa Fe?"

"It's a great Mexican restaurant on West Seventy-First."

As always, the warm terra-cotta of the restaurant's walls cheered Faith up. So did the first sip of her margarita.

"Okay, start at the beginning. Who are you looking for?" She'd ordered the masa-crusted shrimp, succulent jumbo ones dredged in corn flour and quickly fried. They came with a dipping sauce, but she liked them plain. She also ordered a wild mushroom quesadilla for Francesca, knowing she would share, and asked for some guacamole and chips right away. Although she'd had the omelet not all that long ago, she was starving.

"His name is Gus Oliver."

Faith was surprised. "That doesn't sound like a typical Italian name, unless it was changed."

"Maybe it was. I never thought about that. He's an American, not Italian, but lived in my village after the war."

"The Second World War? Then he's a very old man."

"Yes. Maybe ninety."

"Are you sure he's still alive?"

"That was one of the things that *bastardo,* excuse me, was supposed to find out."

"I'm assuming you have something besides the man's name?"

"Yes, an address in Brooklyn. It's why I came . . ."

Francesca got very busy with the guacamole and popped a loaded tortilla chip into her mouth.

"Why you came here. To New York. Except your family, or some of them, think you're in London."

The girl's face reddened. The room was warm and the margarita was having an effect, but it was clear she was embarrassed.

"I thought Josie probably noticed those postcards."

Faith waited. Francesca broke the silence almost immediately.

"I have to find him, and if I can't I didn't want anyone to be disappointed, so I let them think I was going to London to take some courses there instead of here. A friend mails the postcards every once in a while. I didn't want my mother or grandmother to worry."

"Finding him is very important?"

The food arrived. Francesca did not look at it, but looked at Faith instead.

"More than anything in the world to me."

Francesca would tell her why eventually, Faith thought, but first things first.

"Then that's what we'll have to do; now eat up before it gets cold."

Faith's grandmother was used to delegating, citing the prerogatives of old age, but Faith knew it had been an established pattern many years earlier. She loved Nana dearly, but she muttered to herself, "I don't have time for this," as she headed for the Queens Midtown Tunnel and a lightning visit to The Cliff. Mrs. Lennox's bridal gown had been right where she thought it was, carefully stored in her apartment's cedar closet, but the extra lace was out in Long Island, she remembered after searching through her other closets and drawers. Faith's protests of work, and what she called "The Francesca Project" to herself and wasn't about to mention to Nana, fell on deaf ears—not that Mrs. Lennox was hard of hearing.

"You simply cannot expect Bergdorf's to rush on something like this. Imagine how you'll feel if it's not ready in time!"

Faith had protested that the wedding was still months away and that she was coming out with her mother for a tasting with the caterer in a week. She could pick up the lace then.

"Not months. A little over two months—nine weeks, to be precise. No time at all."

Picturing the worst-case scenario—walking down the aisle in sweats—Faith agreed to borrow her parents' car and drive out to Long Island. Nine weeks! That was what, sixty-three days! No time at all was right.

Of course Nana was too busy to accompany Faith, but gave her instructions as to the probable location, one of the wardrobes in the attic. So Faith had called Uncle Sky, who was delighted, but would have to leave soon after her arrival.

"You might see Tam if you stick around. I've been batching it while she's being covered in Tibetan mud or some other expensive stuff out at Canyon Ranch, and she's due back."

"I'm sure Mrs. Danforth has been taking very good care of you," Faith had said. It was well known that the housekeeper, who, legend had it, accompanied Sky to Harvard and took an apartment nearby so she could be on hand to keep him in comfort, had seen that he wanted for nothing, wife away or in residence.

The morning rush hour was over and traffic was light. Driving up along one arm of Long Island Sound, Faith felt herself relax. This bride business was definitely something she only wanted to do once. It was, of course, because she adored Tom and would never want to be married to anyone else, but in addition, who knew getting married would be so much work? As was fast becoming a new habit, she went over a mental wedding checklist. Dress—check, well, once she located the family lace. Check also beside invitations. Her mother had taken that on and they were ready to go out at the end of next week. Caterer booked and only the tasting to be done. No problem finding someone to perform the ceremony. Tom was coming on Monday, ID in hand, and they'd go down to the Manhattan Marriage Bureau on Worth Street to get the license. She'd thought it would be romantic to take the ferry and go to the bureau on Staten Island, but Tom could only stay until the following morning, and they had to pick out china and silver. Both Faith's grandmother and mother had been adamant about this, saying that it was a great nuisance when you were giving a wedding gift and didn't have any idea what the couple liked. Besides, if you didn't register you might end up with twelve fondue pots. Faith thought they'd register at Tiffany, Crate and Barrel, and Bridge Kitchenware. She liked the thought of furnishing a nest. Tom had suggested giving the stores a quick once-over together, then she could return later at her leisure. He had other plans for their limited time.

Faith pulled into the long drive that led to the house. The Cliff would have been at home in Newport, Bar Harbor, or any of the other watering places popularized in the late nineteenth and early twentieth centuries. The exterior combined fieldstone and shingle, both weathered to a soft gray. The house had a commanding presence—it was a grande dame, a dowager of a dwelling—and she loved it. She turned the wheel. The drive curved sharply at the foot, and leaving The Cliff, you'd plunge straight into the ocean if you didn't curve as well. She parked behind the house, went in the back door and down the hall. Her uncle said he'd leave it open for her in case he had to leave. She didn't see his car, but it could be in the garage. He rarely trusted his 1971 Rolls Corniche convertible to even the mildest elements.

"Uncle Sky," she called. "Mrs. Danforth, it's Faith."

She heard a door open and her uncle came out of the library to meet her.

"A treat for sore eyes, my darling. Let me get you something. Too early for drinkies?"

He gave her a hug.

"I think I'd better keep my head clear to tackle the attic, but I'd love something cold."

They went back into the library and Schuyler rang for the housekeeper.

"Danny, we're thirsty," he said when she arrived. "I'll have some Perrier with a twist and, Faith, what about you? I believe we have all the customary soft beverages."

"Perrier sounds fine, thank you."

Mrs. Danforth soon reappeared with the drinks and a plate of homemade shortbread. It was still warm.

"You do spoil me, Danny. Now leave us alone. Faith and I have much to discuss." Mrs. Danforth gave him a slight smile, the expression vanishing as she nodded to Faith and left.

"I want to hear all about the arrangements you've made so far. It *is* my house, you know." He laughed heartily to take away any possible sting his words might have left. Faith had occasionally wondered whether he minded the way the entire family used The Cliff. She had no idea whether his sisters contributed to its upkeep—and it must be an extremely expensive proposition. But there seemed to be plenty of money. Sky loved parties and gave a major one each year on his birthday, which was in early September. Last year Faith and Hope had gone together, getting to the house toward the end of the evening. A band was playing Gershwin tunes in the ballroom. People were dancing. People were also in the pool, happily splashing in the moonlit water. Hope had turned to Faith and said, "I feel as if we've wandered into one of Gatsby's parties and that if I walk down to the shore I'll see the green light." There was plenty of foie gras, caviar, and the like, but Sky had also hired one of the city's preeminent sushi chefs. Faith had never tasted any better before or since. Her uncle always had his finger on the pulse of a new trend.

She settled in to tell him what had been planned so far, and he suggested they walk outside to consider where the tent should be placed before he had to leave. Faith said she would be going back to the city soon, too—it shouldn't take long to find the lace given Nana's detailed instructions. They walked out the front door and around to the back of the house.

It was a beautiful day and Faith crossed her fingers, wishing that the weather would be the same, only a bit warmer, on June 9. She was sure that the saying "Lucky is the bride upon whom the rain doth fall" was invented by a medieval party planner to soothe a client with a large fiefdom, and Faith would not be happy if this was the form her luck took come the big day.

Sky tucked Faith's arm through his.

"You're my favorite niece, you know. Oh, the others are quite charming, but you're like me. We're two of a kind. We know what we want and we go for it. I fully expect you to name your firstborn for me, girl or boy."

"I will," Faith promised, hoping it would be a boy: otherwise there would be the Sydney-type problem. "I promise."

"Good. Now, we want to be away from the big oak. How about here." He walked to a spot in the middle of the spacious lawn.

"The beds don't look like much now, but we'll take care of that."

He pointed to the broad swaths on either side that the gardeners had been tending, clearing away the detritus of winter. Schuyler Walfort had been a handsome man in his youth and was handsome still. He was tall and slender, and kept his thick white hair just a bit long—a streak of rebellion or to show that he had it. He'd been a college athlete, rowing crew and wrestling. Despite the passage of time, he continued to move like one and kept fit with tennis and squash. There was an indoor court at The Cliff. Today he was dressed for town. Savile Row pin-striped suit and a Sulka tie. Sky loved Sulka ties. Faith had seen them hanging in his closet, an aviary of bright silk plumage.

He walked back toward her, pulled her into his arms, and spun her around. "We'll need a big dance floor. I do like to dance."

Faith laughed. He was in his element. He always was.

An hour later Faith was ready to leave. The lace, which was exquisite and plenty for a Juliet cap as well, had been exactly where her grandmother had said it would be, but Faith had lingered in the attic. It was the size of most people's houses, with windows that overlooked the grounds and, from the front, the sea. There was a chair next to one of those windows and Faith sat down wondering who had pulled it into the spot—Sky, Tammy, perhaps Mrs. Danforth? Or had it been here for years and she hadn't noticed? What thoughts had run through the sitter's mind? Happy, sad, confused? She was happy, very happy, but she couldn't ignore the tremor accompanying it all. The one produced by the thought of leaving New York, her family, her friends, her business. Tom. Tom was coming soon. It would all be all right then. She'd take him to the Russian Tea Room, the roof of the Metropolitan Museum of Art overlooking Central Park, and the other museums—MoMA, the Guggenheim, the Whitney. Blintzes at Grand Dairy in the Lower East Side. She always had the same ancient waiter, and she was pretty sure he was wearing the same ancient, somewhat streaked apron that he'd had on every previous visit. She stood up, aware suddenly that she wasn't introducing Tom to the city as much as she was saying farewell to it.

She went back into the library, where she had left her jacket and purse. A whiff of Uncle Sky's aftershave, Penhaligon's Blenheim Bouquet, lingered. He was a complete Anglophile. She smiled to herself, thinking of him no doubt on his way to his club, the Century, and then on to dinner at the Palm or one of his other beloved steak houses. He served exquisite and exotic food, but often proclaimed he was a meat-and-potatoes man. Faith knew that meant prime and au gratin, specialties of these venerable restaurants where he was well known. Maybe she would take Tom to one of them instead of the Russian Tea Room. Like Gallagher's. The restaurant had started out as a speakeasy in the 1920s, complete with a secret password. It had endured, serving

Broadway and sports stars over the years. He'd like the history—
and the steak.

No sign of Mrs. Danforth. Faith made a mental note to thank
her next time. Truth to be told, she was a bit intimidated by the
woman. As children, she and her cousins had been flat out afraid
of her. Something about the fact that she rarely spoke, just fixed
you with a look. A look that pinned you to the wall.

She opened the back door and glanced straight up at the sky.
No clouds, but to her horror a huge chunk of brickwork was falling straight toward her. She ducked and it shattered on the walk.
For a moment she wasn't sure what had happened. She felt her
legs tremble and sat down on the stoop, not sure they'd support
her. For an instant she realized that she had never felt so physi-
cally afraid before as she had when she saw the brickwork coming
straight at her. It must have come from one of the house's many
chimneys. Impossible to tell now. She looked over at the debris.
There was some rope attached that a workman must have left.

She stood up. The moment had passed. The sky wasn't falling.

But she ought to leave a note of some sort. They'd wonder
what the brickwork was doing here. Better to call. But what to
say? I was almost killed? While she was deciding what to do, a cab
pulled up in front of her and Great-aunt Tammy got out.

"Faith, honey, Sky said you might come out today. I'm so glad
I didn't miss you. But is something wrong? You look like you just
saw a ghost!"

Tammy walked the few steps to Faith's side. The cabdriver was
getting the bags.

"What on earth . . . ?" she said, looking at the ground. She put
an arm around Faith. "I swear this place is going to tumble down
around our heads. You come in and sit down. I'll get you a drink.
I'm parched myself. Nothing but carrot juice for days. No toxins."

Faith allowed Tammy to lead her back into the house. Mrs.
Danforth was standing in the hallway watching them.

"I did not know that Miss Sibley had returned," she said.

Faith started to tell her that she hadn't left, had stayed longer than intended in the attic. The housekeeper somehow made you feel as if you should continually be apologizing. Tammy cut Faith off.

"Get someone to clean up that mess outside. Faith here was almost murdered to death by our chimney. And we'll have drinks on the sunporch. Bourbon and branch for me. Faith?"

She shook her head. "I really have to get back."

"Don't worry. I know just how you feel. I almost got hit by lightning on the way back from Mardi Gras when I was sixteen. Momma said it was God's punishment since I went without telling them and was gone for two days, but she knew where I was, all right. Just wanted to yank my chain a little. Anyway, after it missed me by inches all I wanted was to get home and crawl under the covers. So, you go on. You're coming out for a tasting soon, right? I'll see you then. *And* I'll make sure there are no more accidents."

Faith said good-bye, went to the car, and collapsed in the front seat for a moment.

What if she hadn't looked up?

All Francesca had to go on was an envelope. It was addressed to Mrs. Augusto Oliver at 1740 Battery Avenue in Brooklyn, New York. It wasn't postmarked. There was nothing inside and the envelope itself had been crumpled.

"My grandmother found it. He must have meant to throw it away. It's all he left."

This was the clue Francesca had shown Rinaldi. Faith doubted that the individual who wrote the address and the intended recipient were still at it—or even alive—but going there was the only thing she could think of to do, even though there were no Olivers listed at that address in the phone book. It was doubtful the detective had bothered.

Battery Avenue was in Bay Ridge. Bay Ridge immediately conjured up the image of John Travolta walking down the sidewalk at the beginning of *Saturday Night Fever,* those long legs, sexy disco shoes keeping time to the irresistible Bee Gees beat. A stable, family neighborhood. Faith knew this from a Norwegian-American friend who had taken her to the annual Norwegian Constitution Day parade one year, a remnant of a time when more Norwegians lived in Brooklyn than in Oslo.

Armed with a map, the two women set out, boarding the Fourth Avenue line's R train on Sunday afternoon, figuring that would be a time when people would be home.

It was Palm Sunday and Faith had taken Francesca to church with her so they could leave immediately afterward. The weather was beautiful, and when they emerged onto the street, the sidewalks were filled with pedestrians enjoying the first real spring day.

The address was a well-kept three-family attached brick house. A railroad flat from the look of it—those narrow apartments designed at the turn of the twentieth century to cope with the problem of urban overcrowding. The rooms were laid out like a railroad car, one behind the other off a long hall.

There were three separate doorbells. None of the last names beneath them was Oliver. There was no reply when Faith rang the first two and she pushed the third. The intercom crackled and a male voice asked what they wanted, adding if they were selling anything to please keep walking.

"We're not selling anything. My name is Faith Sibley and I'm here with my friend Francesca Rossi. We're trying to find out whether someone by the last name of Oliver who lived here in the nineteen forties and maybe later is still alive, and if so if you have an address."

"I don't know the party in question. But come on up. I might be able to help you."

They were buzzed in and heard a door at the top of the stairs open.

"I'm Benny—Benito Lombardo."

He pointed at Francesca. "You look like a fellow countryman, or I should say, woman."

Benny appeared to be in his forties. His hair was thinning, but the rest of him was a testament to someone's way with pasta. He was wearing a wedding band, so it was probably Mrs. Lombardo's.

"Sit. You want something? Coffee? The wife left biscotti. She went to church with her sister, and who knows when she'll be back? After they worship our Lord, they do a little, you know, retail worshipping."

"Thank you," Faith said. "We're fine. About the Oliver family. Did you ever hear of them?"

"I heard the name. My family has been here since the nineteen fifties. I was born here. Not in this very room, but at Victory Memorial. My mother could have told you what you want, God rest her soul. My wife and I moved in to take care of her ten years ago. The Olivers were gone by then."

Francesca started talking to him in Italian and he looked serious. From her intensity Faith knew she must be telling him it was very important that she find Gus Oliver. He answered, got up, and patted Francesca's hand.

"I told your friend that my aunt still lives next door, and what she doesn't know isn't worth remembering. I'll give her a call. She doesn't answer the door. Her name is Maria Corelli."

They all moved toward the door, which he opened. As they left he shook his finger at them.

"And you'd better not turn down *her* biscotti!"

The last thing they heard as they headed out was his laughter.

They didn't have far to go and were soon ushered into a cookie cutter of the house next door. One look at Signora Corelli told

Faith that the woman had not been putting away much of either her own baking or her pasta. A good strong wind would carry her straight across the Verrazano-Narrows Bridge.

"Come in, come in," she said.

Francesca immediately started addressing her in Italian, and Faith followed them down the hall to the kitchen in the rear, where the smell of coffee and baked goods beckoned. She realized she was hungry. Somehow they'd forgotten about lunch.

Faith managed to say, "*Ma non parlo l'italiano.*"

"No problem! We'll speak English. Now, *mangia*—that you know, I'm sure." She was as outgoing as her nephew, and Faith did not need to be urged to eat. In addition to several kinds of biscotti, there were *pizzelles,* those crisp waffle cookies with a trace of anise.

"I knew the Oliver family very well. We were all newlyweds here before the war and our men went off together. They were Italian, too, and at that time there weren't so many of us in this part of Bay Ridge. A lot of Norwegians. They had their own shops, newspapers. Good neighbors. I never had a complaint. We used to play cards with the Hansens. You think these cookies are something? You should have had hers. Melted in your mouth. And what she did for Christmas you wouldn't believe. Started in October, but I'm getting off the track. I do that a lot." She laughed.

"So, the Olivers. It was Oliveri, but someone changed it. You're interested in Gus? A lot of us were!" She laughed again. "Like a movie star. That good-looking. People would mistake him for Victor Mature. Really.

"So the war is over and our guys came home, but Gus stayed in Italy doing something for the military, so he was the last. It was hard on Angela, his wife. At least she didn't have to worry about keeping food in her kid's mouth the way the rest of us did. They hadn't had any yet. She had a job working as a secretary to some big shot and always looked like a million bucks. Gus put a stop to that when he got back. He wasn't about to have people thinking his wife had to go out to work. Anyway, she'd get pregnant the moment he laid his pants across the bed, so it was just as well."

"What happened to them then, Angela and Gus?" Faith asked, taking just one more cookie.

"Nothing much. Just life like for the rest of us. She died, and he didn't want to stay on in the apartment, so he went to Jersey to live with one of his daughters."

"And when did he pass away?" Faith took a biscotti that was slightly smaller than the others. This cookie would be her last.

"Gus died?" Maria crossed herself. "I'm about the only one left of the crowd now."

"No," Faith corrected hastily. "I should have said do you know whether he's still alive or not? We don't know anything about him."

"I had a card at Christmas. So far as I know he's alive and kicking in Verona. That's in Jersey," she repeated, giving the word a slight inflection, as if she were speaking of another country, not merely a state. A state just across the river.

"Would you mind giving us the address? It's very important to Francesca."

"So I gather." She paused for a moment. "You're not planning to cause him any trouble? I always liked Gus."

Francesca shook her head. "He visited my village often after the war and made a lot of close friends. Everybody wondered what happened to him. He must have been called away suddenly by the army. One day he was there and the next day not."

Maria nodded. "I can understand. I've had people move from here and I never know whether they're still with us. Okay, I'll get my address book."

She returned and gave them his address. Francesca wrote it down.

"I don't have a phone number for him and I'm not sure what his daughter's married name is, but my card to him didn't come back. If you do find him, tell him to give me a ring. On the phone that is." She laughed some more. "My husband was a saint, but once is enough."

On that note they left, promising to relay her message.

Outside Francesca gave Faith an impetuous hug. "You are a genius! I should have told you right away instead of going to that crook!"

Faith was feeling good herself.

"So, next stop Jersey. But it will have to wait awhile."

"My family has been waiting for many, many years. A little longer won't matter."

On the subway ride home, Faith looked over at Francesca, who was still glowing from their success. She sincerely hoped the young woman hadn't been lying when she'd told that nice old lady she wasn't going to cause any trouble for Gus Oliver.

"Happy?" Tom had arrived just before eleven o'clock, having gotten an early start. They were back in the apartment after a day spent at various bridal registries and were about to leave for some much needed protein at Gallagher's.

"Sublimely," Faith answered, noting that they seemed to have been designed by a cosmic being with a jigsaw. Her head fit perfectly on his shoulder.

As they went from place to place that day, she had told Tom about Francesca's quest, and she was happy to note that he didn't tell her she shouldn't get involved. Involved was what she did. He did, too, of course, otherwise he would have holed up in an ivory tower and just written about God.

"What are you thinking about, future Mrs. Fairchild?"

"You. Us. And how much I don't want you to leave. You?"

"Same. Plus the image of a rare slab of beef too big for the plate, although I'd forego even that if you say the word, and stay in with whatever you have in your fridge."

"You'd get terribly hungry," Faith said. Tom had still not cottoned on to the fact that although she was a caterer, her own provisions were Spartan in the extreme. He was assuming she had the makings of a four-star repast. What she had in her larder was enough for breakfast plus some wine, crackers, and cheese.

"Let's go." She was getting hungry now with all this food talk, and Gallagher's creamed spinach was the kind of dish she imagined she'd crave when pregnant.

They did, eventually, but not immediately. When she was finally grabbing a jacket, Faith thought to herself that while she had shared everything about Francesca and all sorts of other things, she hadn't mentioned the fact that she had almost been beaned by a very large chunk of stone and that this was no Chicken Little story. On one level she didn't want him to think the house was unsafe for the wedding—Tammy was having a structural engineer go over the place—and on another, a more basic level, she didn't want him to worry about her. Now or ever.

Jane Sibley picked her daughter up at work Easter Sunday evening. Have Faith had catered an Easter brunch and a cocktail party that had nothing to do with either the Resurrection or pastel bunnies, although from the way the crowd was drinking, pink elephants were making an appearance. Faith and Jane were on their way to The Cliff for a tasting appointment with the caterer the next day.

"Get the car blanket from the backseat, darling, and get some rest," Jane said after Faith had joined her. "I'll drive. You must be exhausted."

"I *am* tired," Faith admitted, reaching for the army blanket, a relic of her father's service during the Vietnam War. It had become the car blanket in her childhood sometime and she welcomed its warmth. It was magically soporific and she knew she'd be asleep soon. Her mother was a good driver, although she pushed the speed limits knowing that every time she'd been pulled over, she'd only received a warning. She'd once told her daughters that the day she got a ticket would be the day she'd know she'd lost her looks. They'd been amused at the streak of justifiable vanity; Jane Lennox Sibley had always been a beauty.

"It must be hard. Starting to pack up the business. You've been such a marvelous success," Jane said.

Faith thought about her mother's comment for a moment. Josie was coming soon for some of the equipment the caterer who'd be taking over didn't want. She was on schedule for Josie's opening and Faith planned to be there. Today's events were among the last scheduled for Have Faith, and she'd be devoting herself full-time to getting married and moved by mid-May.

"It *is* hard—and the days are rushing by—but seeing Tom last week made me want them to rush by faster."

Her mother nodded. "I remember feeling that way, too. I couldn't wait to get married."

"I'm glad Marian will be able to come down for Nana's tea. It feels a bit odd to be marrying into a family that you and Dad haven't met. Well, you did meet Betsey . . ." Faith's voice trailed off.

"Yes, I did meet Betsey, and you have your work cut out for you there. She wants Tom to marry that other girl. The neighbor. It was so obvious."

"I know, and the funny thing is that I'm pretty sure Tom has never thought of her except as one of the guys."

"Men are so clueless."

Faith laughed. "What a thing to say! Not Daddy!"

"Him most of all. You've seen the way certain unattached females in the congregation bring him his coffee at coffee hour and a plate of treats, hinting not so subtly that they could be a much better helpmate than the one he saddled himself with, and they might be correct, but encumbered he is and he's not getting out of it."

Faith had a sudden flash of what lay in her future and decided to take a nap until they reached their destination.

"That's odd," Jane said. "I thought Tammy was here. Sky is away on business."

The Cliff was pitch dark except for the outside lights. They pulled around to the back, grabbed their overnight bags, and went down the path.

The door was ajar. Faith began to feel uneasy. Sky and Tammy were pretty casual and might have left the door open, but Mrs. Danforth wasn't. She would never have left it like this before turning in for the night.

"Mom, I don't think we should go in. We should go somewhere and call. Wake up Mrs. Danforth and make sure everything's all right."

"Don't be silly. What could be wrong? Tammy may not have been feeling well and went to bed early. Mrs. Danforth always does. One or the other may not have shut the door all the way and it blew open. I have a PenLite in my purse we can use, although it doesn't look like a power failure. All these lights are on." She motioned to the ones by the walk.

Faith followed her in and down the hall. Jane snapped lights on as she went.

"See, nothing's been disturbed," she said, pointing to an ornate Georgian tea service displayed on a hall table.

From the foot of the dramatic double staircase in the front foyer they could see light from upstairs.

"You go check on Tammy. That looks like her room. I want to crank up the heat. It's as cold as a tomb in here," Jane said.

Faith went up the curved staircase, and as she approached the light coming from Tammy's open door, she called out to her.

There was no reply. She hesitated. "Aunt Tammy?" she called again and moved to the door. Again, there was no answer.

She stood and looked into the room. Jane's words had been eerily apt. Her aunt was slumped forward onto the boudoir's dressing table, but Faith could tell from the way Tamora Baines Wayfort's arm was hanging that the woman dressed in a ruffled cerise negligee, her head wrapped in a bath towel, wasn't in any shape to answer.

Great-aunt Tammy was dead.

CHAPTER 6

Someone was screaming. Faith realized it was her own voice and clamped her hand over her mouth, stifling the sound.

There was a smoldering fire in the fireplace. The room seemed insufferably warm and the air was filled with the scent of a cloying perfume. Everywhere she looked all she could see was red. The embers, the room's crimson décor, Tammy's flamboyant outfit.

And the towel that was wrapped in a turban around the dead woman's head was red, too—blood red.

Faith started toward her to feel for a pulse. What could have happened? The open door. An intruder—a murderer! A murderer who might still be in the house! But there hadn't been a car outside. A murderer who had come up from the shore or across through the woods! She heard footsteps coming up the stairs and started to run toward the door leading to the bath on the left. Someone shoved her to one side.

"What the hell is going on here?"

Faith started to scream again, stopped, stood still, and looked wildly from the corpse to the figure next to her.

"Who's in mah boudoir, wearing mah negligee?"

Tammy Walfort couldn't be dead, because she was very much alive—and as if to prove it, her accent became more pronounced. Faith clung to her side in disbelief as her aunt crossed the room and yanked at the lifeless figure balanced on the dressing table's stool. Tammy let out a screech.

"It's Danny!"

As the body fell to the floor, the towel slipped, revealing a bludgeoned head, and indeed it was the housekeeper. The back of her skull resembled Humpty Dumpty's. It was the second dead body Faith had seen in the last few months, and that was two bodies too many. She grabbed a wrist, confirming what she had suspected—no pulse. No sign of life at all. She tried not to look at the corpse.

"Call 911," she said. There had to be a phone in the room, although none was obvious.

"Darlin', she's gone. Nothing anyone can do. Poor Sky. He's going to take this hard. Go round the bend, in fact." Tammy allowed herself a moment before returning to her initial reaction. She began walking around the room angrily plucking at her bed, which had been turned down. "Sleeping here. Playing dress up!" She opened the bathroom door. "And using my tub! And candles! Smell it. That's Rigaud, Faith. Ninety dollars apiece. The big ones are three hundred!" Indignation appeared to be the woman's overriding emotion and Faith generously decided her great-aunt must be in shock.

"I think we should go downstairs to call the police. We mustn't disturb anything here."

Tammy had opened one of her closets.

"My sable is missing. Two guesses who's been wearing it and the first one doesn't count. Let's go search her room. I thought some of my things had been moved around, but figured it was the cleaners. Danny didn't dirty her hands with housework, you know."

Considering the woman's age, which had to be about the same as Uncle Sky's, and considering the Walforts' income, Faith thought Mrs. Danforth had earned a toilet-bowl-free semiretirement.

She urged her aunt again.

"We have to call the police. Now! And Mom is downstairs alone. The house may not be safe."

This did it and Tammy looked alarmed.

"There have been a number of break-ins in the area lately. But we don't have to waste time calling from downstairs. Use the phone here." She pointed to what Faith had assumed was a decorative cloisonné coffer on the Louis Quinze commode next to the bed. She opened it and pulled out a gold-plated phone, or maybe it was brass. In any case, it had a dial tone. She got through to the police immediately and, as she'd thought, the dispatcher told her to leave the room. An ambulance and a squad car would be there as soon as possible.

Jane Sibley was in the library and reacted with astonishment, then sorrow, at the news.

"I hope she didn't know what was happening. What do you think, Faith?"

"She wasn't facing either the door to the hall or the bath, so I don't think she could have seen the attack." Unless she was looking straight into the mirror, Faith added to herself. No need to mention the thought to the others.

Tammy had poured herself a drink and was pacing back and forth.

"What was she doing in my room? What was she doing here at all? She's supposed to be at her sister's in Bridgeport for the holiday weekend. We told her to stay until Monday. I know she left the house yesterday. Called the car service myself since Sky took my car. His is in for kid-glove servicing, as usual. Finds a speck of dirt on the hood and off it goes. He's supposed to be hammering out some kind of real estate deal over in Westchester at one of Trump's resorts, but I know these guys and I'll bet they've been spending more time on the golf course and in the bar. He left Friday and is due back tomorrow."

"Mrs. Danforth must have come back sometime today," Faith said, reflecting that neither her uncle nor Tammy were ardent churchgoers, or much for things like Easter-egg hunts.

"I wouldn't know. I'd planned to be here, catch up on a few things. You know how it is when your husband is away. Well, you will know, Faith. Anyway, Saturday morning the idea of staying here alone began to give me the creeps and I decided to go into the city. I left when she did. Omigod, what if I hadn't!"

She poured herself another generous shot of bourbon—and no branch—tottered over to the couch, and sank into the cushions.

Faith was still trying to get everyone's whereabouts straight.

"So the two of you took the train to Penn Station and she caught one for Connecticut?"

Tammy sat up straighter and looked askance. "I don't take the train. The driver brought me into the city after dropping her off at the station out here."

Faith and her mother exchanged glances. They knew there was no love lost between mistress and housekeeper, but not to give her a ride . . .

"I know what y'all are thinking, but you didn't know what she was like. So far as she was concerned I was trailer trash and she didn't hide it. Wanted me to get fed up and leave—like some of the others, I'm sure. I tried to tell Sky what she was doing, but gave that up quickly. If it had come down to her or me, well, you know it would have been Danny. Always going on about Caroline. Wife number two, or three? The one from that rich Philadelphia family. Maybe if she hadn't died so soon after they were married, she wouldn't have been promoted to sainthood. Oh, I can tell you everything about Caroline's perfect taste in clothes. The elegant dinner parties she gave. Her famous friends. And pedigreed ancestors. It's a wonder the *Mayflower* didn't sink."

Sirens outside interrupted Tammy's soliloquy.

"Thank heaven!" she said.

"Tam, dear," Jane suggested gently. "It might be a good idea not to let the police know how much you disliked Danny. I mean, of course we understand, but someone else might misconstrue your words . . ."

Tammy paled visibly. "You don't honestly think they'd suspect me of bashing her head in! If anything, it would be the opposite. Believe you me, when we were alone in the house together when Sky was away, I locked my doors. I wouldn't have put it past her to creep in and smother me with a pillow so she could—"

"Hush now," Jane cautioned. "Faith, go answer the door."

Faith was relieved to see the police and EMTs, although with a dead body upstairs in her aunt's boudoir, she was aware that the emotion was a fleeting one.

She was also aware of two questions that occurred to her as Tammy spoke. Why had the housekeeper returned to The Cliff and when? Aware, too, of the one that had sprung to mind the moment she'd realized who had been murdered. Dressed fit to kill, had Mrs. Danforth been expecting someone—and been killed instead?

Faith led the way upstairs then returned to the library. She'd told the officer in charge the name of the victim, realizing that she had no idea of Mrs. Danforth's first name or any other salient information—age, permanent address, next of kin. Tammy had mentioned a sister and she told them that. She'd also mentioned the open back door before returning downstairs.

She walked into the room at the same time as her aunt.

"I called and left a message for Sky," Tammy said. "Just said there had been an accident and to come straight home."

"We'd better call my mother—and Aunt Frances."

"No, Jane." Tammy sounded firm. Either the shock was wearing off or the bourbon was kicking in. She seemed in complete control now. "We'll wait until Sky comes. He can break the news to them."

"They'll want to be here."

"And that can wait, too."

It was the calm before a storm of activity that only Faith had witnessed previously when police had arrived at Emma Morris's apartment in the aftermath of her ordeal in December. The ordeal Faith had fortuitously interrupted, or she would have come across three bodies in these last months.

Her mother and aunt looked askance at the number of uniforms who began to stream into The Cliff carrying all the equipment necessary at a crime scene. An officer, who appeared to be still in his teens, came down from upstairs shortly and informed them that the chief as well as the Nassau County medical examiner would be there soon. Would they mind remaining where they were? And refrain from using the phone? He took a seat near the door. Tam poured herself another drink.

Upon arrival, the chief, Matthew Johnson, turned out to be a jovial-looking man in his late fifties, Faith guessed. He was in plain clothes, as was the man he introduced as Detective Willis, "helping us out from Manhasset." Chief Johnson greeted Tammy warmly, asking solicitously if she was all right. In a town the size of the one in which The Cliff was located, it would have been odd if the police chief *didn't* know the Walforts and every other inhabitant.

"I'm fine, Matt, but as you know, something dreadful has happened and our treasured Mrs. Danforth is dead."

"I remember seeing her at some of your lovely parties. A great loss to your family. My condolences."

Faith began to feel as if she were watching a surrealistic drawing room play. All the niceties were being acted out while above their heads was a chamber of horrors.

"Sky's been away since Friday and I left word for him. He

should be calling soon—or on his way already. I told him to come home immediately."

The chief nodded and the detective took out a notebook. He looked less like a regular on the North Shore social circuit—the chief was wearing a tie that, Faith recognized, sported the local country club logo—than someone just dropping in from much meaner streets.

"I understand the dead woman was your housekeeper," he said, and began working his way through a list of questions, eliciting Danny's vital information from Tammy, although she often answered by saying he'd have to ask her husband. She had no idea how old Mrs. Danforth was or other relatives' addresses. She did know her first name.

"Mabel."

He nodded and closed his notebook. "They should be about finished with the photographs upstairs. I'll need some more information about the deceased's movements this weekend, but I want to have a look at the scene now. Matt?"

The chief had settled in next to his hostess and jumped up, apparently recalling the matter at hand.

"I understand the back door was open when you arrived," he said. "Any signs of forced entry? Broken glass? The lock jimmied?"

"No," Faith said, shaking her head. "When Mother and I got here the entire place was dark, except for the outside lights. The door was ajar, but nothing indicated it had been forced open."

"Okay. We're checking around in back, and over the rest of the grounds."

Faith thought of something. "There were no cars in the garage. And with the house dark, anyone casing it would assume it was empty."

"She's so smart." Tammy beamed. "And she's going to be a beautiful bride. Right here in June. Y'all have to come, Matt."

On that note the men left.

Bride. She was a bride, Faith thought, and she desperately wanted to talk to the groom. She didn't know if she'd be able to erase the picture of Mrs. Danforth in Tammy's frilly, feathered, totally incongruous outfit from her mind by the time the nuptials took place. Whenever she looked up at those windows—they'd be facing the house during the ceremony—she'd be reminded of the body in the boudoir.

Elopement was beginning to seem extremely attractive.

When had they arrived? Around nine thirty? Faith was losing all sense of time. Looking at her watch, she was startled to find it was only a little after eleven. It was going to be a long night. The detective had mentioned the photographers. They'd be taking pictures of the victim as well as every corner of the room. And Faith knew they would also be covering every surface with fingerprint powder besides looking for anything else that might give them a clue to the identity of the murderer. Hairs, threads from fabric, dirt from the sole of a shoe. There wouldn't be anything like a matchbook or a receipt dropped—it would be a much too Sherlockian piece of luck. But she hoped they'd get some kind of lucky. Hoped this would be solved immediately. She needed a swift arrest to lift the shadow that threatened to destroy all their wedding plans.

Tammy was uncharacteristically quiet. And for once Faith didn't suggest food as a panacea. She wasn't hungry and she doubted the other two women were. Besides, the kitchen was Danny's domain and Faith didn't want to be reminded that the woman who had prepared Uncle Sky's favorites all these years was dead. Favorites that tended in the direction of nursery food—jam roly-poly, rice pudding, custards, crumbles, and ones Faith suspected Sky favored for the British names: toad in the hole, bubble and squeak, bangers and mash. Danny kept two cookie jars filled—one for Sky and the other that visiting children were allowed to pillage. They may have been terrified of her, but all of them regularly risked her steely eye for the oversize oatmeal-raisin and chocolate-walnut cookies, the lemon squares and treacle tarts.

"When are they going to leave? And why isn't Sky here yet? Why hasn't he called?" Tammy sounded fretful. The lack of activity was getting to her.

Faith didn't have an answer to the second two questions, but she addressed the first. "I wouldn't count on their leaving anytime soon—and they'll be here tomorrow in the daylight. I'm sure if you want to go to bed in one of the guest rooms, that would be all right. I'll wake you when Uncle Sky arrives."

"Bed!" she exploded. "That's the last place I want to be! Not until I can get my own room all cleaned up as if none of this had ever happened. I know I sound just like Scarlet—'I'll think about this tomorrow'—wanting to put it all out of my mind, but it's obvious what happened. A burglar came in, panicked when he saw Danny, killed her so she couldn't identify him, and took off. As to what she was doing in my things, I cannot think and I certainly do not want to."

She stuck her chin out and then lowered it. "Where the hell is Sky?" she said again. "And why hasn't he called?" She was wringing her hands. It was a gesture Faith had only read about in books and, oddly enough, it looked very natural. At least in this case.

At midnight they brought Danny down the staircase, zipped into a black body bag, and out the front door.

"Mrs. Walfort, would you mind coming up to your room? We'd like you to see if anything is out of place or missing." It was the adolescent-looking cop. He seemed to have aged a bit over the course of the evening, to the point where he might be starting to shave.

Tammy grabbed Faith's arm. "You come, too. I don't want to go back there alone."

"Is that all right?" Faith asked.

The officer looked slightly discomfited but said, "I don't see why not. Anyways, if it isn't, the chief will say something."

Without the macabre figure at the dressing table, Tammy's boudoir looked much as it always did save for the black finger-print powder everywhere and the number of people milling about wearing gloves. It wasn't a lurid scene. Perfect servant to the last, the towel Mrs. Danforth had wrapped around her head had kept her blood from splattering.

No one said anything about Faith's being there, and in any case, it would have been difficult to loosen the grip her aunt had on Faith's arm.

"Tammy," the police chief said. "Anything out of place? Missing? Walk around in here and the bathroom. Sky's room, too."

Right away Tammy pointed to her bed. "One of my Delorme pillowcases is gone!"

"Typically, thieves grab a pillowcase and fill it with whatever they spot," Detective Willis said.

Tammy rushed over to her dressing table. "I left a few trinkets out, the good stuff is in the safe, I assume—we'd better check—or at the bank. Let's see. There were a couple of those Jean Schlum-berger enamel bracelets—I couldn't decide whether to wear green or blue yesterday—and I'd taken out some blue topaz David Yur-man earrings, which I left because I *did* wear green, but put the gold Schlumberger cuff bracelet on instead. What else? A Piaget watch, but an everyday one. Mikimoto pearls. I always leave a few different sizes of strands out. They go with everything. Oh, and an amusing little Kenneth Lane vintage butterfly brooch like the Duchess of Windsor wore."

Both the chief's and the detective's faces registered bewilder-ment at the onslaught of names. Faith was struggling to keep something like bewilderment from hers. Trinkets! The Schlum-berger bracelets started at $20,000 and went up from there. Either

Tammy or Sky or both had a great deal more money than Faith realized.

"I think we can assume this was a break-in gone tragically wrong," Chief Matt said ponderously. "Have a look around the other two rooms, although I think the thief panicked before he could go any further."

The detective spoke in a speculative tone. "He may have only meant to knock the old woman out, stun her."

"Have you found what was used to hit her?" Faith asked. Tammy was pawing through a bureau drawer.

"No. Whatever it was, he took it with him. We'll know more after the autopsy. More about the time, too. With the fire keeping the room so warm, we can't make a guess at the time of death." He turned toward Tammy. "I know it's late, but we do need to ask for some more information, Mrs. Walfort."

She wasn't listening. "Ha!" she said triumphantly. "They didn't get my charm bracelet! Daddy gave me a new charm on my birthday every year from the time I was five until I married Wade. See this little bride? Isn't she the cutest thing? Daddy gave it to me on my wedding day. I'd die if anything happened to this bracelet. That's why I keep it here."

Faith had heard that thieves went straight for your underwear drawer after they'd emptied your jewelry box and from there to the toes of your shoes and the pockets of your bathrobe—the traditional "safe" hiding places all women employed if they didn't opt for the fridge's freezer. She wasn't surprised at Tammy's most precious possession. She'd had several friends who'd been robbed and their charm bracelets were lamented more than their diamonds by the yard, if they had them. But she was a bit surprised by Tammy's timing, but once again generously decided her aunt must be in shock—still. Plus, there was the bourbon. Meanwhile, her aunt was busy putting the bracelet on. Faith led her into the bath and Sky's room, where a quick look revealed nothing unusual except for the fact that Danny had apparently used up the last of Tammy's La Prairie bubble bath.

Back in the library, before Detective Willis came to ask the rest of his questions, Faith decided it was time for food and announced she was making omelets and coffee for them all. There was only so much a body could take.

The detective took them through their various arrivals and then asked whether there had been workmen at the house recently.

"Not just individuals who might have had occasion to enter the house, but window cleaners, for example. We broke up one ring when we realized that the break-ins—they were daytime break-ins—all occurred when it was raining and the thieves couldn't work at their other job."

Tammy shook her head. "No, and everyone who's done work for us—the gardeners, the cleaners—have all been in our employ for years."

"We'll still need to check them out. If you could make a list of names and get it to us tomorrow, we'll start right away," he said. "The fact that the perp, or perps, knew to go directly to your room where you kept some jewelry indicates some familiarity with the home."

"I've checked the safes," Tammy said, "and nothing has been disturbed. There are two. A big old one in the butler's pantry, where we keep the silver, and one that Sky says I'm not supposed to mention the location of, where things not at the bank are kept."

Detective Willis closed his notebook.

"Now we'll let you people get some rest. Do you have any idea when Mr. Walfort might be getting here?"

"It's an hour and a half drive, shorter this time of night. He should be here soon." Tammy had called again and was told the message had been delivered two hours earlier. Mr. Walfort had been out to dinner.

"Chief Johnson and I will wait back upstairs for a while, then." He left the room.

"I'm as tired as a mule, but I won't sleep a wink until Sky gets here."

"I think I'll go stretch out on the couch in the living room," Jane said. "Faith?"

"I'll stay here with Tammy." She was slightly amused at Tammy's discretion regarding the location of the safe for valuables. She, Hope, and most likely the entire family knew it was behind a violently pink genre painting of cows grazing at sunrise, purchased at an estate sale by the Walfort who'd selected it for the express purpose of disguising the safe, which was in what had become a little-used guest room.

Schuyler Walfort arrived a half hour later, opening the front door with such force that it crashed against the wall. Faith ran to him.

"What's going on? Why are there police cars outside? Who's been hurt?"

"I'm afraid it's bad news, Uncle Sky." She led him into the library. Tammy threw her arms around him.

"I'm so glad you're here! It's been a nightmare. Danny's been killed!"

Faith thought her uncle was going to pass out.

"Danny? You say Danny's dead? Danny?" He looked wildly about the room as if he expected her to appear. He pulled away from his wife. "Not Danny, noooo . . ." He began to sob uncontrollably. Jane came in from the living room.

"I'm so sorry, Sky."

"It can't be Danny! Not Danny!" He collapsed against his niece and she was able to move him onto the couch. Tammy sat on his other side and took his hand.

"She didn't suffer, the police said. Faith found her. She was in my boudoir of all places, wearing—"

Faith interrupted her aunt. Now was not the time for this particular litany of grievances. She handed her mother a box of tissues from the adjoining half bath and Jane started dispensing them, murmuring words of comfort as Sky continued to give way to his overwhelming anguish.

The noise brought the police chief and the detective into the room.

"Don't you worry, Sky. We'll find the animal who did this," Matt Johnson said. "Some hopped-up junkie looking for easy pickings. Your wife is giving us a list of what's missing, and we'll have it out to every pawnshop in the Northeast." He was speaking rapidly, trying, it seemed, to stem the tsunami of grief. Sky wasn't bothering to use the tissues; the tears flowed unchecked.

"I don't care!" he wailed. "It won't bring her back!"

Faith looked at his face. It was the saddest she had ever seen.

By 5:00 A.M. the police had left after taking everyone's fingerprints for elimination, and the business of death began. Sky asked Faith to call Mrs. Danforth's sister in Connecticut. He didn't think he could handle it. He called his own sisters and broke down all over again. He told them not to come out. Tammy had remarked that that was not going to happen and Faith had privately agreed. Jane had let her husband know and he was on his way. No one went to bed. Sky began toasting his beloved Danny with Laphroaig scotch, apparently her favorite tipple.

Taking Sky's address book, Faith went into the breakfast room to use that phone. A man answered. Faith apologized for the early call and asked for Gertrude Todd, the name next to the notation "Danny's sister" in the book.

"What's this about? I'm her husband. Gert's asleep." He sounded irritated.

"I'm very sorry to tell you that her sister, Mabel Danforth, is dead. She was the housekeeper for my uncle—"

"Dead! What's that you say? Mabel's dead? Was it her heart?"

"No." Faith took a deep breath. "She was murdered sometime yesterday. A burglar, we think. She was alone in the house at the time."

"Murdered! My God! What am I going to tell my wife?"

Faith could hear the disbelief in his voice. Things like this weren't supposed to happen to people you knew, to relatives.

"She wouldn't have felt anything. He came up behind her—"

He interrupted again, "So the cops have the guy?"

"Not yet, but they're hoping to soon. Would you like me to talk to Mrs. Todd? Tell her? We were all so fond of her sister."

"No, I'll tell her," he said.

Before hanging up, Faith gave him The Cliff's phone number and the numbers the police chief and Detective Willis had left. She paused a moment and then dialed the number she'd been aching to call ever since she'd first walked into Tammy's room.

"Tom?"

"Hey, you. What are you doing up at this hour?"

Faith could picture his slightly teasing smile.

"Oh, Tom, something horrible has happened!"

She went on to describe the events of the night before and with difficulty restrained him from driving straight down, much as she wanted him by her side.

"What happens now? You'll be staying on?"

"Yes, for as long as they need me. And as for what comes next, I have no idea. Sky wants her buried in the family plot here. He says the Walforts were her family. She wasn't close to her sister, her only sibling, and there are no nieces or nephews."

"Was there a Mr. Danforth?"

"That's a good question. I have a feeling not, or if there was, the marriage ended a long time ago."

They talked some more. Tom kept insisting on coming down, but Faith said there really wasn't anything he could do other than hold her hand, which would be lovely, but she'd be trying to comfort her uncle and keep people fed. The last thought reminded her of another.

"I almost forgot. I have to call the caterers and cancel the tasting. Mother and I are supposed to go there at noon. I'm afraid the wedding is the last thing on my mind right now."

"The wedding, but not getting married."

"No, dearest Tom, not getting married."

Faith's grandmother Eleanor and her sister, Frances, arrived late in the morning. Like their brother, both women were tall, and age had not caused either spine to bend, literally and figuratively. Eleanor was slender; Frances, the eldest, was a different story. All her life she had been what was referred to as "broad in the beam" and she had the shoulders of a linebacker. She wore her hair, white as snow, in a plump bun. With a slight change in period dress, she could have assumed the role of Wilde's Lady Bracknell. And it was the voice so like the character that announced her presence.

"Where's Schuyler? Where is the man? Prostrate with grief, I imagine, and of course we're all terribly sad, but how on earth did Danny manage to get herself murdered?"

"I don't think she had much of a choice," her sister said dryly. "And yes, where is our brother?"

"Tammy called their doctor and told him what had occurred. He came by and gave Uncle Sky a mild sedative. He's sleeping now."

Frances looked disapproving. "I don't believe in this sort of thing, but as the bard says, 'sleep knits up the ravell'd sleeve of care,' and after the way Schuyler's depended on that woman his entire life, he's going to need a lot of shut eye."

Great-aunt Frances had never married. It would have been hard to find a match for her oversize personality. She was known for always saying what she meant and saying it in a unique manner.

Faith noticed neither woman had asked for their sister-in-law and took it upon herself to mention Tammy. After all, it had been Tammy's boudoir—and Tammy's dressing gown. She wasn't sure whether Uncle Sky had mentioned the latter, but he would certainly have told them where the murder occurred.

"Aunt Tammy is resting as well. She's in one of the guest rooms."

"Do you think I should go see her?" Faith's grandmother asked hesitatingly, her reluctance confirming what Faith had always observed. The sisters didn't know quite what to make of their brother's colorful spouse.

"Let her be, Eleanor. She'll come down when she's ready." Frances cast the deciding vote. "Faith, could you make us some tea? And, Jane, come tell us what's happened. Dreadful, just dreadful."

Faith had everything ready, knowing her grandmother would immediately require a restorative cup of Earl Grey. There was also a platter of sandwiches and another of assorted cookies and pastries. They had arrived from the caterer, who Faith had called earlier to postpone the tasting due to a death in the family. There was no need to get any more specific. In a community this size, it would be all over the place soon enough. Sending over the food had been a much appreciated, thoughtful gesture and Faith was glad she'd chosen this firm for her wedding. The wedding! Should they pick another spot? Get married in her father's church and have the reception someplace in Manhattan?

She brought the tea and food into the living room, where they had moved after the police left. The library had become much too familiar.

"I hope you're not thinking of changing your plans, Faith," Aunt Frances boomed. "Danny would have hated to cause any trouble, and there's no reason why this unfortunate incident should upset your nuptials."

"The invitations haven't gone out," Jane Sibley said. It was clear she was leaving the decision up to her daughter.

"I want to do whatever Uncle Sky wants and I don't want to mention anything about it now."

Her grandmother nodded. "Of course, but I agree with Frances. I'm quite sure Schuyler will want the wedding to proceed as planned, but let's let it lie for now."

The front door opened and the voices they heard in the hall were Faith's father and sister.

"There's that yellow plastic police tape all over the back door! Is that how the killer got in? I assume it was all right to come in this way." Hope walked into the room followed by her father.

Faith was extremely glad to see them. After the Reverend Lawrence Sibley greeted everyone and learned that Sky was sleeping, he went upstairs to Tammy with no hesitation. "The poor woman! Such a shock."

"Ask her if she wants something to eat or drink," Faith said. "And would you like me to bring something up on a tray for you?" Like other members of the clergy she'd observed, her father's meals were often sketchy and interrupted, causing him to adopt a grazing pattern for sustenance.

"That would be kind, but let me see how she is first."

He returned a few minutes later. "Could you make up a tray with coffee and perhaps some sandwiches for us both?" Lawrence said.

Hope went to the kitchen with Faith.

"I'll bet you haven't been outside since you got here, or slept. Which would you like to do—take a walk together or lie down and I'll man the ship?"

"A walk would be heavenly. Take the tray up and I'll tell Mother. They're all set for now. I'll just bring some more hot water for the pot."

It felt glorious to be outdoors even though the sky was appropriately overcast. A brilliant, sunny day would have been jarring. Without discussion, Faith and Hope headed for the familiar wooden staircase at the top of the cliff that led to the beach. And without discussion they walked along the sand to the large flat rock that had been their favorite spot since childhood, serving as a table for dolls' tea parties, picnic spreads when they were older, and occasionally a refuge—a place to stretch out, look up at the sky, and think. It was a refuge now, and the sisters sat close together. Hope put her arm through her sister's.

"Fay, I hope you're not going to postpone the wedding or move it someplace else. This is where you've always wanted to get married."

Her sister was right. The Cliff *was* where Faith had always pictured herself as a bride, but first the falling brickwork and now a murder—not exactly propitious omens.

No, she told herself firmly, not omens—coincidences.

"I think it will be all right. It's just too soon to think about anything to do with the wedding now. I'm leaving it up to Uncle Sky in any case."

"That's all right then. He's so over the moon about having you get married here that you'd think he was the groom."

Faith smiled. There had been ever-widening age differences between her uncle and his wives, but even if Tammy wasn't the keeper she appeared to be, she doubted Sky would be stooping over a cradle as low as hers. She'd asked him to give her away after discussing it with her parents. Hard for her father to walk her down the aisle and then do an about-face at the altar. Tom's brother Craig had asked her what she was going to do, joking that her father would have to be a quick-change artist. Faith could have

come down the aisle alone or Tom could have met her halfway—
she'd been at a wedding where the bride and groom had done this
and it was very moving. Her mother had flatly refused to walk her
down. "I'm not that liberated. At least not in this respect," she'd
added. Being given away was an odd notion in many respects, but
Faith was a traditionalist. Uncle Sky had been delighted. He'd
already ordered full morning coat regalia from his London tailor.

"This has been a nightmare for you," Hope said. "What did
your honey say? You have talked to him, right?"

She filled her sister in, including Tom's offer to drive down,
which Hope agreed should be put off.

"You have enough on your plate. Let him come next week,
when I'm afraid the shock of all this will hit you. Right now,
you're too busy."

Faith agreed and turned the conversation to Hope's current
work dilemmas. She felt a bit guilty at not having gotten back to
her sister after the most recent client departure, the one who was
not, technically, a client but was in the bag.

"Any more desertions? And any ideas about the sudden concern for your health?"

"Nope and nope."

Faith needed to express a thought, though, and aimed it carefully.

"Who do you discuss your clients with? I mean, is there someone at work you ask advice from, or maybe Phelps, since he's in
the same sort of business?" Phelps was the target.

Hope straightened slightly to look her sister in the face. "Heav-
ens no, Fay! Client confidentiality, duh!"

"So, no pillow talk?" Faith said.

"Not that kind." Hope gave a slightly wicked smile and they
both laughed. Faith was relieved. She was still dubious about
Phelps Grant, but at least he wasn't using her sister to poach clients.

"We'd better go back. Uncle Sky might be awake, and the police were going to call or stop by after the medical examiner finished the autopsy," Faith said.

"Is this really happening? Murder? Autopsies? Here at The Cliff? I always thought that when people said on the news they couldn't believe something had happened it sounded so fake," Hope said, "but it isn't at all."

"No, it isn't," Faith said sadly, and the two sisters set out for the house over the glistening sand, still wet from the ebbing tide.

In their absence both their uncle and aunt had gotten up. Everyone was in the living room. As Hope and Faith entered, Schuyler Walfort stood and went over to Faith, placing one hand on her shoulder. The sleep had done him good. He looked much better, although his face was still pale and drawn.

"I won't hear of any change in plans for the wedding. Jane says the invitations are ready and were to go out at the end of the week. I insist you stick to the schedule. And you were out here for the tasting, which I can understand you needed to postpone, but call them and do it tomorrow. Danny would have been devastated to think her death had done anything to upset what she always called 'her family.'"

Faith gave him a quick hug.

"Thank you. It's hard to think about it now, but we won't change anything, and I'll see if Mother and I can go tomorrow."

Privately she wondered if Mrs. Danforth had ever called any of them other than Sky her family, but it was what he believed—and needed to believe.

"Tamora is finishing a list of stolen items to fax to the police," Great-aunt Frances said. "There's been no word from the medical examiner's office yet, but the police chief called to say that unfortunately all the fingerprints they found have been identified as some of ours and that the miscreant must have worn gloves." Frances had appointed herself the town crier.

"There." Tammy flourished a sheet of paper. "Done. All jewelry. Nothing else. I remembered that my sable is having the lining repaired, so it's accounted for, and there was nothing in Danny's room that didn't belong to her." As the woman was not here to object, Tammy was using the name she never dared use when the housekeeper was alive.

She continued, "The agency is sending over someone for now and I'll start interviewing for a replacement tomorrow."

The room grew silent.

"Well, y'all aren't going to do laundry, wash dishes, cook dinner—although, Faith could do that—and everything else that keeps this place running, and I'm not, so the sooner the better."

"Of course, Tamora," Frances said. "You are to be commended for your foresight."

Faith was standing next to her aunt and heard Tammy mutter, "Who talks like that, for God's sake? It's almost the twenty-first century."

And then the phone calls began. Faith and Hope took turns. The local grapevine had passed along the news faster than the speed of light and they fielded prurient calls disguised as condolences as well as genuinely sympathetic ones. There were also nuggets of information. A house farther down the road had also been broken into last night, albeit unsuccessfully. The glass in a rear door had been shattered, but the thief or thieves had been unable to turn the dead bolt. There had been several reports of a black utility van in the neighborhood on Sunday. A neighborhood noted for luxury vehicles, these vans were around only on workdays. It was because of the possibility that someone might have real information as well as hoping the police would call with some that kept Faith and Hope jumping up at the first ring, although it was tempting after some twenty calls to let the machine pick up.

The family remained in the living room, leaving for various reasons, but returning to stay together. Conversation was determinedly steered to the weather and the various cultural activities the Lennox sisters had recently attended. Both Great-aunt Frances and Faith's grandmother Eleanor were lifelong patrons of both Mets, the opera and the museum.

At about four o'clock the doorbell rang, followed by the sound of the front-door knocker.

"It must be the police. Will you let them in please, Faith?" Frances said. Sky's sisters, especially his oldest, had taken charge.

But it wasn't the police. When Faith opened the door, two elderly people were standing outside. They were carrying suitcases.

"I'm Gertrude Todd and this is my husband, Herbert. We've come for Mabel's things. I always knew you people would kill her."

CHAPTER 7

"Please come in. Our hearts go out to you at this terrible time of bereavement." Tammy was behind Faith at the door, and unlike her, not at a loss for words. A Southern gentlewoman through and through, she was dealing with the awkward situation to the manner born, speaking gently and with apparent sincerity.

"Would you like to go straight to your sister's room or may I get you something to eat or drink? It must have been a long drive."

Herbert Todd opened his mouth. "That would be—" But before he could finish, his wife snapped, "We're not hungry. We just want to pack her things and go."

She was a terrier of a woman, a bit smaller than Mabel Danforth and, it seemed, younger. Was this rapid appearance on the Walfort doorstep due to grief—wanting reminders of the dead woman—or avarice? Sky had always been generous to his Danny, and Faith had observed the housekeeper had some good, albeit understated, jewelry and dressed well. She may not have had a sable coat, but she had a nutria one that she wore for best. Did her sister covet it? Then again, the venom with which Gertrude Todd had spoken indicated that she did not simply dislike her sister's employers but suspected them of criminal behavior—the way she'd spat out the word "kill" did not suggest "kill" as in "overwork." Could she really suspect that one or more of the family was a murderer, and her arrival might mean that she believed they were thieves as well?

Uncle Schuyler had said the two sisters weren't close, but Faith wondered whether he was correct. There was more going on here than making sure the nutria didn't get spirited away by someone who was not entitled to it. Or perhaps that was it. Gertrude *wasn't* entitled to Danny's belongings. Sky would have made sure Danny had a will. He was a stickler for detail in legal matters. Who inherited and what did the housekeeper have to leave? Was there another relative, a cousin perhaps, and the Todds were quickly putting the good old "possession is nine tenths of the law" into action?

Sky came forward into the hall from the living room with his hand outstretched. "Mrs. Todd, Gertrude, I cannot tell you how upset we all are, and the police are moving swiftly to find the person who committed this heinous act." He was starting to cry again.

Gertrude ignored his hand and his sympathy. "Like I said, we want to get her things and get out of here." Her intonation suggested that any lingering on their part would only be due to the unlawful kinds of duress used to extract confessions—branding irons, splinters under fingernails, waterboarding.

"Her room is upstairs. I'll show you and leave you to it," Tammy said, still speaking as graciously as if the Todds had dropped by to vet the house for a photo spread in *Town & Country*. Faith was not surprised by the way her aunt was dealing with the situation. Hope and Faith regarded her not just with affection but with admiration—she always seemed to have her bases covered. At the moment, Faith was noting that the offer to leave the Todds to it was not due solely to Tammy's discretion in a time of sorrow, but owed more to the fact that she had gone over the housekeeper's suite with a fine-tooth comb once the police were finished. She'd told Faith that her search had merely yielded some cosmetic bonus samples that Tammy had thrown into her wastebasket. Apparently, Danny made free with Tammy's clothing and other belongings only within the confines of the bath and boudoir.

"She kept some things in a closet in the kitchen, so when you're finished upstairs, I can show you where that is. And at least let me give you some coffee while you're performing this sad task."

Tammy's accent had migrated from the Delta to someplace in the British Isles. It seemed to have a positive effect on the Todds. Gertrude said they *could* use a cup of coffee and Herbert looked positively genial as they followed her up the stairs. Sky, having been so brusquely ignored, stood staring after them until Frances came out from the living room, took him by the arm, and said they should all take a walk.

Faith rightly assumed the coffee was her job and she added a plate of sandwiches with a few cookies, the ones sent by the caterer. The jars in the kitchen were still filled with Danny's handiwork, which her sister might or might not recognize.

She knocked on the door and Herbert answered, opening it just wide enough to admit the tray, which he took from her hands with a quick thank-you. She had time before he shut it, however, to catch a glimpse of the room and suppressed an audible gasp. It looked as if it had been tossed. Clothing and a number of pocketbooks were spread helter-skelter all over the bed; the drawer from the nightstand and one from the bureau were upside down on it. Gertrude was by the desk at the window and taking some papers from an accordion file.

Faith seldom had an occasion to be in this part of the house. Mrs. Danforth wasn't the type to invite you up for a cozy chat. She did know, though, that Danny's quarters weren't a shoe box of cast-off furniture—a Spartan straw mattress on an iron bedstead. The rooms—there was a separate small sitting room with a balcony off the large bedroom—were beautifully furnished and looked out over the ocean. But then, Danny had been at The Cliff for many more years than Faith had been alive and it was appropriate that she had such a nice place to live.

She stood for a moment staring at the door that had been firmly closed. Gertrude's activity suggested that what they were looking for so frantically was some sort of paper—a letter, a document, maybe a photograph? And the fact that they were searching the room with such thoroughness must mean they suspected it had been hidden.

On her way downstairs she continued to run through the possibilities—what could the housekeeper have had of such value? And whatever it was, its existence was known to her sister, but not its exact location.

The group had moved back to the library, where Sky kept his liquor cabinet. He had opted for more scotch instead of a walk. His sisters were drinking sherry. Faith was struck by the realization that times of crisis alternated between intense periods of activity and equally intense stretches of inactivity, which was unsettling—like not knowing whether you were stepping onto firm ground or quicksand.

Faith's father got up when she entered the room.

"I'm afraid I have to go soon. I promised Dan West a game of chess this evening. There won't be too many more."

Faith gave her father a hug. "Of course." Daniel West was not only a parishioner but also one of her father's closest friends and had refused further treatment for the pancreatic cancer that was killing him. He wanted to die at home surrounded by his books, listening to his favorite operas, and, he'd told Lawrence, losing one last chess game, but only to the grim reaper, no one else. When Faith had heard this she'd pictured Daniel in the Swedish filmmaker Ingmar Bergman's *Seventh Seal,* courageously facing Death's final checkmate.

Her sister came over to her and said softly, "I can stay if you like."

"No, Mother's here, and everybody else. You need to get back to work. Circle your wagons and make sure no one raids your client list. I expect I'll be busy supplying everyone with food and drink, although the drink part doesn't seem to be a problem at the moment. I'll go see if the Todds want more coffee in a little while."

Faith had debated telling her family about the search going on over their heads and decided it wasn't something she ought to keep to herself. And maybe Uncle Sky knew what it was they were after, Danny's will most likely.

"The Todds seem to be making a very through search of Mrs. Danforth's belongings before packing them."

"What do you mean?" Tammy said. "Searching how?"

"Turning over drawers, going through papers, and her clothes were scattered all over. I thought it could be that they wanted to find her will."

"Nonsense," Sky said. "Her will is with my legal documents in a safety-deposit box at the bank and the lawyers have the other copy. Her sister gets everything, and she's known that for years. Danny doesn't have a large estate, but I've always advised her on how to invest prudently and the Todds won't be disappointed." He said this last acerbically.

"Maybe they're looking for money," Tammy said. "When Aunt Sister died, we found hundred-dollar bills all over the house— tucked between plates, in books, even a bunch at the bottom of her sewing basket. We didn't dare give a single pot or pan to Goodwill until we'd examined everything. 'Course it was all Confederate currency. Her granddaddy told her it was a fortune and the poor thing would just *not* believe otherwise. Fortunately her husband believed in the other kind of moolah and kept it all in the bank."

"Which is where Danny's is, too, so what that harpy and her

husband are doing is a sacrilege." Sky was fuming and made for the door. "Rummaging through her things before she's even cold in the ground." The sudden change in tone from grief to fury was startling. Even his face looked completely different, Faith noted. She repressed a slight Jekyll and Hyde shudder.

"Sit down, Schuyler," Aunt Frances said. "You can't stop them now. They're in the house—we let them in, as was proper—and getting yourself into a tizzy won't change anything."

Her sister added, "Tamora is no doubt correct that they suspect Danny had a rainy-day fund tucked away under the mattress or somewhere like that. Older people sometimes do this." Her tone made it clear that she was not one of them.

Sky sat down again. Faith walked her father and Hope out the front door. As she waved good-bye, Faith suddenly felt very alone, enveloped by the bizarre nature of the last twenty or so hours. She'd found a corpse in the ancestral home from which she would soon be married, after which horror it had been crawling with police and now was host to relatives of the deceased who seemed to be putting a new twist on Kübler-Ross's anger stage of grief. Time to bring another carafe of hot coffee and see what they were up to.

She knocked on the door before entering, but it wasn't necessary. They were gone. The room was empty and still a mess, although the pile of clothes was diminished. There was no sign of the nutria coat—or of any of the housekeeper's pocketbooks. Shoes were another matter—dumped out of their boxes and the wooden shoe trees removed, they were in a heap by the closet. Faith went over to the windows and was in time to see the Todds pull out into the road. They were traveling fast, but not, she suspected, light. They wouldn't have left this soon if they hadn't found what they were looking for—*and* they had wanted to slip away with whatever it was without the family's knowledge. They must have gone down the back stairs and come around the house from the rear to their car parked in front.

Faith picked up the tray—every last crumb had been consumed—and went downstairs to tell the others. The harpies, if
that was what they were, had flown away.

"I see, yes." Uncle Sky was on the phone and the room was quiet,
all ears intent on what he was saying—and hearing. "Yes, yes. No,
we had no idea. Most unfortunate. Yes. Thank you. I'll let my
wife know. Good-bye."

He turned wearily. "That was Matt. He's received a prelimi-
nary report from the medical examiner's office, emphasis on 'pre-
liminary,' but it's clear that Danny died instantly from a blow to the
back of the head." He paused to pull himself together. "She . . . she
had an unusually vulnerable skull, possibly they think because of
something called osteogenesis imperfecta, brittle bone disease. It's
hereditary and she must have had it all her life. I never knew," he
said sorrowfully. "Matt thinks the blow was just meant to knock
her out. When it was apparent they had killed her, they took off
with what was on the dressing table without going through the
rest of the house."

"Oh dear," Faith's grandmother said. "Danny wasn't one for
the outdoors, not active in that way—and she did break a bone at
least two times that I can recall, but she *looked* fit."

"She was," her brother retorted. "This other business was an
anomaly. Anyway, they may be releasing the body as soon as tomorrow."

"We have to let her sister know, Schuyler," Aunt Frances said
sternly. "I know how you feel about keeping Danny with us, but
it's Mrs. Todd's decision as next of kin."

"I am *not* calling that woman!" he shouted. His emotions were
appearing not just close to the surface but on it.

"I didn't say that, dear. I'm sure Faith will do it. She called
earlier, didn't she?"

I seem to be having all the fun, Faith thought as she said, "I'll call in a while. They won't be back in Connecticut yet." It would give her time to think about how she should phrase this latest news—"Your sister would be alive if she hadn't been soft in the head" didn't sound right.

"Matt also said they're finished with the house and we can use those rooms now."

Tammy jumped up. "I'll call the cleaners. They can be here in the morning and get rid of all that nasty black powder! I'll sleep in the blue guest room. You're staying, Frances and Eleanor, I assume, I mean, we hope?"

They were, and after a flurry of assigning beds, Tammy left.

The day crept on in its petty pace into evening. Faith put together a hearty soup from chicken broth she found in the freezer; kale, onions, and chorizo that were all in the fridge; plus cans of chickpeas and stewed tomatoes and some orzo in the larder. No one seemed to want to eat at the same time, so she was kept busy ladling it out and serving it with Parmesan grated on top until close to nine o'clock, when Sky announced after consuming two bowls that he was going to bed.

"I doubt I'll sleep, but I'll see you all in the morning," he said, making it clear he needed to be alone. Faith hugged him hard. "I'm so sorry, Uncle Sky," she told him, producing another onslaught of tears. The soup would help, but she grabbed two of the water bottles the caterer had included, placing them in his hands. Dehydration was a definite possibility.

After some desultory conversation, the Walfort sisters turned in, as did Jane Sibley.

"Faith, you must be exhausted. Come to bed," her mother said.

"I will. I just want to try the Todds again. I haven't been able to reach them." She'd called twice.

Third time was a charm and after a brief and extremely unpleasant conversation with Gertrude, who answered the phone,

Faith returned to the library. Tammy was its only occupant and was heading upstairs carrying a nightcap.

"They'll be making the funeral arrangements, and they're private," Faith told her.

"Sky will be upset, but I can't say I am. The plot is getting pretty crowded, plus I had enough of her dirty looks when she was alive without suffering them through all eternity. Guess I won't have to worry about minding my *p*s and *q*s so much now."

One thing about Tammy. She could always make you laugh.

Faith went around and turned out the lights, making sure the doors were locked. It was what Danny would normally have done. Why hadn't she locked the back door last night? The question kept returning. The housekeeper was a stickler for details like this and would never have been careless about something so essential. As far-fetched as it seemed to Faith, it had to be that Mrs. Danforth was expecting someone. But who?

Even with the extra guests and the need for its mistress to vacate her boudoir for the night, the house offered a wide range of choices for Faith to bed down. She selected the room she and Hope loved best. It was on the top floor in one of the turrets that graced The Cliff's four corners. She'd spent many rainy days curled up on the curved window seat reading the old-fashioned books left by young females from previous generations: *What Katy Did, The Little Colonel,* and *Elsie Dinsmore.* Tonight she didn't need reading material to fall asleep and drifted off as soon as she pulled the covers up.

What she hadn't pulled were the drapes, and when she turned over in her sleep toward the windows, the moon's bright rays shone directly on the pillow, forcing her eyes open. She got up to block the light and instead stood looking out, entranced by the scene in front of her. She could just make out the shore below and was filled with a sudden impulse to go see more of it from the attic.

A terrible thing had happened, but the moon, the sea, and the shore were still there, unchanged and unchanging. She was filled with a mild euphoria. She was going to be married to her true love on this very spot. They would watch moonrises, and sunrises, for the rest of their lives together. She slipped on her robe and slippers, opened the door quietly, although she was the only one sleeping in this part of the house, and made her way to the attic. Still, she tiptoed. Halfway up its stairs she heard something and paused, listening. It wasn't coming from above. A door closing, a footstep? Whatever it was, it had stopped. She waited a bit longer and then continued, chiding herself for being spooked by what was probably a tree branch blowing against the side of the house or some other act of nature.

The moonlight eliminated the need for any other illumination. She squeezed past boxes, trunks, wardrobes, a rocking horse, and a dressmaker's dummy for a full-figured gal to the chair that had been placed at one of the front windows. She sat down as she had done the week before, enjoying the vista spread out beneath her. It was like being in a treetop. She felt her body relax as she thought about bringing Tom here, as well as showing him the rest of the house and grounds. Her eyelids began to get heavy. In a moment she'd fall asleep in the chair, even though the seat was caned and the back hard as a rock. She leaned forward on the sill for one last parting look, her mind filled with pleasant reveries. Her foot grazed the baseboard, picking up what she thought at first was a large dust bunny. Bending over to pull it off her slipper, she saw that it wasn't dust but a feather. A bright red feather. A fluffy marabou feather. It hadn't been here on the floor on Thursday. She would have spotted it, as incongruous in this setting as it would have been anywhere else in the house save Tammy's boudoir.

Chilled, she pulled her robe more tightly closed.

Danny had been here. When? Last night? Sitting in the chair alone with her thoughts? Sitting in the chair keeping watch?

Or had it been Great-aunt Tammy? She'd been at the house until Saturday.

Could the simplest explanation be the right one? That one woman or the other had felt the same urge Faith had and wanted to gaze out at the landscape from the house's highest point?

Quickly moving to the switches by the stairs, Faith flicked on all the lights. Shadowed forms took reassuring shapes. She began to circle the entire floor, going from window to window, slowly working her way around the attic. No more feathers. At the rear, there was a large window that opened out, high above the back door. Unlike the other sills that were in need of a spring cleaning, this one showed signs of activity, as if someone had been here recently. Faith unlocked the window and pushed. It swung freely on well-oiled hinges. She examined the oval frame carefully. There was a small, frayed piece of rope, like the kind used for clotheslines, caught in a crack in the outer sill where the bottom of the window rested. She worked the scrap free and looked at it in stronger light, noting a faint streak of orange dust that rubbed off on her fingers.

It was the same kind of rope that had been around the brickwork she had so recently dodged. Attached to it was a minuscule piece of fishing line. She almost missed the transparent filament. The chunk she had barely avoided hadn't fallen from a chimney. It had been dropped from here.

Someone was in her room. The drapes were opening. Sunlight streamed in. Faith sat up, completely wide awake.

"I didn't mean to startle you, darling, but it's almost ten o'clock and I thought you might not want to sleep too late, although you certainly needed it."

It was her mother and she was holding a steaming cup.

"Coffee. And when you're ready, come down for breakfast. There's an extremely pleasant lady in the kitchen who will make whatever you want. I had poached eggs."

Her mother always had poached eggs—two instead of one on special occasions—with wheat toast and marmalade.

She handed Faith the mug and sat down on the side of the bed. It was infinitely comforting seeing her there, and Faith wished they could stay like that all day, her mother making forays for something to eat on a tray and more up-to-date reading material than *Highlights* magazine, but sequestered as if she'd been transported back to a childhood bout with the flu. She had a sudden craving for flat ginger ale and cinnamon toast, her mother's sickroom staples.

The coffee was good and strong.

"How is everyone?"

"As you might expect. Mother and Aunt Frances have been up since dawn and already taken a walk. They're going to go back with us later this afternoon. I admit I suggested it—Sky and Tammy need some time to themselves after all this. I haven't seen Sky this morning, but Tammy has been a whirlwind, organizing the cleaners and interviewing housekeepers by phone. She's got two coming in person this afternoon, and she's also considering hiring the woman the agency sent. The one who's here now."

Faith finished her coffee, set it down, and stretched. When it came to organizational skills, you couldn't beat those Delta women.

The rest of the morning passed quickly as Faith showered and had a light breakfast. The tasting was scheduled for one o'clock, so she didn't want to eat much. Her visit to the attic the night before had taken on the quality of a dream, no, make that a nightmare.

And there was no one to tell. She put on a smiling face and went off with the mother of the bride to the next town, where the caterers were. The tasting was a pleasant interlude. Nothing more stressful than deciding between things like raw shrimp or lightly battered (they decided on both). When they returned, everyone was in the conservatory and things seemed, on the surface, to be back to normal. Uncle Sky got up and kissed her.

"Are you going to be well and truly fed as well as well and truly wed?"

Faith was happy to see the change in his mood. If he was up to a bad rhyme, he was definitely over the worst of his grief.

"It will be both a palate pleaser and pleasing for the eye." He tended to elicit this kind of remark in others, too. She *had* been impressed at the tasting, however. The food was even better than she had hoped it would be and the presentation perfect—attractive without being silly, four slivers of something on a tray gussied up with orchids from the Amazon.

Sky rubbed his hands together. "Good, good, good. And remember, as 'father of the bride,' I'm providing the potent potables. Don't want the caterers to palm off some Cold Duck disguised as champagne. The horror!"

Feeling bridal indeed—the caterers had presented her with a lovely nuptial nosegay—Faith went upstairs to get the small overnight bag she had brought, never imagining what that night would bring. When she returned, her mother, her grandmother, and Aunt Frances were in the hall saying good-bye.

"Now don't forget about my tea for Faith, Tammy," Nana said. "And it's ladies only, Sky. Don't try to crash the way you did at Faith's shower."

"Poppy would have been happy to let me stay. Rules like this are made to be broken! Faith is a modern bride."

"That may be, but I am not a modern woman and I'm the

one giving the engagement party." Her grandmother tempered her words by kissing her brother's cheek, a demonstrative gesture in this family akin to a bear hug and busses on both cheeks in another.

Back in the city after dropping the others off, Faith refused her mother's invitation for dinner—the ubiquitous nice piece of something and salad—planning to indulge in carb-laden Chinese takeout. Garlic lo mein with plenty of veggies and pot stickers. Comfort food.

The phone was ringing as she opened her door and she ran to answer it. She'd talked to Tom when she'd gotten up this morning and he said he'd call her apartment around now. Never had she been so in need of hearing his voice. Another kind of comfort food.

"Hello?"

"Darling," he said. "How are you? Have you been home long?"

"I just walked in. Literally."

"Good. I'll be there in less than an hour."

"Tom! Where are you?"

"At a rest stop in Connecticut. Not sure what town."

"You're crazy."

"No, I'm not. And let's eat in. Should I stop and pick something up?"

Faith laughed. She couldn't imagine what Tom would bring and was almost tempted to say yes just to see, but told him she'd been about to order Chinese and would order a whole lot more. She made a mental note to nix the garlic and go for ginger.

"Get me some spareribs. Oh, and sweet-and-sour something. I love that stuff."

Clearly there was work to do here, but she'd indulge him with the cloying red dye #2 dish for now—and probably later as well. Faith was a food snob and proud of it, but she realized with a

slight shock that she would jettison all her strongly held culinary
principles for the man she loved. Well, maybe not the one about
canned bread crumbs.

The timing was perfect; Tom arrived a few minutes after the
food had been delivered. As they ate, Faith started at the beginning and told him everything that had happened over the last few
days, only omitting her visit to the attic and the piece of rope. She
hadn't told him about the falling brickwork. She was still trying to
figure out what it meant herself. When she'd returned to her room
last night, she'd lain awake thinking about Thursday's incident.
Aunt Tammy hadn't arrived home yet from her spa vacation and
Sky had left before Faith did, which meant only the housekeeper
was in the house. Was this some kind of *Jane Eyre*/madwoman-
in-the-attic scenario? Danny heaving the rock down at Faith in a
crazed fit of jealousy, never having been a bride herself? But why
had she tied the rope around the missile? Had it all been rigged up
earlier and suspended out the window, scheduled somehow to fall
on a different victim? One of the Walforts? Who else used that
door?

No, there had been enough drama to last a lifetime and she
didn't want to add to it, spoiling any more of her precious time,
this beautiful unexpected time, with Tom. And it didn't.

The next morning Tom made a few calls and decided that First
Parish could spare him for one more day and night. Faith was ecstatic, and besides, she pointed out to him, the parish would soon
be getting a kind of twofer—and the work she would do wouldn't
cost them anything.

"I've told you that this is *my* job, Faith," Tom protested. "I'd
like you to come to church on Sundays, but that's it."

Having been on-site all her life, Faith knew better, and at this point, she welcomed her new role. Except for the church school Christmas pageant. There were limits.

"I have to drop off a fabric sample that I picked out for Hope's dress at her office, and it's a nice crosstown walk. And maybe my father is free. We could stop at the church before or after and talk some more about the ceremony."

"Sounds perfect," Tom said, reaching into his pocket and pulling out a Day Runner. "I've jotted down a few possibilities for readings."

"We don't want too many; people will get restless," Faith said. "We're going by the book, yes, the King James one?"

Tom laughed. "Absolutely. I've been at those weddings where if one more person gets up to read from Khalil Gibran, I begin to wish I hadn't held my peace at the start. And don't worry, honey, I haven't changed my mind about our vows. I'm not going to stand on the seashore and describe you as a lighthouse, your beacon of light shining through the fog of my life, or some other maritime metaphor."

"And in return I promise not to say you're the wind beneath my wings."

It wouldn't be sung either. Faith had already engaged the string quartet Have Faith used for events. Now all Tom and she had to do was choose the music. Definitely the Pachelbel Canon, and she was also leaning toward "Jesu, Joy of Man's Desiring." Both pieces regularly caused a lump in her throat when she heard them at weddings.

They were in luck and Lawrence Sibley had time after a lunch meeting.

"I never officially asked your father for your hand in marriage," Tom said as they walked down Central Park South toward Fifth Avenue.

"Too late now," Faith said, holding up her left hand. The ring caught the light and sent tiny rainbows across her fingers. "But judging from the cheers that came roaring through the phone when I called to tell them, I'd say he would have given you my hand and anything else you wanted—a lock of hair and I think they have the first baby tooth I lost."

They arrived at Hope's office in the Citicorp Building on 53rd Street between Lexington and Third Avenue a few minutes later. The building was one of Manhattan's tallest, with a dramatic sloped roof that, when it went up in 1977, had originally been intended for solar panels until someone realized the angle was wrong—it wouldn't face the sun. Instead, it became a design element, almost as distinctive now as the venerable Empire State and the Art Deco Chrysler buildings. Tom was suitably impressed.

Hope was finishing a phone call and they waited outside her office. Faith was amused to note that Tom elicited much more attention from Hope's assistant than she had—"May I get you some coffee? Bottled water? Today's paper?" She was still trying when Hope emerged and introduced them.

"Jennifer, you remember my sister, Faith, and this is her fiancé, Reverend Thomas Fairchild."

Faith could scarcely keep from laughing out loud at the crestfallen look on Jennifer's face. Whether it was the word "fiancé" or the word "reverend" that placed the man off-limits didn't matter, although looking at the striking woman and the provocative smile that quickly returned, Faith doubted any man was off-limits for Jennifer.

Hope liked the swatch—a soft moss color that would make her eyes look even greener and go well with her dark hair.

"Has Mother decided what she's wearing yet?"

"Anything but mauve lace. I don't know where she got the idea that this was a mother-of-the-bride thing, but she has. Oh dear, Tom, I haven't asked *your* mother what she's wearing. It may be mauve lace."

"I don't even know what that means, but don't worry. It will be some shade of blue, her favorite color. Right now she's not thinking about the wedding, but about this tea your grandmother is giving. She has the idea that everyone there will be dressed to the nines and she'll look like a hick."

"I'll call her. My grandmother doesn't travel in an Oscar de la Renta crowd."

Tom looked puzzled. When it came to names and faces, he often had no idea what his beautiful bride was talking about.

"A designer popular with society ladies. Anyway, the Cosmopolitan Club bars jeans, shorts, and athletic apparel. As long as she doesn't jog in wearing any of those, she'll be fine. And your mother could wear a burlap bag and make it look good." Marian Fairchild was still an extremely attractive woman, tall like the rest of the family. Tom had inherited her velvet brown eyes and her thick hair, now so white it looked platinum. Faith was glad Tom's mother and one of his aunts were coming. She'd arranged for them to stay at the Morrises' as Poppy was away with Emma on their trip. Jason Morris had moved to his club, but the house was still staffed. Marian had confessed to a passion for seeing other people's houses. She'd told Faith she loved house tours and walking by places at night, feeling a bit like a voyeur as she looked into lighted rooms. "Not such a failing considering Dick is in real estate, but I'd be like this if he was a butcher," she'd said. Faith shared this enthusiasm. Looking at and talking about real estate was not just a pastime in Manhattan but an obsession.

After leaving Hope, they stopped for lunch at the Brasserie in the Seagram Building, also on East 53rd Street.

"I'm definitely getting the architectural tour this time," Tom had said as they crossed the plaza toward the Mies van der Rohe international-style structure, one of Faith's favorite buildings. Outside it was a sleek bronze box; inside it exploded with light. Erected in the 1950s, it was timeless.

Tom had mussels and frites, addictively crisp fries, and, as usual, shared. Faith opted for the onion soup that was as good as the ones she'd tasted in France, maybe better. Not too salty or too cheesy and plenty of caramelized onions. They skipped dessert. Faith knew there would be coffee at the church offices, and on the way they stopped at an Au Bon Pain, the closest bakery, for her father's favorite *pain au chocolat* as well as some of their *pain raisin,* which was a decent version with yummy almond cream.

The church was a short walk farther and soon she was munching away between the two men she loved most in the world—if only Uncle Sky was there, it would be three. Faith was very happy. It was going to be a beautiful service. And she was basking in the affection the two men already had for each other. There wouldn't be any in-law problems for either the bride or the groom. Lucky. She was a very lucky girl.

Her father's office at the church was lined with glass-fronted bookcases and wooden file cabinets. It was neat, in sharp contrast to his office at home, where the floor was covered with teetering stacks of books and papers that all, save him, were forbidden to touch. "I know where everything is." During Faith's brief visit to Aleford, she had noted that Tom's public and private offices followed the same pattern. The only difference was a computer in his cluttered workspace compared to Lawrence Sibley's preferred manual typewriter.

The phone on her father's desk rang.

"Will you excuse me?" he said, reaching over to answer it.

They stood, preparing to leave the room so he could talk in private.

He held up a hand and motioned for them to sit back down.

"It's your mother," he said, and after telling her that Tom and Faith were there, turned his attention to what his wife was saying.

"Very sad," he said. "That poor family. Oh, no children? Well, a tragedy all the same."

He listened quietly.

"I'll be home early. No, I don't know what their plans are. I'll ask. I do know that Tom is staying until tomorrow morning." There was a pause. "I rather think that's your and Faith's department, my dear. But I'll mention it. Good-bye."

He hung the phone up. "There was a fire at the Todds' and neither Gertrude nor Herbert has survived. A neighbor noticed smoke coming from the house early this morning, and even though the fire department arrived quickly, it was too late. The house was an older one and it's been a battle to keep the flames from spreading to the houses on either side."

"Do they have any idea what started it?" Tom asked.

"Yes," Lawrence said. "It was unseasonably cold last night, and they were in the habit of using a propane space heater they'd had for years in their bedroom when the temperature dropped. The same neighbor who reported the fire told the police she had been after them to replace it because her own sister had barely escaped a fire started by one."

"How did Mother find out?" Faith had a too vivid picture of the couple, lying now forever asleep. Why were those heaters still on the market? All winter there had been headline after headline about tragedies like this one.

"Their car was in a detached garage and the crew pushed it out into the street. The police found directions to The Cliff, including the phone number in the glove compartment, and called Sky."

Tom put his arm around Faith and she leaned her head on his shoulder.

"I know what you're thinking," he said, "but God is not a puppeteer and our wedding is not jinxed. It's a coincidence that the two sisters died so close together and so unfortunately. A coincidence that you knew them. Otherwise the fire would have just been a small item in the paper about a couple you didn't know."

He was right. "Still, I wish it had been a warmer night."

"So do I, darling."

Faith sat up. "What was that last bit about? What did Mother want you to mention?"

Her father smiled. "Wardrobe concerns. She asked me to be sure Tom, his best man, and his brothers are all set."

"You can tell her to cross that off her list—and yours, Faith. Morning coats it is. I'm only getting married once and plan to do it in style. I have your Uncle Sky to thank for suggesting it. We've all been measured at a very nice rental place and are set. Craig wants to buy his to wear on campus afterward."

Faith was going to enjoy this brother-in-law.

"We're having dinner at the Russian Tea Room," she told her father. "I've been giving Tom a taste of all my favorites, a crash course. We'd love you to join us. I can change the reservation. I made it for eight o'clock. But we can eat earlier if you like."

"I think we'll pass this time, thank you. You enjoy your blinis." He knew Faith always ordered the same thing: the caviar tasting, three varieties, and warm buckwheat blinis. "It's rare that I can get home early, and I think we'll make it an early night all around."

"I could get used to this. Your New York, I mean," Tom said. "This place is like a set for *The Firebird,* a very opulent one."

"Exactly right. The restaurant was started in the nineteen twenties by former members of the Russian Imperial Ballet, homesick, obviously, although I doubt they had *this* many golden samovars. With Carnegie Hall next door, it's always been a hangout for musicians, actors, show business people. When I was a little girl, Aunt Chat would take Hope and me here and we always thought it looked like Christmas decorations all year round."

It was Wednesday and that meant the Russian Tea Room's special Siberian *pelmenis,* the Russian version of kreplach, pot stickers, raviolis—all those wonderfully stuffed doughs, steamed or fried in countries across the world—was on the menu. This version was filled with ground meat and served with peas, sour cream, and dill. Tom ordered the special and Faith stuck to her usual. They were both drinking vodka, and the shimmering red and gold room was beginning to feel very toasty warm, she thought.

"Boston is going to be hard put to come up to any of this." Tom looked slightly worried.

Faith hastened to reassure him. "'Whither thou goest,' remember? And New England offers plenty of good stuff to eat. Lobster, for one."

"Which reminds me. Are you sure a clambake is a good idea for the rehearsal dinner?"

Dick Fairchild had come up with the proposal and had even checked with his favorite spot, Woodman's, up in Essex, on Massachusetts's North Shore, to see if they could ship their lobsters, steamers, chowder, and even the bibs. They could and would. Faith thought it was a wonderful idea. The last thing she wanted was a stuffy country club–like dinner the night before the wedding. It would just be the family and the wedding party. An informal gathering would give everyone a chance to get to know one another best.

"It's perfect, and the only thing I have to do before we nail it all down is talk to Uncle Sky. Having it on the beach sounds romantic, but means sand and maybe sand fleas. Yet having it indoors is too formal. I'm hoping we can use the barn."

"Barn?"

"My great-grandfather liked the idea of having milk close at hand, so in addition to the stables he put up a barn for a small herd of Guernseys. The next generation discontinued the practice and the barn stood empty. When Sky inherited, he converted it into a kind of playhouse for grown-ups, with billiards, Ping-Pong, a large room with a bar and fireplace where the stalls had been. There's even a small kitchen and bath. It hasn't been used in a while, though, so I don't know whether he wants the bother of opening it up."

After sharing the Russian Tea Room's famous cheese-and-cherry blintzes for dessert, they continued to discuss wedding plans over coffee, reluctant to leave the restaurant's fairy-tale setting.

"Since Phil's heading off to Africa with the Peace Corps, I think cuff links or a money clip are out as a gift. I found a watch that does everything except make a phone call—waterproof, shockproof, worldwide time zones. I'm trying to think of something appropriate to have engraved on back. What do you say to the man who just happened to cause the best thing that ever happened to you?"

"You'll think of something. As I recall, you're very good at thinking of things to say on the backs of watches." They were holding hands across the table and hers was in plain sight. Tom smiled.

"Cuff links for Robert and Craig, I thought. And I don't want Bets to feel left out, so I'm getting her the same ones as earrings—they're silver knots. Mom spotted them at Shreve's."

Bets. Betsey. No, we don't want her to feel left out—or anything that might produce any harder feelings. The only thing that would make her future sister-in-law truly happy, Faith had realized weeks ago, was if Tom married Sydney, and she was definitely not prepared to go that far to ensure Betsey Fairchild Parker's well-being, real or imagined.

Tom left early the next morning. Ever since her father had told her about the Todds, the juxtaposition of the deaths in that family kept pushing its way into her thoughts and Faith was very glad that Tom had been able to stay—and very glad that whatever sad news might arrive in the future, he'd be by her side permanently.

There were still several events before she closed Have Faith's doors for good. Thinking of the *pelmeni* at the Russian Tea Room, she and Francesca made and froze several varieties of ravioli and tortellini. Her favorite filling was the simplest: finely chopped fresh spinach, lemon zest, ricotta, and a pinch of nutmeg. While Francesca finished the ones she was making, Faith called The Cliff. The woman who'd been working Tuesday, and had either been hired or was still filling in, answered the phone and soon Sky picked up.

"Hello, beautiful."

It was his standard greeting and never failed to charm whatever woman he was addressing. Sky Walfort was a connoisseur.

Faith described the proposed rehearsal dinner plans, and before she could even broach the subject of using the barn, he suggested it.

"Such fun. We'll have some long tables set up and cover them with newspapers or some such stuff. Drip melted butter all over the place. We'll get Tam to sing 'It Was a Real Nice Clam Bake,' you know, that song from *Carousel*."

Great-aunt Tammy had channeled Ethel Merman at some point in her life and was known for belting out show tunes, especially Rodgers and Hammerstein's.

"I'll go out and take a look at the place this afternoon," he said. "You leave it all to me."

"I feel as if I'm leaving everything to you, Uncle Sky. You're doing so much. I can't thank you enough. And I know this must be a hard time for you. And the news about the Todds was terrible."

Her uncle was silent for a moment.

"Foolish people. House was a firetrap. Danny mentioned it often. No mystery why they perished. You're not trying to make one out of all this, are you? Or Danny. She was in the wrong place at the wrong time. I've heard all about your solving Emma's little contretemps in December from Poppy. So, stop meddling, Miss Faith Schuyler Sibley. Put away your no doubt very fashionable deerstalker and magnifying glass accessories."

Almost being murdered the previous December by a crazed madman who was also blackmailing you wasn't what Faith would term "Emma's little contretemps." His last words had taken some of the edge off the prior ones, but his tone was uncharacteristically stern. Clearly, he didn't want her to mention any of this further and she changed the subject.

"Are you sure I can't help with the barn? I could come out and start cleaning up."

"That's very sweet of you, but unnecessary and not what the bride should be doing herself. If you want to drop by to see it— and more important, *moi*—that would be divine. Tomorrow perhaps?"

"I wish I could, but Francesca and I will be tied up here all day getting ready for a dinner Saturday night and a brunch on Sunday. Another time soon, though."

"Not to worry. I know you need to earn as much pin money as you can now. Tom won't want his wife to work."

Faith avoided the topic. Her uncle was very old-fashioned both about working wives and pin money. The income from the catering business was Faith's livelihood, and any pins accrued went into a savings account. But the mention of Tom's name triggered a thought.

"I'd love to bring Tom out when he's here next."

"Perfect. Just let me know and we'll roll out the red carpet."

They said good-bye and Faith returned to work. Danny had been in the wrong place at the wrong time, the emphasis in Faith's mind at the moment was "wrong place." What *was* the woman doing in Tammy's boudoir, in Tammy's clothing? Sky wouldn't be providing any answers—that was clear. It wouldn't stop Faith from trying to figure it all out, though.

❋   ❋   ❋

"There. Done." Saturday's dinner was a small one, only twenty guests, who Faith would seat at two round tables in the host couple's spacious SoHo loft. They had asked for a seafood entrée and loved the idea of paella. The wife was an art dealer and Faith had worked hard to create a colorful meal. The grilled radicchio with balsamic vinegar and shaved pecorino cheese that Francesca had suggested as a first course would bring in deep red, and the saffron rice in the main course would add a splash of bright yellow.

They had been working all day, alternating between food preparation and more packing up. Josie had called at noon asking Faith whether she could fax the menu for Faith to look over one more time before it went to the printer. Josie's grand opening was only a month away. When the fax came through, Faith and Francesca had taken a break. Faith had called Josie back as soon as they finished reading it.

"We want to order everything! And the layout is great, easy to read and attractive. The logo is perfect." Josie had had a designer create a kind of crest with a crossed knife and fork below the restaurant's name.

"Okay, off it goes. Are you still going to be able to make it? You won't be tied up with wedding plans? And Howard and Francesca?"

"By that time, everything except the knot will be tied—or better be. The last big item I've been worrying about is off my plate. Hope found a photographer who will not make the whole thing into a photo-op circus but will discreetly snap away. And yes, both Francesca and Howard plan to be at your opening."

They talked a bit more before saying good-bye. Both women had made major life-changing decisions and both would result in being married—Josie's would be to a restaurant, but the commitment, particularly the hours, would be the same.

Francesca was heading downtown to meet friends for dinner

and Faith was heading home. They were taking the same subway and walked out together, descending belowground a few blocks away. From the stairs Faith could see that the combination of Friday and rush hour had made the platform more crowded than usual.

"I want to try to get the next train," Francesca said. "I'm a little late. Let's get closer." They worked their way to the front and soon heard the sound of the approaching cars. Faith took a step forward. Tom had said he'd call before he had to go out to a talk at the Harvard Divinity School that evening and she didn't want to miss him.

The train was getting closer and the crowd lunged forward. Faith was used to being jostled, even pushed, but what she was experiencing now was very different. She started to panic.

There were two hands on her back, hands shoving her directly toward the tracks in front of the oncoming train.

CHAPTER 8

Arms flailing wildly, Faith fought to keep her balance. She could smell the train—oil, grease, something noxious—and feel its heat. Her purse slipped from her shoulder onto the tracks. The conductor caught sight of its movement and looked over toward the platform ahead. His face was now close enough for Faith to see the sudden horror cross it and hear the deafening screech as he applied the brakes. Applied them too late. She was falling—and the train wasn't stopping.

She felt a viselike grip on her shoulder, wrenching it, thrusting her to one side and then down onto the ground. The floor was hard, cold, but it wasn't the tracks, the tracks with the third rail—instant death even before the train hit. She became entangled with her savior, a teenage boy, as they clung together, the cars speeding past close enough to touch before coming to a halt in the station. The doors opened and crowds streamed out; crowds streamed in—stepping around the two prone figures, ignorant of what had almost been a headline in tomorrow's *New York Post:* "Caterer Cooked in Transit Tragedy." Stepping around them, barely looking down, and avoiding eye, or any other, contact as every New

Yorker learned to do if not at birth then shortly after moving to the city. It wasn't callous or uncaring, but simple common sense. A survival mechanism.

"Things can't be that bad, miss."

The boy looked about seventeen, and dreadlocks hung down the back of a T-shirt that proclaimed FEAR NO ART. The Jamaican lilt in his voice attested to the hairstyle's authenticity. He was helping her stand up. She was wearing her work clothes and the only damage to her apparel was a tear at her checkered knee where she'd scraped against the concrete when she fell.

"No, no. I wasn't going to jump. Someone was pushing me!"

She looked around for Francesca. She had been standing next to Faith. She must have seen what was happening. Where was she? The station was beginning to fill up again, but the girl was nowhere in sight.

"This city is crazy," he said, shaking his head slowly. "You sure everything's cook and curry?" He had large round eyes, like chocolate marbles, and they were searching her face for an answer. "I mean, are you okay?"

"I like the other way you asked the question better," Faith said. "That's what I do for a living. Cook. But yes, I'm all right." She'd have major bruises, but nothing was broken. Her legs felt wobbly and she knew she had to sit down. "I owe you my life." At those words, she really *did* have to sit down and he followed her to a bench by the turnstiles.

"My name is Faith Sibley. Please let me do something to thank you—"

He held up his hand to interrupt her and then offered it to her. She shook it, grateful for the memory of its strong grasp.

"I'm Marley Clarke, and, yeah, named for the man. My parents were big fans. Me, too. And saying 'Thank you,' that's enough. Anyone would have done the same, Faith."

"How long have you been in the city?" She was smiling. She

could still smile. As soon as she'd sat down, everything around her seemed to come into sharp focus. She felt as if she was seeing, hearing, sensing ten times more acutely than usual. And this young man next to her was the most beautiful person in the world right now.

"Two years. Going on three. Maybe because of my name, but I can sing, play some instruments. My parents sent me to live with my auntie here so I could go to a school for my music. I'm at LaGuardia. Know it?"

Faith knew it well. LaGuardia High School of Music & Art and Performing Arts was one of the city's specialized schools that combined academics with other programs, in this case those for future actors, musicians, composers, directors, and so forth. It was on the Upper West Side and known as the *Fame* school because of the movie loosely based on it. It was extremely hard to get in. Marley must be very talented. She knew now how to thank him. She'd give to the school's scholarship program in his honor.

"Of course. And, as the song said, I'll 'remember your name,' so when it's up in lights or wherever it may be, I can say I met you. That you were my guardian angel."

He laughed. "Come to one of our performances now, and then be the judge."

They exchanged information. Faith found herself telling him she was getting married in June.

"So that makes it for sure. You don't want to be jumping on the tracks until *after* you're married I hear."

They laughed and said good-bye. Faith needed to sit a bit longer, and he was getting on the train that was now approaching. The sound gave her a moment of fear and she briefly held on tight to the bench.

"You need a band at that wedding of yours, get in touch," Marley called over his shoulder.

"I just might!" she said as he disappeared into the crowd.

But where was Francesca?

And, noting the absence of its familiar weight hanging from her shoulder, she recalled her purse was gone, too. After the train pulled out, she crept cautiously to the platform's edge and peered at the tracks. Her purse had fallen directly below and the contents hadn't spilled out. It looked pretty flat, but her wallet with all her identification, credit cards, and cash might have survived intact.

Survived. She'd survived. She went to find a transit worker and soon a stocky man was fishing around with a pole, trying to loop the purse strap onto it.

Faith was watching from a safe distance, but could hear him muttering. "Drop all kinds of trash. Their pocketbooks, wallets, coats, hats, baby bottles. What am I? The Lost and Found?"

He held the pole up and slid her purse toward her, dropping it at her feet, still muttering. "Gotta stand close. They *always* gotta stand close and drop stuff. Packages, lunch. A bowling ball." He shook his head and left.

The purse, a Coach saddlebag, was a testament to the company's workmanship. It was grimy, but it was usable. The apple she'd tucked inside to eat later was sauce, but her wallet was in one piece. She decided to go back up to the street and take a cab home. There was no way she could stand and wait for another train right now. Mounting the stairs, she turned around to look back once more at the station.

Where was Francesca? Now—and when Faith had been pushed?

She'd missed Tom's call and for once she was glad. She didn't think she'd have been able to keep her voice from betraying her brush with death and she'd already decided not to mention it to anyone. It happened, it was over, and she was fine. Wasn't she?

Besides the tear, her pants were filthy from the litter on the platform floor and she tossed them, put the jacket in the hamper, and got into the robe her mother had given her. A nap. Yes, she was exhausted. She started to take the decorative pillows from the couch. It was too much trouble to do anything but stretch out on it for the moment. Much too early to make it up and really go to bed. She slipped off her shoes and lay down. Her eyes were closing.

The sound of the buzzer startled her. She wasn't expecting anyone. Her heart was racing. Ordinarily she wouldn't be reacting with alarm—the sound meant a friend, her sister, or a takeout delivery was downstairs and she'd go to the intercom with eager anticipation. Stop it! she told herself and went to the door.

"Yes?"

"It's me, Francesca. Are you all right? *Mio Dio!* I was so frightened . . ."

"I'm fine. Come up and see."

She pressed the button to release the front-door lock. In the minutes before Francesca arrived at the apartment, Faith stood still trying to think what might have happened. The crowd could have pushed the girl onto the train when the doors opened and she hadn't been able to get off before they closed. That was the most likely scenario. The most unlikely? That for some bizarre reason Francesca herself had pushed Faith. From the ease with which she picked up a heavy pot filled with stock, Faith knew the girl was strong.

She still didn't believe that the girl had told the entire story about why it was so important that she find this Gus Oliver. Why was it so crucial now after all these years? And was it something she didn't want anyone else to know about? The corollary being that Faith already knew too much? She shook her head. Her imagination was running wild. This wasn't a detective story, a *romanzo poliziesco.*

Francesca had run up the stairs. Red-faced and breathless, she threw her arms around Faith and held her tight. When she let go, Faith saw she had tears in her eyes.

"I'm fine," she said. "A teenager grabbed me in time."

Francesca nodded. "I saw him and you both fall away from the train together."

So, she had been close enough to witness the rescue. Then what did she do? Faith wondered. She waited. Francesca still seemed to be struggling to calm herself. She stood twisting her hands together, and just as Faith was about to suggest they sit down, she blurted out, "Someone tried to kill you! I saw them!"

"Them? There were two people?"

"No, no, I'm stupid. I mean her. A woman. Very large, with those sunglasses the movie stars wear to keep the paparazzi from taking pictures of their faces. And a hat, like for the rain." Francesca was talking rapidly and gesturing, her fingers made large *O*s around her eyes, then darted to her head and formed a visor.

As Faith had made her way closer to the edge of the platform, she had seen the woman out of the corner of her eye. She wished she could remember more. The hat and sunglasses, yes. And she was big—tall, well padded, but that was all. Nothing that could help the police or anyone else track her down. Wait! Beige. The woman had been wearing a beige Burberry raincoat, like the hat. She closed her eyes, willing more details, but none came.

"I'm making tea," Francesca said, moving toward the stove and sink. "Do you have *camomilla*? Very good for a shock."

Faith went to one of the cabinets and took down a box of chamomile tea. It was good for all sorts of ailments: stomach upsets, sleeplessness, and now this new one—potential loss of life.

Francesca was filling the kettle and her words continued to pour out as well.

"Someone pushed between us, but I could see you. Then the train was coming and I kept looking at you because I was afraid we'd get separated. I wanted you to come with me to dinner, and if you got on another car I couldn't ask you. I should have said something before, at work. I was thinking all these things and then I saw her! The woman had her hands on your back and I was screaming at her to stop and for someone to help. Then the boy grabbed you away and the woman ran onto the train. I knew you were safe, so I jumped on the train, too. I thought I could get hold of her. And then pull the cord. Stop the train so the police would come."

It was Faith's turn to do some hugging and she put her arms around the girl, the dark thoughts she'd been having earlier evaporating like the steam rising from the kettle's spout.

"That was so brave."

Francesca tossed her hair back over her shoulders. Getting ready for her dinner, she'd loosened it after work. The gesture suggested defiance and a willingness to embark on any chase again. Once more Faith wondered how she could have doubted her employee.

"She knew I was after her, oh yes, and ran into the next car. I ran, too, but then the how do you say it, the *conduttore,* stopped me and said it was forbidden to go when the train was moving. He didn't see her. I stood at the door and at the next stop I ran out. But I couldn't find her. She must have kept going to the other cars and was staying on the train. I got back on a car farther up, but still she wasn't there. I did this a few times at each stop. I never saw her get off, but she wasn't in any of the cars. Finally I came back uptown. It was hard to get on the trains. So many people this time of day. But I didn't stop looking. A fat woman like that could not vanish, I was thinking, only poof! She was gone. Just gone. I'm so sorry, Faith."

They took their tea over to the couch.

"You were wonderful. I wouldn't have known who it was if you hadn't been with me. And pursuing her like that!"

"But I didn't catch her."

She looked so downcast that Faith hugged her again.

"Here I am. Having a nice cup of tea with you. Everything's all right."

"But she wanted to kill you! She was pushing you in front of the train!"

There *was* that.

There had never been any question about where Eleanor Lennox would host her granddaughter's engagement tea. The Walfort sisters had been active members of the venerable Cosmopolitan Club, the "Cos Club," all their adult lives, as had their mother before them. In turn, their female offspring, including Faith, had followed suit. Founded in 1909 as a club for working women, governesses to be precise, the club quickly expanded its membership to include, according to a 1910 *New York Times* report, "women interested in the arts, sciences, education, literature, and philanthropy or in sympathy with those interested." That pretty much covered everyone in Manhattan with two X chromosomes, and by 1917 the club had six hundred members with another four hundred on their waiting list. They moved to larger quarters and then moved again to the present location on East 66th Street. Faith loved reading the early membership list—Willa Cather, Helen Hayes, Marian Anderson, Margaret Mead, and Eleanor Roosevelt—as well as the descriptions in the club's records of various performers and speakers: Sergei Prokofiev, Robert Frost, Nadia Boulanger, Lotte Lenya, Count Basie, Edward R. Murrow, Padraic Colum, and Dorothy Thompson. Even the von Trapp family had stopped by. Picasso exhibited at the club in 1917. But Faith's favorite description was the one detailing an early event, "An Evening in a Persian Garden." Club members donned costumes, listened to a reading of Persian poetry, and, no doubt mesmerized, watched exotic snake dancers. Today's tea, in the Sunroom on the clubhouse's top floor, would be very tame in comparison, although you could never tell with these ladies, Faith reflected. They'd been in the vanguard of Votes for Women and ahead of their time in exploring national and international affairs during several wars, expertly raising relief money, all the while keeping up with classes in everything from exercise to computer literacy nowadays.

The incident in the subway had been a little less than a week ago and Francesca had been sticking to Faith's side like mozzarella on pizza. She'd had difficulty persuading the girl that this constant vigilance wasn't necessary and had almost persuaded herself. It was an accident. She tried hard to ignore the little voice that reminded her the falling brickwork had been an accident, too. And Danny's death? The Todds'? In addition, the event today, another of the rituals leading up to her nuptials, reminded her of her shower and the as-yet-unexplained food poisoning. Entering the club, she put all of it firmly out of her mind. Nothing more untoward was going to happen. Not here or anywhere else.

She was wearing a pale lemon sleeveless linen sheath with the pearls her grandmother had given her on her twenty-first birthday and she was carrying a light raincoat since an April shower had been predicted for later. Before going upstairs, she went to hang it up in the club's cloakroom. Aunt Tammy was headed in the same direction. Faith helped her off with the beige Burberry she was wearing and assured her they weren't late.

"Aunt Frances was here when I came in and she told me that Nana and my mother had arrived just before her. We have plenty of time."

"I hate to be the last one, but Sky kept dawdling. Men take so much longer to get ready to go out than we do. I don't know how that whole thing about us being the ones keeping our near and dear waiting started. We weren't even leaving together, but first he couldn't find his keys, then it was his wallet. Finally, I told him he was a big boy and could get himself off alone. I swear, Danny just plain ruined him."

And his mother and sisters before her, Faith said to herself. Her mother had often told her that every woman related to Sky or in his orbit thought he hung the moon, catering to his every whim. Well, Faith thought, she counted herself among them.

"He had to go to Manhasset to pick up Danny."

"What!"

Several women turned in Faith's direction and she lowered her voice.

"Aunt Tam, what on earth are you talking about?"

Tammy was giving her hair a final pat, although it would take a cyclone to disturb a single strand, and was taking out a tube of lipstick from her voluminous purse.

"Her ashes, silly. What did you think? The police released the body to some funeral home there and it took a while to be sure no relative was coming forward to claim it. Sky's putting her in a beautiful Ming porcelain container, which to my mind is a complete waste. It's going in the ground where only the worms will see it. Now I ask you, isn't that going too far?"

Faith decided the question was rhetorical and avoided giving an opinion. Whatever her uncle Sky wanted was fine with her if it lessened his grief. She supposed the rare antique was the equivalent of a mahogany casket with Florentine gold handles if the housekeeper had been embalmed instead of cremated. It certainly seemed that Sky wasn't about to spare any expense for his beloved Danny's interment. And it was his call.

She'd known there were no relatives, unless they were very distant ones. A brief article in the paper about the Todds' house fire had stated that there were no next of kin. It had also listed Gertrude's name as "Mrs. Gertrude Danforth Todd," which meant her sister's "Mrs." was bestowed by convention. There was not now, nor ever had been, a Mr. Danforth, except for the sisters' father and so on.

"You look adorable, Faith, like a buttercup. Now, let's go up.

I'm as dry as dust. I told Eleanor to put me at the same table as your future mother-in-law. I just know we're going to get along."

The club's Sunroom lived up to its name and light was flooding in on three sides from the floor-to-ceiling windows overlooking the city. It was warm enough, so a few guests had wandered out to the terrace. The women looked like butterflies, or spring flowers, mimicking the tulips and daffodils on Park Avenue's median strip or the beds in Central Park. There was a steady hum of conversation. Faith went over to her grandmother, who was talking to one of the servers. It was a high tea and the round tables were covered with crisp white cloths that matched the rattan-type chairs. The room's walls were a soft blue-green decorated with trompe l'oeil rose-covered lattices and topiary. Each table had a different arrangement of seasonal blooms.

"Nobody wants to stand up for hours balancing a plate and something to drink," her grandmother had said. "It's going to be sit down."

"The bride is here," Eleanor called out, giving Faith a swift peck on the cheek, not quite an air kiss, but one calculated not to leave a smudge of the coral lipstick she always wore.

There was slight applause, smiles were directed at Faith, and then the ladies returned to their conversations.

"Where's your sister?" Jane Sibley asked. "Did she call you to say she'd be late?"

"No, I spoke with her last night and she said she'd blocked out the time and would even try to get here early to help put out the place cards."

"She needs to find a man." Aunt Frances had joined them. "Not that namby-pamby whatever his name is. Phelps something. Then she wouldn't bury herself in her work this way."

"I don't think that's it," Faith said, surprised since her great-aunt was a close friend of Bella Abzug's and had worked on her various campaigns, as well as other women's. She'd done many a needlepoint pillow with A WOMAN NEEDS A MAN LIKE A FISH NEEDS A BICYCLE for NOW fundraisers. Surely she understood what Hope's career meant to her—and it was the kind of career that demanded every waking hour, and very few sleeping ones.

She added, "To stay in the game, Hope has to work the way she does. And she loves it."

"All right, but she should still be able to make it to her sister's engagement tea."

Hope arrived a few minutes later and stood in the doorway scanning the room. The guests hadn't sat down yet. She spied Faith and waved her over. Faith was only too happy to go. She saw at once that Hope looked terrible.

Faith pulled her sister out of the room. "What's wrong? What's happened?"

"I don't know. Things have been so weird at work and they just got even weirder. My boss came by as I was getting ready to leave and handed me this."

It was a legal-size envelope with the name of the firm in the upper-left corner and addressed by hand simply, "Hope Sibley."

"He actually patted me on the shoulder. Not the male-bonding pat they give one another—that punching thing—a pat like, 'There, there,' and said I might want to consult the doctor whose name he had put in the envelope and he was sure everything was going to be all right."

"But you're not sick."

"I *know* that, and I told him I was fine and thanked him for his concern. He said, 'That's what I admire about you, Hope. You're a trouper.' Now what the hell is that supposed to mean and what the hell is going on?"

"It has to be tied somehow to the client stuff, don't you think? He'd know about it, right?"

"Yes, but he hasn't said anything before."

Faith had a sudden thought, one that she'd raised out at The Cliff with Hope, but she wanted to make sure again.

"I know how confidential your work is, but besides him, who else would you have told about your transactions? Who has access to them?"

"Only Jennifer, and I trust her completely. Besides, what could she do?"

Faith sighed. This wasn't going to be an easy fix, but at least she knew where they should start.

"The first thing we have to do is find out what kind of doctor this is so we know what's supposed to be wrong with you."

"No," her sister corrected her. "The first thing we have to do is have a wonderful time at Nana's tea. I'm going to fix my face and then be the life of the party. Maybe they have some of those snake-charmer costumes hanging around."

Eleanor Lennox was clinking a teacup and asked everyone to find her place. When all were seated, she clinked again.

"I'm not going to make a big speech. You all know how hopeless I am at it. Didn't some survey come out that said people feared public speaking more than death?"

There was general laughter—and agreement.

"But this speech is no chore. I'm devoted to both my granddaughters and proud of them. We're celebrating Faith's engagement and upcoming wedding. Please raise a glass or cup to the bride, but let's add my dear Hope, too."

"Hear, hear," Frances said, and the toast was made. "To Faith and Hope," the room chorused, clinking in turn.

Faith had always known her grandmother possessed special gifts, but how had she managed to divine that Hope needed this affirmation especially today?

The afternoon passed by pleasantly, and too quickly, as the guests table-hopped in between courses—field greens salads with

Maytag blue cheese and toasted walnuts, followed by small lobster pot pies, and petit fours decorated like wedding cakes for dessert. There was plenty of tea and champagne, too. It struck Faith that in future years, whenever she thought back to this happy time before her wedding, she'd remember the champagne that kept appearing at every turn. She felt positively awash in it—like Cleopatra in her asses' milk bath, only much, much better. She'd always wondered how that ancient skin treatment would have smelled. Maybe the perfumes of Araby played a part.

"Are you feeling overwhelmed, dear?" It was Marian holding a glass of champagne, and she had even more of a sparkle in her eye than usual. "Hard when the groom is in another part of the country and so busy on top of that."

"Maybe I'm missing something, but I think it's all pretty much done. And we still have almost a month and a half to go. One of the last things on my list was the dresses for my attendants. I found the dearest eyelet ones for the little girls. White with different pastel-colored linings and moiré sashes to match them. They can use them as party dresses afterward. We were going to have boys, too, but my cousins, who have infinitely more experience, told me it was safer to stick with their daughters since their sons might head for the beach and show up strewing seaweed instead of rose petals."

"I agree completely, and I also speak from experience. I can't imagine any of my boys in a wedding party at that age. I just hope Craig behaves himself in this one! He was in a wedding last fall and I believe he was the ringleader for the trick the ushers played on the groom. They got hold of his shoes and wrote 'Save' on the bottom of one and 'Me' on the other. When he knelt, everyone couldn't help laughing. Fortunately it was just the rehearsal and they scrubbed the paint off for the real thing."

Faith laughed, but also resolved to keep a firm eye on her mischievous soon-to-be brother-in-law.

Great-aunt Tammy was waving to her from across the room and Faith made her way over.

"I knew I would adore Marian. She is such a hoot!"

This was not the way Faith would have described Tom's mother, but Tammy tended to bring the "hoot"ness out in people.

"Imagine. She's never been to Mardi Gras! I'm taking her along next year. She told me she's lucky if she can get that husband of hers to go to Cape Cod. Thank goodness Sky isn't like that. Well, if he had been, I wouldn't have married him. Marian seems happy with her husband, though. Wouldn't be normal if he didn't have something wrong with him. Mark my words, sugar, a man who seems perfect is going to have some major flaw that he's hiding. Like bodies in the backyard."

There *were* bodies in Tom's backyard, but to Faith's best knowledge they all had headstones.

Eleanor had asked several of her friends' teenage granddaughters to come after school and be "floaters," graciously moving about to see that everyone had what she needed. Their main task was to help departing guests with their wraps and make sure each left with a favor. Faith's grandmother was not to be outdone by Poppy Morris. The floaters were carrying pretty white wicker baskets filled with Tiffany signature blue boxes containing an Elsa Peretti heart bookmark. A lovely sentiment, and appropriate to the party's setting. Cos Club members were readers.

Faith lingered in the foyer saying good-bye and thank you to everyone. She was waiting for Marian and her sister so she could take them over to the Morrisses'. This evening they were all having dinner at Faith's parents'. She'd offered to get tickets for a show or concert, but Marian said they would much rather spend this time getting to know each other better. "We can go to shows anytime," she'd said. They had to be back in Massachusetts for the weekend and were taking a late afternoon train the next day. Marian had made her wishes clear for the next day, as well. "You're busy, but too polite to say so," Marian had told Faith. "Besides, we want to explore on our own, so don't worry about us."

She had definitely lucked out in the mother-in-law department. Whatever Marian wore to the wedding, it wouldn't be the black outfit complete with mourner's veil that the groom's mother of one of Faith's friends appeared in at the church, weeping copiously. Or the one who declared she was boycotting the ceremony only to show up at the reception with a number of uninvited guests—a Hell's Angels gang she'd managed to corral. The newlyweds left for their honeymoon a bit sooner than planned by the country club's back door.

Dropping the two women off, Faith got out of the cab, too, deciding to walk across the park to her apartment. The predicted shower had come and gone, leaving a bright sheen on the city. She needed a breather and it was a walk she was going to miss, this shortcut from the east to the west side through Frederick Law Olmsted's masterpiece. Tom had told her there would be plenty of the landscaper's work to explore in the Boston area, but she was dubious. Especially since she'd heard from Hope that major portions of his "Emerald Necklace," Olmsted's green space along the Charles River, had been paved over to create Storrow Drive, the city's main artery.

Hope! Faith was very worried about her sister. She'd left right after dessert appeared and it had to be because she didn't want to waste a moment trying to discover what the recommended doctor's specialty was. And when Hope found out, Faith assumed she would be the first to know.

But know what?

As soon as the invitations had gone out, wedding gifts started to arrive, and some of those attending yesterday's tea had brought more. Faith had been raised in the send-a-thank-you-note-no-

more-than-ten-minutes-after-receiving-the-gift school of manners and the next morning she was busy catching up before leaving for work. She'd written "Both Tom and I deeply appreciate
the exquisite [fill in object name]" so often that she was sure she
must be mumbling it in her sleep. It *was* lovely of everyone to
think of them and she was extremely touched, but once more she
thought how nice it would be to be married as opposed to get
married, with all that entailed. Two more notes to go and she'd
post them on her way uptown. The phone jolted her from her
task. It was Hope.

"Any news?"

"Well, the word on the street, and I mean 'the Street,' as in
Wall, seems to be that I am suffering from chronic fatigue syndrome, also known as 'yuppie flu' and 'shirker syndrome.'" Her
bitterness was as strong as vinaigrette with too much mustard.

"What!" Faith had heard about CFS, considered to be a fad by
an alarming number of people and a serious illness by others more
knowledgeable.

"Yup, that's his specialty. I didn't call my own doctor. He
might think I was avoiding him, consulting someone else. I called
Becky Havers. Remember her? My class at Dalton? She's doing a
residency in internal medicine at Mount Sinai. I figured if I said
I wanted to find out what his specialty was for a friend, she'd assume it was me, so I told her it was for you. I mean, you're moving
and you never really knew her anyway. I told her it was in confi-
dence, don't worry."

"Glad to be of help."

She was, but she also wished Hope had come up with a better
cover story. Manhattan was such a small village. She had to trust
that Becky, whom she recalled as a skinny teenager with an over-
bite, took her Hippocratic Oath seriously.

"I'm really freaked out, Fay. How did all this get started? Obviously that's what the flowers and other stuff meant. Why? I asked

myself. Well, I know why. Someone wants my job and all he or she had to do was whisper six little words to enough people—'Don't you think Hope looks tired?'—to start a tsunami of rumors that ended with this diagnosis."

"What are you going to do?"

"As soon as I get off the phone, I'm going to tell my boss that there's absolutely nothing wrong with my health and I will happily bring in a doctor's note to that effect."

"Can't hurt. Used to work for gym."

"Then I have to find some charity run and go around getting people to sponsor me."

Running was how Hope kept in shape. She claimed it took less time than a health club. She'd entered the New York Marathon for the last six years, finishing with more than respectable times.

"Put me down and I'll spread the word, too. But, Hope, we have to find out who started this."

"I know, I know. The problem is that in my biz, it could be just about anyone."

They hung up, and Faith finished her thank-yous and walked out into the city, which was looking a little more grim today than yesterday.

Somebody was out to get her sister.

"There are four messages on the machine from somebody named Max for you," Francesca said. "He sounds upset about something."

"I'll call him right away. We met at the ICE and he started his company at the same time I started mine. He does mostly corporate work, has a steady job as the private chef for one of the large brokerage houses. Nice guy. He's probably just heard that I'm leaving the city, although I don't know why he'd make so many calls." She played them back and they were all the same, terse, somewhat frantic-sounding messages to call him as soon as she could.

Crossing to the phone, she said to Francesca, "I haven't forgotten about going to New Jersey. Maybe Monday?"

"I know this has been a busy week for you, it's okay. Monday would be good. How will we get there? Train?"

"I'll borrow the car from my parents. We don't have the great railroad system like you do at home."

Faith had thought about trying to find a phone number for Gus Oliver, but without knowing his daughter's married name, it would be difficult. And maybe arriving unannounced was a better idea in any case. Francesca was determined to find the man, but it might turn out that he didn't want to be found. They'd have the advantage of surprise.

She called the number Max had left.

"Hi, Max? It's Faith Sibley. What's up?"

"Thank God you called. My wife went into labor this morning. This is the pay phone at the hospital. It could be anytime. I'm going to be a dad!"

"That's terrific—and you'll be terrific."

Joyful news, but Faith was wondering why Max was calling *her*. They were close, but not that close.

"I'm desperate. I have a reception tonight. It's a meet and greet with some stockholders in the firm's private dining room. My sous-chef could handle it, but she's sick. Everything's all set. Food, and my waitstaff knows the drill. But I need a chef there. I heard you were shutting down and I thought maybe you'd be free. By the way, congratulations. Whoever he is, he's a lucky guy."

Max sounded breathless. Maybe he'd been doing the labor-breathing thing with his wife.

"Shutting down," there were those words again. Yes, she was free, as opposed to every other caterer he might have called in the city at the last minute, Faith thought. And with her fiancé out of town, she wouldn't have a date either.

"It would be a pleasure. Glad to help, and you don't even have to name the baby after me if it's a girl. You sure you're okay for staff?"

"Well, if Howard's available, maybe another bartender would be good. This is a cocktail crowd, not white wine—they really suck them up. And nobody can turn out martinis like Howard's."

As well Faith knew. The firm taking over her quarters wanted him, as did a dozen other caterers in town, not to mention another dozen restaurants. He was basking in his popularity for the moment, having told her, "You have to understand what this feels like after always having been picked last for kickball."

Max gave her further particulars and then suddenly said, "My God, I've got to go!" and hung up.

Howard wasn't doing anything and was up for the job. They met early downtown to have a look at the setup.

And it was quite a setup. The top-floor private dining room had pocket partitions, which had been recessed, opening the area to its full size, the space alone guaranteed to impress. Plus Faith was pretty sure the Chippendale and other furniture weren't repros, nor were the Orientals on the floor. There were a few obligatory oils of the founders, but the rest of the artworks were landscapes and still lifes—investments that had accrued many times over in value since leaving Sotheby's or Christie's. There was a very faint smell of some kind of lemony polish that must have just been used—or it may have been the omnipresent, ineffable smell of money. A lot of money. Of course it was a million-dollar view, straight out to the Statue of Liberty. The full-service kitchen boasted top-of-the-line appliances and the guests would be drinking from Baccarat and eating from Wedgwood with sterling flatware, nothing vaguely commercial. Max's staff hadn't arrived yet.

"Since nobody's here, I'm going to explore, unless you need

me. The men's room is probably the size of my apartment," Howard said.

"Go ahead. There's nothing for you to do yet, but I need to go over everything. Max said they'd prepared yesterday and all that was left to do was heat the warm hors d'oeuvres and bring the cold ones to room temperature, but I don't want to have to send someone out for lemons or something else essential to your mixology once the guests arrive. I'll make sure all your garnishes are here."

Faith began taking down serving platters. Max had also said the menu was in the kitchen, on the counter by the phone, next to a pad with reminders to himself. She was happy to see both items were there. And it was a great menu. Like Faith, he was avoiding the current craze for things on skewers—overcooked tortellini and cherry tomatoes were ubiquitous these days. And Faith didn't even want to hear the words "chicken satay" ever again. Instead he had a broad range of interesting choices. She might steal the tuna tartare on endive with enoki mushrooms, as well as the potato nests filled with crème fraiche and caviar—the crisp "nest" would make a nice change from a soft blini. He wouldn't mind sharing the recipes, she was sure. They had traded in the past. Past! She wasn't doing this anymore, wouldn't be for the foreseeable future. Still, she filed the ideas away.

Howard was back in a few minutes, sooner than she expected. "Everything locked up?"

"No, just the opposite. There's a full gym and spa down the hall."

Howard seemed to hesitate.

"Is your sister still seeing Phelps Grant?"

"Yes, why?" Faith was taking fondant blossoms that looked almost more real than real out of the fridge. She'd use them to decorate some of the trays. Max had also left some carved vegetables, large sprigs of herbs, and some banana leaves. "Oh, how stupid of me. This is his firm. I mean, he works here, not owns it."

She wasn't surprised that Howard had remembered about Phelps. Besides being a bartender extraordinaire, he had a Rolodex of New York and beyond's *Who's Who,* with all their information implanted in a frontal lobe and never forgot a face or name.

"I think you'd better see this. But I warn you, it's not pretty."

He led her down the lushly carpeted hallway, pile so deep it would silence a bear *and* a bull. Faith's heart was sinking. Whatever was behind door number two or three wasn't going to be an all-expense-paid trip to Hawaii or a brand-new car.

Halfway down the hall, Howard opened a door. It was the fitness area, and Phelps was getting quite a workout, every move reflected in the mirrors lining the walls. Neither he nor the young woman moaning, "Oh, Phelps! Yes! Yes!" in rapture beneath him heard the door open; Howard started to close it silently, but Faith flung it wide, sending it banging against the wall. The couple using a broad treadmill for that which it was not intended—it wasn't moving, for one thing—looked over, wild-eyed. Phelps pulled at his trousers and rolled off. It would have been funny if it hadn't been so depressing and infuriating. He tried to stand up and tripped.

Recognizing her, he said, "Faith! What are you doing here? I can explain everything! This isn't what it looks like!"

"I think it is, Phelps. You're doing to Jennifer, my sister's 'trusted' assistant, exactly what the two of you have been doing to Hope."

CHAPTER 9

There wasn't time to be gentle. As soon as Hope answered her phone, Faith said, "You've got a mole. It's Jennifer. Change the password on all your files immediately. And I'm really sorry, sis, but Phelps is your poacher. She's been feeding him your information."

"That can't be! They don't even know each other!"

"I just caught them having a nooner, so I'd say they know each other intimately. I was worried about *your* pillow talk, but it was Jennifer's." As she said this, Faith reflected that treadmills and the other spots the couple might have grabbed—they obviously couldn't be seen together—did not have pillows, but the concept was the same.

"Omigod! How could he do that to me? I introduced him to the guy who hired him. And Jennifer! That snake! Fay, I feel like such a fool!"

"We'll talk later. But I think little Phelps couldn't cut it and was getting pressured. He had to bring in some big fish, so he took your fish. And aside from what I suspect is just a case of evil personality, Jennifer is looking to land her own fish and saw Phelps as her ticket to Greenwich, Connecticut; a Gucci charge; and two point five children with straight teeth in private school. I realize I'm mixing a lot of metaphors, but you know what I mean."

"But where are you? Phelps should be at work now."

The notion that her boyfriend was not only fooling around but blowing off work was obviously compounding Hope's distress. How could she have misjudged him so totally? Didn't he live and breathe billable hours the way she did?

Faith explained and then said, "Max's staff is coming. I have to get off. I'll call you as soon as I can take a break. Now go do what you gotta do."

The event had gone well, and when Faith returned to her apartment there was a message from Max on her machine. He was now the proud father of a bouncing baby boy, name still to be decided, but they were leaning toward Nicholas. His wife was doing fine. He thanked Faith profusely for stepping in and would call again to see how things went. There was also a message from Tom and he sounded excited. "Good news. Call me. I love you. Very much."

She punched in the number that she suddenly realized was going to be *her* new number, the home phone at the parsonage. He was there.

"A meeting I had on Monday has been canceled, and Tuesday is clear, too. I thought maybe we could meet out on Long Island and you could finally get to show me the spot where we'll be pledging our troth. I can take the ferry from New London to Orient Point."

"Oh, Tom, that's wonderful. Uncle Sky has been wanting us to come out. He'll be so pleased. I was going to do something with Francesca, but I know she'll understand. We can put it off to another day easily."

They talked some more about the logistics and Faith asked, "Did your mother and your aunt have a good time here?"

"You know the old song, 'How Ya Gonna Keep 'Em Down on the Farm After They've Seen Paree'? Well, change 'Paree' to 'New York City' and you'll get a vague approximation of how much they enjoyed themselves. I think they're going to be regulars on Amtrak."

"I'm so glad, but not surprised. Your mother is a very special person. I watched her at the tea fitting in with everyone, all the while clearly having fun herself. I know you think I think New Yorkers are perfect, but if we have a fault it's that we tend to be a little jaded and often go to a party with low expectations. Your mom is the kind of person who goes expecting it will be great, so it is."

"That pretty much sums her up. And, my beloved, she adores you, too."

They talked some more, each loath to hang up, exchanging foolish nothings until finally Faith looked at the time and realized that she was keeping her fiancé from much-needed sleep. He'd confessed to her early on that his sermon-writing pattern was to wrap it all up by Thursday and then spend Friday agonizing over whether it was good enough, followed by rising at dawn on Saturday to completely rewrite the thing. Faith was rather in awe of the process. She regarded her father's weekly task in the same way, although he seemed to have his finished before the weekend drew nigh. Imagine always having a paper due. And one you had to read aloud. No way you could wing it—or get an extension.

Faith called Francesca and they debated going to New Jersey the next day or Sunday, but decided to stick to a weekday.

"Weekends are family time. On a weekday, an old man like that will be alone," Francesca said.

Faith agreed and they settled on Thursday. As she made up

her bed, Faith wondered why it was so important for Francesca to see him alone. Once more it struck her that she really had no idea what she was getting into. What was it that made tracking down Gus Oliver so important? Bringing greetings from people he hadn't seen for sixty-some years had always struck Faith as a little far-fetched.

She'd called Hope earlier during a lull in the evening. Max's staff was the veritable well-oiled machine and all Faith had to do was keep the food coming out. Hope gave her a report. The first thing she'd done was get one of the firm's techies to secure her files and help her change her password.

"He told me not to use my birthday, one, two, three, four, et cetera, or the beginning of the alphabet. Apparently, that's what most people do, and it's the easiest to hack. He said to stick a few numbers in and make them as long as I could reliably remember."

When Hope had mentioned this, Faith thought, Not a problem. Her sister had been memorizing numbers—how much the DOW was up or down, especially—since she was a kid. The multiplication tables had been child's play and she'd never looked back.

While the guy was working on her computer, Hope had gone up to her boss's office.

"The moment I told him what had happened, it was like Vesuvius! I didn't know a person could erupt like that. He picked up the phone and called Phelps's boss. As we speak, Mr. Grant is looking for work someplace else, someplace like Guam. It's not just a question of never eating lunch in this town again, but never walking the sidewalks. A big no-no. Stealing somebody's wife or husband, maybe, but a client . . . *And* an even bigger sin, he got caught."

Her voice trailed off in a satisfied sigh. There was occasionally justice in this world.

She'd then informed HR about the reason for Jennifer's immediate dismissal; the young woman would be entitled to an outtake interview with the firm, but she wouldn't be getting a reference from Ms. Sibley or anyone else.

"I had the pleasure of shoving all the stuff from her desk into a carton, and the techie is taking her computer to go through. She just might have been stupid—or arrogant—enough to have sent information to Phelps from here. I told the guy even one personal e-mail to Mr. Grant would be golden.

"Her desk had the usual, Fay, you know, tampons, breath mints, Tylenol, plus a ratty-looking hairbrush, but what was the final nail in the coffin was a little cache of the brand of condoms Phelps likes *and* his favorite chocolate bars. I mean, all the time I've wasted looking around for Godiva's dark chocolate with raspberry!"

Faith had made some sympathetic noises, while wondering about the way the other find had encroached on her sister's time, keeping her from meeting someone else—someone with a heart and a conscience.

The conversation had ended on a happy note. Hope told Faith she had taken scissors and neatly cut all the packets into pieces—a small act of revenge, but satisfying.

Faith sank into sleep. As she succumbed, the image of Phelps and Jennifer on the treadmill flashed in front of her closed eyes and she burst into laughter.

Tom had said he was going to get the seven o'clock ferry. The trip across the sound took about an hour and a half; the drive to The Cliff would take about the same amount of time. When Faith called her uncle he urged her to come the night before, and she did not take much persuading. She seriously doubted she would ever be able to change her biorhythms to match her soon-to-be spouse's. Since Tom would have his car, she took the train out and it was Tammy who met her at the station, driving the large Range

Rover SUV that she referred to as her "whale" since the color she'd selected was Beluga Black, with all the bells and whistles. A luxury car with a leather interior that she insisted was for the "country."

"Darlin'," she said once Faith was settled in the passenger's seat. "You haven't seen Sky for a couple of weeks and I don't want you to be upset. He'll be fine, but he's taking Danny's death hard, hard, hard."

Tammy was a good driver—she'd once told Faith her daddy had let her drive on back roads since she could reach the pedals—but she was not a stickler for speed limits. The Long Island countryside, in the first blush of spring, dissolved into an impressionistic blur outside the car window.

"We should have put the visit off. I can still call Tom."

"Oh no, he'd hate that worse than anything, and I'm counting on you and all the wedding talk to cheer him up. He put Danny in the ground just yesterday, so it's all very fresh. Wanted to be alone. Well, there was a man from the cemetery to dig a hole, but I gather he went off to another part and left Sky to himself. Danny wasn't a churchgoer, so I suppose whatever he said is all the service she's going to get. Now, when it's my turn I want a lot of wailing and rolling around on the church carpet with everyone draped in yards of black. Lots of hymns. Maybe a choir. And a really good party afterward. I have the instructions all written out, attached to my will. I'll be planted next to Wade, down home. Sky doesn't mind."

There was a small cemetery in the village nearest The Cliff, and the Walforts had a plot there. Faith knew this was where Sky had wanted Danny interred and intended to be himself, rather than at Woodlawn, the garden cemetery in the Bronx where there was a much larger, and grander, family plot complete with a McKim, Mead, and White memorial. It was hard to believe the Bronx was farmland in 1863 when the cemetery was founded, but walking through it now, past the beautiful monuments among the flowering trees and shrubs, was a step back in time.

"Your people will be my people." Ruth's famous Old Testament words. Faith supposed she'd be buried in Massachusetts, an odd thought—so far she'd only been there a handful of times—but her demise was a long, long way away and she intended to go at the exact instant Tom did. The idea of life without him was unbearable.

"And we're having a slight disagreement about the housekeeper," Aunt Tammy said. "I love her to death—she's from Kentucky! But Sky wants to replace her with some old friend of Danny's. A Mrs. Tingley, oh, that's not right, but something like that."

She hit the brakes. A chipmunk was crossing the road. Tammy braked for animals. It didn't interrupt the flow of her conversation.

"Poor Danny was so old I had to keep asking the cleaners to do more and more. And this woman is even older! No, I'm putting my foot down." She sped up slightly. "It's my house, too, although you wouldn't think so. I told him he could take her salary out of my money, not his. That may do the trick."

They pulled into the drive and Tammy parked behind the house.

"There he is, looks like he's walking to the barn. Go after him. That's a good girl."

Faith got out and opened the rear door to get her overnight bag. Tammy grabbed her arm. "Leave your things. I'll take them." Faith looked down at her aunt's hand, large, like the rest of her. Her long nails were painted scarlet and she had a strong grip. For a brief moment the hand looked more like a talon.

Faith obediently trotted off, thinking about Tammy's words, "It's my house, too." She realized she had always thought of the house as Uncle Schuyler's—and the rest of the family's. Yet it was Tammy who kept the place running, that was now clear.

Her uncle heard her approach and stopped to wait for her. She was shocked at how much he had aged since she'd seen him last—the day after the murder. He had seemed to be dealing with everything as well as could be expected. She remembered that he'd even made one of his terrible rhyming jokes, but she realized it was adrenaline and the reality of what had occurred hadn't set in. It had definitely set in now. He hadn't shaved this morning, and maybe not yesterday either. Schuyler Walfort was fastidious about his appearance, and this more than anything signaled the depth of his grief. His eyes were watering and Faith did not think it was due to the stiff breeze blowing across the field.

"My dear. Good of you to come. And the bridegroom cometh also." He took her arm.

"I'm so sorry about Danny—it's still very hard to believe," Faith said. They had all slipped into the habit of the nickname that never would have crossed their lips when she was alive. "Have the police made any progress?" She knew she would have heard, but she thought talking about it might help. He shook his head.

"I'm afraid this is fast becoming what they call a cold case. Matt has been in touch a few times, but I think that's because I sponsor the police and firemen's ball every year. No, that's too cruel. He does care, but apparently home invasions, even deadly home invasions, are all too commonplace and almost never solved, after this amount of time has passed, unless by chance."

"We can still hope. They could get careless, or greedy. Pawn the jewelry and nabbed on the spot."

He smiled wearily. "It won't bring her back."

"I know," she said, "but maybe we should get everyone together to pool information. The police did say there had been other break-ins at the time. I'd be happy to help organize a meeting. Find out whether there were things in common—lawn services, delivery people looking for an address. We could present any findings to Detective Willis."

Her uncle didn't reply, but seemed to be turning the idea over in his mind. They walked on, passing the short path to the barn. There didn't seem to be a destination. Finally, he spoke again.

"You and me. Two peas in a pod. I knew it from the moment you were born, and when Jane gave you my name and made me your godfather, I was as happy as if you were my own child. Yes, we've always thought alike. You feel things, I know. Just the way I do. It's almost uncanny. I know exactly what you're going to do sometimes. Just as I know what I'm going to have to do, too. Two peas . . ."

Faith gave his arm a squeeze.

"Thank you, Uncle Sky, I'll always remember these words."

She was back in the turret room after an early and subdued dinner. Her uncle had excused himself immediately afterward, saying he had some things he needed to go over in the library. Tammy looked after him.

"I believe those things are called 'Mr. Scotch' and 'Mr. Water.' I hate for him to drink alone. It's too sad, but as you know, Sky does as Sky wants."

Faith was surprised by her aunt's bitter tone. This marriage had lasted longer than any of their brother's previous ones, Great-aunt Frances had remarked to Faith at the tea. Had the housekeeper's death caused irreparable friction? Was the fact that Danny dressed up in Tammy's clothes and made free with her toiletries going to be grounds for divorce?

"I think I'll make it an early night, take a good soak, but you stay up. There are lots of movies to watch in the TV room." This was not a small den with a set on top of a TV stand, but a state-of-the-art media center with comfy chairs and recently installed surround sound.

"Thank you, but I'm going to turn in, too," Faith said.

"Get lots of beauty sleep for your beau," Tammy said.

Earlier she had told Faith to choose one of the large guest room suites.

"No need for Tom to go creeping around from another room. You'd better know by now whether you're compatible in the bedroom department with the wedding so close. Don't want any nasty surprises at the start of the honeymoon. My father had a third cousin, Desiree—whitest wedding you ever saw—and her 'he' turned out to be a 'she.' Des never got over the shock, even though she did marry a nice boy from Tupelo. Believe you me, I know for a fact that she checked first before she said 'I do' the second time."

Faith had laughed and said she'd move, but wanted to spend one more night in her old room. She always felt a little like a princess in a tower, and tonight was no different. I *am* getting horribly sentimental, she thought. Tomorrow my prince will arrive and in June, I'll sleep here one last time as an unmarried woman. "Married woman." It sounded very grown up.

There was a thin sliver of moon, like a silver-crescent pendant, and the sky was bright with stars. She loved Manhattan, but bright lights, big city meant the Milky Way was skim. Out here it was as if a large cereal bowl filled with constellations had been overturned directly above one's head.

Once again she felt pulled toward the attic for the view over the water and she got out of bed.

This time, reaching the top of the stairs from the light in the hall below, she had to turn on the attic lights to make her way across to the chair by the front window. She sat, entranced by the scene stretched out below. The wind had picked up, and the moon made the whitecaps look like bits of frosting. The long drive from the house to the top of the cliffs sparkled from something—mica?—in the gravel. She was feeling drowsy, her eyes losing focus. She could sleep now. Out of curiosity she looked for the feather. She had left it where she had seen it and now it was gone. She got up and bent down, pushing the chair back. No feather anywhere. The floor didn't appear swept, though, and she imagined that a turnout of the attic was a yearly event, not part of the house's regular upkeep. Mice? To feather their nest? She made her way to the rear of the attic and the large window overlooking the back entrance. She'd left what she'd found there, too. Hard for anyone other than a human being to dislodge.

The small piece of rope and fishing line had disappeared as well.

If not with the birds, Faith was up uncharacteristically early the next morning, which meant she had a long wait. She had some breakfast, started to take a walk—it was a beautiful, sunny day—but Tom might call and besides, she planned to take a long one on the beach with him. Finally she asked Shirley, the new housekeeper, if she could use the kitchen to make some muffins. Tom would be hungry. He was always hungry.

"Sure, honey, you cook anything you want. Got to feed your man."

The doughnut muffins had just come out of the oven when Faith heard the front doorbell. Perfect timing! She had to let them cool a bit before dipping the tops into melted butter and sprinkling them with cinnamon sugar. She'd show him to the guest room in the meantime.

"This is just like in the movies," Faith said. As soon as she'd opened the door, Tom had scooped her up in his arms for a long kiss. "Better."

"I hate being apart. Do you realize it's been eleven days since I've seen you, almost wife of mine?"

"And how many hours? Oh, and minutes?" Faith felt that it had been much too long, but the way things were going lately she was lucky to know how many days there were in a week. At least everything with Hope was straightened out, and as Tom ate muffins she filled him in on Friday's denouement.

"I wish I had been there. Although I might have had to smack the guy a little."

Tom was obviously a believer in Muscular Christianity.

"It was all I could do to keep Howard from going for his jugular. Hope is one of Howard's close friends. When I started the business he heard about the bartender opening from her."

Both Walforts slept in and had their breakfasts on trays, Sky while he perused the *Wall Street Journal* and Tammy while she chatted on the phone. They rarely appeared downstairs before eleven. On the dot, Sky came into the dining area off the kitchen and whisked them both away to see the barn. He seemed to have had a good night's sleep and looked much better than he had the day before. He had still been in the library with the door closed when Faith went up to bed, yet he didn't seem hungover. Faith had once remarked on his capacity for alcohol to her aunt Chat, who explained that it was not uncommon among men his age who had honed this skill on the three-martini lunches of the 1950s.

When they got back to the house, Tammy was waiting for them and said they should feel free to make their own plans. In any case, both she and Sky would be out most of the day. They could all have dinner together if Tom and Faith wished. And they very much did.

It was happening. From the moment Tom arrived, Faith knew that the wedding would be wonderful. Having him here finally at The Cliff made all the lists and preparations—words on paper and in the air—concrete. The wedding was as vivid in her mind's eye as if she were looking at the photographs months from now.

"The first thing we're going to do is go down to the beach," she told her aunt, "then I thought we'd have lunch at that café the caterer runs on weekdays so Tom can meet her."

They parted ways and as they walked down to the beach Tom said, "I can see why you wanted to get married here. I've been up and down the New England coast, but I've never seen a more beautiful spot."

"I knew you would love it."

They walked for a while, picking up shells and beach glass. The cliffs that gave the house its name ended in a series of several good-size grassy spots and flat rocks that sloped down to the water. The tide was out. Tom took off the cotton pullover he'd been wearing and spread it on the grass.

"Have a seat," he said.

Faith looked at her watch. It was past noon. Lunchtime.

"Hungry?" she asked.

"Oh yes, I'm very hungry."

They got to the café an hour later. Tom ordered the day's special, a portobello mushroom and Asiago cheese panini, while Faith decided on a cup of their lentil soup and chicken salad with dill on a multigrain baguette. She wouldn't be able to finish it all, especially since she had her eye on one of their famous oversize macaroons for dessert, but Tom in the present and future would be there to make sure no food would ever go to waste.

The owner came to their table with a plate of cherry tomatoes stuffed with fresh ricotta and basil to go over the wedding menu for Tom. She would use local foods whenever possible. Faith had given him a rough idea of what she and her mother had selected. He'd said it sounded terrific and repeated his opinion, more enthusiastically after he'd finished his and Faith's lunch. The owner came back again, this time with a plate of pastries.

"I just had an inspiration," she said. "How about adding strawberries Romanoff? We could serve it in martini glasses." (See recipe, page 245.)

Faith loved the idea. The combination of the slightly macer-
ated fruit, orange liqueur, and cream was perfection. Maybe crème
fraiche instead of whipped cream.

For the reception Faith and the caterer had both hit upon using
the strawberries that would be at their peak on the island to accompany a traditional wedding cake for dessert. The fruit would
appear as strawberry mousse, sorbet, strawberries dipped in dark
chocolate, tiny tartlets with one perfect fruit and larger tarts with
the berries on top of pastry cream. And there would definitely be
shortcake. The real kind, with a biscuit and masses of whipped
cream. The offerings would cover several buffets to make it easy
for people to choose and return for seconds.

The addition was approved and the couple lingered over coffee. Tom told Faith how much he liked the caterer and how getting married was turning out to be a spectacular idea in so many
ways. Faith took this last as a reference, in part, to the hazelnut
éclair he was finishing. She was beginning to think Tom's French
gastronomic experiences heretofore had been limited to Dunkin'
croissants and maybe Boursin cheese from Stop & Shop.

Observing him settle into a pleasant postprandial haze, Faith
decided now was as good a time as any to bring up the one subject
she'd been reluctant to discuss with him.

"Okay," she said. "So what's the deal with Sydney? I mean, did
you date? There has to be some reason your sister thinks you two
are the ones who should be walking down the aisle."

"Lord, Faith. It would practically be incest if Sydney and I ever
got married. We've lived next door to each other all our lives and
been in and out of each other's houses so much they're like our own."

"Never anything but rafts on the river, tree houses, and the
garage band? And I want to hear more about that phase, too."

"Let's draw a curtain over that one. Think the Stones meet
the Osmonds. We were neither country nor rock and roll—some
truly horrible hybrid all our own."

He was avoiding the question.

Faith wasn't. "She's beautiful now and she must have been beautiful then. Do admit."

"Well, I might have taken her to our proms," he said somewhat sheepishly.

"Aha, I knew it! And you were crowned king and queen, right?"

"Something like that, but honestly, we never thought of each other that way. Like boyfriend and girlfriend. At least I didn't."

This Faith *could* believe. Men were indeed clueless. She'd bet that Sydney had shed many a tear on big sis Betsey's shoulder over Thomas Fairchild. And recently. But she had her answer as far as her fiancé was concerned. He was not now nor ever had been in love with Sydney Jerome.

All too soon Tom was dropping her off at the train station before heading for the ferry. Dinner the night before had been everything Faith had hoped it would be—Tom and her uncle had hit it off—although the conversation took an unusual turn. Tom was finishing his doctoral thesis on the thirteenth-century Albigensian Crusade against the Cathari sect, considered heretics by the church for their belief in two gods, one representing the world of the flesh, the evil physical world, and the other pure, embodying the world of the spirit. Tom was exploring the heresy, as well as one of its major outcomes, the Medieval Inquisition. The newlyweds were honeymooning in France's Languedoc, the Cathar stronghold, so that he could gather more information, as well as imagine Raymond-Roger facing the pope's troops from the fortifications at Carcassonne. Faith was eager to experience a different Languedoc: cassoulet; *saucisse de Toulouse; pélardon,* a particularly toothsome goat cheese; oysters from Bouzigues; and lovely fresh fish from the Mediterranean, some of which she planned to consume in one of the region's famous *bourrides,* a garlicky fish stew, cousin to bouillabaisse. Tom had held forth on occasion about the ascetic Cathars, and while Faith applauded their belief in equality of the sexes, she was dumbfounded by their practice of suicide by starvation—life being evil, get it over with quickly—in such a succulent region.

They were flying into Paris, lingering for only a few days before renting a car for the drive south, then continuing on into Spain for five days before leaving from Barcelona.

They had barely outlined their plans and Tom had started to briefly explain his area of interest when Sky interrupted him, exclaiming that he was fascinated by the period himself and had made his own modest study of it, particularly Simon de Montfort, the leader of the crusade and father to "my" Simon de Montfort who took on Henry III in England during the Barons' War. Faith had been surprised that Sky knew so much about this period in French history, but once he explained how he got there, she understood why. All roads led to Westminster for her Anglophile uncle and he had the complete works of P. G. Wodehouse bound in leather with the Walfort crest where they cohabited nicely on the shelf next to Agatha Christie, as well as Shakespeare, similarly adorned. He also had several editions of Debrett. So should a contingent of British nobility arrive for a meal unexpectedly, Schuyler Walfort would know exactly who belonged below the salt and whom above.

Tom had spent a long time with Uncle Sky looking at his collection in the library, imbibing some of his good port as well. Joining Faith upstairs, he had pronounced her beloved relative "unusual, but delightful." Or that may have been the port.

Morning came all too soon.

"It's been heaven, Faith." Tom was waiting on the platform with her as the train approached. If he noticed that she was standing much farther back than the other riders, he didn't comment.

"I know. Fifty-three days until the wedding. You're not the

only one counting! I looked at the calendar in the kitchen this morning."

"Too long. But I'll be down again and you'll need to come up. To choose paint colors, for one thing."

The church was repainting the interior of the parsonage as a wedding present. It would be done while they were in Europe. Also, Faith had not yet broached with Tom her plan to bring the kitchen into the twentieth century, at her own expense. This called for her presence, tape measure in hand, too.

"I'll be there as soon as I close up here in two weeks. Probably the Tuesday after the weekend in Richmond for Josie's opening."

"Maybe I can come to the city before then."

She was in his arms, intent on holding on to the feeling, and the idea of seeing him soon was a happy one. "I'd love you to come, but I don't want you to tire yourself out."

They went back and forth, and finally, since the conductor was blowing his whistle, Faith boarded, sitting by the window, waving good-bye for as long as she could see Tom. She felt terribly lonely already.

Francesca met Faith the following Thursday and they went across town to pick up the car. Armed with a map and instructions from her aunt Chat, who now lived in Mendham, New Jersey, Faith figured it would take about forty-five minutes to get to Verona from Manhattan. The suburb was located in Essex County and over the years had become a commuter town for New York City.

"Don't even think of going during rush hour," Chat had said, and so they had waited until ten o'clock before heading for the Lincoln Tunnel.

Francesca was quiet, and after pointing out the New York/ New Jersey state line on the tile in the tunnel under the Hudson,

Faith lapsed into silence herself. Part of it was her desire to con-
centrate on the route she'd memorized. She didn't want to get
lost. She knew only a few things about Jersey, but one of them was
how easy it was to find yourself on the wrong highway, unable to
get off. All she needed was to end up in the Pine Barrens, in the
southern part of the state, lair of the Jersey Devil, the real one, not
a member of the hockey team. There had been too many sightings
of the creature since the monster first appeared in the 1700s not to
take it seriously.

"How will we find this address?" Francesca asked. They had
made it safely to Verona Center. Faith pulled over by a large bronze
statue of a World War I doughboy in front of the town's civic center and consulted her notes. Chat had a New Jersey atlas and had
given her precise directions. The house wasn't far away and they
had no trouble locating it. Faith parked at the curb.

"This is it. Now what? We just knock on the door?"

Francesca nodded. "No cars in the driveway. That's good."

Faith was about to ask her why, but the girl was already striding
toward the house. It was a good-size brick ranch with a two-car
garage. The windows all had awnings, and most of the blinds were
drawn in addition. Somebody liked privacy. The walk was lined
with yews trimmed to stiletto points. Faith hurried up the front
stairs to the door. Francesca was pushing the doorbell. Chimes
inside played "O Sole Mio." This was the right house.

The door opened a crack and a very old man peered out at
them.

"We're all Catholics here. Go knock on another door."

"Are you Gus Oliver?" Francesca said, putting one foot on the
doorsill.

He opened the door a little wider.

"Why? What do—" A gasp cut off what he'd been about to
say. "It can't be. She's dead, or old like me!" He crossed himself

and Francesca stepped in, forcing the man to take a step back. Faith was close behind.

"Go away," he said. "Get out of my house." He was clearly extremely upset, pale and trembling, as he waved at the door.

Francesca broke into her native tongue, and it was clear she wasn't going anywhere. Gus Oliver switched to Italian as well. At one point Francesca took a manila folder from her large bag and shook it in front of his face.

"Sit down. I've got to sit down," he said in English and tottered out of the hall into the living room, where the family's roots were very much in evidence. Scenes of Italy hung on the walls, and the large marble-topped coffee table was covered with Murano glass candy dishes and carved Florentine alabaster figurines. The mantel above the fireplace was crowded with photos—wedding couples, graduation head shots, and babies on Santa's lap.

Faith whispered to Francesca, "He doesn't look well. I think we should go."

"No, not yet," she said fiercely. "I won't take long, and he is stronger than he looks. I know the type. He wants us to feel sorry and leave. I need you to be a witness."

"A witness! For what?"

Things were taking an extremely unexpected turn.

"We speak English now. My friend does not speak Italian."

The old man's color had returned and he seemed calmer. He nodded, his face a mask of resignation.

"Is there anyone else home? It's not your house. It's your daughter's family who lives here. Where are they?"

"At work. Everyone's at work." He looked at an ornate phone on a highly polished marquetry table. "I should call her."

"I don't think that would be a good idea for you," Francesca said abruptly as she pulled an ottoman over in front of Gus's chair. She sat down.

"I'm going to tell Faith a story. It's not a nice one, so I'll make it short. At the end I have some papers for you to sign that she will witness and you will never have to see me again."

She pointed to a chair and Faith sat down, too. Whatever was going to happen was happening.

"This Gus here knew me right away, as I thought he would. Since I was a little girl, people have said how much I look like my grandmother Luisa. As I got older, the resemblance became even closer. She is still a beautiful woman. I am proud to hear people say this.

"Luisa was just about my age in nineteen forty-four, during the war, when the Americans came to our village on their way to take Firenze back from the Germans. They used the village as a command post off and on. Everyone was glad to see them and help. One of the soldiers spoke Italian. His mother and father were from Sicily, but had gone to America where he was born. He was very handsome, although you would not think it now." She spat this last comment out derisively.

Things were becoming clear now. Faith knew where it was going. Gus Oliver had been a married man before he was sent overseas. The work that kept him in Italy after the war ended there in 1945 had nothing to do with the army and everything to do with *amore*.

"You don't understand. I was very young. We all were. And nobody got hurt. You're here, so Luisa must have ended up okay. We didn't have any kids."

Francesca jumped up and for a moment Faith thought she was going to hit the old man.

"Nobody got hurt! What about waiting and waiting every day for a letter from your husband! From the man you had planned to spend your whole life with! The one who disappeared one day without a word. And then the shame! Shame for the rest of her life and shame for her whole family!"

Gus lowered his head and mumbled something.

Francesca turned to Faith, pulling some papers and photographs from the envelope she was clutching.

"They were married at the *municipio,* see, here are the pictures!"

She handed them to Faith. Francesca *did* look like her grandmother, both women of rare beauty. In one photo the couple was seated on two chairs before a man who appeared to be the mayor or some sort of other official. Gus was in his uniform; Luisa held a small bouquet of roses and wore a white silk dress made from a parachute, just as Francesca had let slip weeks ago. Both the bride and groom were beaming.

Faith gave the photo to Francesca, who held it up in front of Gus.

"You can't prove that's me," he said, suddenly coming to life. In his day, he'd been a man to be reckoned with, Faith realized.

"Oh no?" Francesca ran to the mantel and grabbed one of the wedding pictures, a formal studio shot of the bride and groom. She'd obviously noted it when she came into the room.

"If this isn't you, who is this and what is he doing on your daughter's fireplace!"

He turned his head away.

The other photos Francesca had brought were taken outdoors. People were dancing. There was food and wine, although Faith was sure it hadn't been easy to obtain. The Germans had laid waste to the vineyards and fields as they retreated north.

Francesca put the photos back in the envelope and took out some documents. "This is the certificate of their marriage," she told Faith. "And these are what I want Gus—Augusto—Oliver to sign. I have a copy in English and a copy in Italian. You need to be the witness for both." She handed the one in English to Faith. It was a straightforward statement saying that Augusto Oliver swore he had been married in the United States both civilly and in the church before entering into the civil union in Italy with Luisa Alberti in September 1945. It went on to further declare that his wife was alive at the time and that there had not been an annulment or any other kind of dissolution of the union. Further, neither Luisa Alberti nor anyone else had known of the existence of his wife.

"Why should I sign this? I don't sign anything. Not unless a lawyer looks at it." He laughed unpleasantly. Faith's heart sank. There really wasn't any reason why he should sign the papers. It was all long ago, and she still wasn't sure why all this was so important to Francesca.

"So I can wait for your daughter to come home from work and tell her about what you were doing after the war? I bet they all thought you were some kind of big hero."

Once more Faith thought Francesca would strike the man, or at least spit at him.

"I have plenty of time and so does my friend," she continued. "I think I'll make some coffee. Faith?"

"Damn you, get me a pen. You don't just look like your grandmother, you act like her, too. Nag, nag. Time to get up and go into the fields. Six days a week and then hours of mass on Sunday. I wasn't used to the country."

Francesca produced a pen, and he signed and dated the copies; Faith did the same as witness.

"I would like to have had two witnesses," Francesca said. "Maybe I should wait for someone to come home after all."

Faith knew she was teasing, twisting the knife in a bit—and she didn't blame her.

"Get out! You got what you came for, now get outta here!" He was purple with rage.

"A pleasure," she said. "I don't want to spend even *uno secondo* more with you."

They got into the car and as soon as she closed the door, Francesca burst into tears, sobbing, repeating something over and over in Italian. Faith caught the word *"Nonna,"* grandmother. She started the car and drove back toward the center of town. They were passing a playground and she pulled into the parking lot.

It was a bit awkward hugging the girl, but Faith did her best and handed her a packet of tissues. After a minute or so, the sobs subsided and Francesca said, "I can never thank you enough for what you have done. My whole family, when they know, will want to thank you, too. I will be going home now and you must come soon."

"I think I understand most of what went on, but why don't you start at the beginning? I know your family thinks you're in England, and obviously you came here to find this man who did such a terrible thing to your grandmother, but why not tell them?"

Francesca mopped her tears. "I didn't want to raise my grandmother and grandfather's hopes. They could not be married—in the *municipio,* and certainly not by the priest. They thought they might be able to, because her marriage to Gus had only been a civil one, so it didn't count in the eyes of God, but the priest refused. All their children weren't, I don't know how to say it in English, legal. You understand?"

"Yes, legitimate." Everything was crystal clear now. If Francesca could prove that Gus Oliver was a married man in the eyes of the state and the church, his marriage to Luisa would be null and void, leaving her free.

"My grandparents can get married now, you understand? What he signed will be enough. After all these years . . ."

Francesca started crying again.

Faith put her seat belt back on and patted the girl's hand. "We need something to eat and then I want to get back to the city." She'd had enough of Jersey for a while. Still, she'd spied what looked like a good place on Bloomfield Avenue, Lakeside Deli.

Breakfast had been a while ago and she was in the mood for pastrami. Actually, she was in the mood for *prosciutto crudo,* but pastrami was closer to hand.

By the time they'd finished eating, Francesca's face was one of pure joy, not a single trace of a tear, although there would be plenty of those—tears of happiness—in her future. No more secrets. No more shame. Francesca's story had brought tears to Faith's eyes as well, and she thought about the kind of love the young woman's grandparents had for each other, staying together and facing the world. They were married in the eyes of God, and now, at last, they could be married before the eyes of the world.

Faith was feeling good. The pastrami had been excellent. Hope's mystery had been solved last week, Francesca's today. She was on a roll.

Two weeks later she put the keys on the largest of the preparation tables. She'd also put a couple of bottles of champagne in one of the refrigerator units for the new occupants. After one last look, she walked out. Have Faith was officially closed.

From now until her wedding day, it would be smooth sailing. All that remained to do was keep up with the increasing pile of thank-yous.

Piece of cake.

CHAPTER 10

The grand opening of Josie's had the down-home feel of a family reunion, one set in foodie paradise. Even before Josie started to advertise, the word was out about the new restaurant and she'd had to schedule three seatings on the big night. Relatives from near and far, friends, new patrons, and hopefully a few soon-to-be-delighted restaurant reviewers packed the dining room. The hum of people having a good time filled the air, reaching Josie as she stirred her pots and checked the ovens. There was no need for canned music; diners were making their own.

Faith was in the kitchen, Howard at the bar. He'd created a new drink for the occasion—a "Josito"—that replaced the light rum in a traditional mojito with Mount Gay Eclipse. He explained that the golden rum with the slight taste of banana, vanilla, almond, and moka was a natural pairing with Josie's food, especially once he added plenty of lime and mint.

"Your food is fresh and deceptively simple, just like the drink. Besides, Mount Gay introduced it in 1910 at another auspicious time—Halley's Comet was overhead that year and there was also a total solar eclipse."

Howard gloried in this kind of bibulous lore. He still hadn't decided on which job to take, but at the moment was teaching a course on the History of Drink at the New School. Faith had sampled a Josito and the pleasant buzz was lasting all evening. It was an inspired creation.

One of the waitstaff came into the kitchen with an order for smothered pork chops, collards, sautéed parsnips, and cheese grits and another one for succotash, deep-fried okra, yams, and fried chicken, dark meat only. The kitchen had been steadily filling orders and reorders for Josie's grandmother's treasured, delectable fried chicken recipe—crisp skin with just the right amount of spices and an extra dash of pepper, fragrant steam from the moist meat beneath escaping with the first forkful (see recipe page 242). There was an endless basket of cornbread on each table, with plenty of butter in small crocks, as well as pitchers of sweet iced tea.

"A woman at a table wants to know if y'all know where the term 'soul food' comes from."

Josie was adding shrimp to her shrimp and grits. "The *food* goes way back—Africa, the Caribbean. Thomas Jefferson is supposed to have brought back macaroni and cheese—which, incidentally, we've almost run out of—from Italy, and 'macaroni pie' was on an 1802 menu in the White House."

"He was certainly an epicure," Faith said. "And grew all those yummy vegetables. Could be Sally Hemings nurtured this taste for things like turnip greens and hominy, which was rooted in her tradition."

"Hmmmm," Josie said noncommittally. "Anyway, tell the diner that the term 'soul food' originated during the civil rights era here, sometime around the mid–nineteen sixties. We had soul music, soul sisters, soul brothers, so it was only natural that we'd have soul food, too—sustenance for the body and the spirit. I wouldn't necessarily call my menu a soul food menu, although if someone wants to that's fine by me. It's just Southern country cooking, using what's in season and mostly what's nearby. Oh, and you can add that my inspiration is Virginia's own Miss Lewis."

Edna Lewis, now in her seventies, had been born northwest of Richmond in Freetown, a farming community founded by freed slaves, including Miss Lewis's grandparents. Her reminiscence of growing up there, *The Taste of Country Cooking*, became a classic the moment it was published in 1976. The book, with recipes arranged by season, predated those by Alice Waters and other proponents of using only the best, local, freshest ingredients. Josie had met Miss Lewis several times and a framed note wishing Josie's great success occupied pride of place in the dining room. Faith thought Howard had described this style of cooking perfectly, "deceptively simple." For example, like Miss Lewis's, Josie's parsnips were parboiled, sliced in half, and slowly sautéed in sweet creamy butter. The only further addition was salt and pepper. They didn't need anything else.

After each seating, people lingered on the front porch and back patio drinking coffee, sipping iced tea and cordials. It was a perfect spring evening. Josie's grandmother had cultivated an old-fashioned garden, and soft lights illuminated magnolias, peonies, irises, poppies, and roses. There was a large smoke tree on one side of the porch, its fluffy pink blooms adding their own fragrance to the others that seemed to have been ordered just for this special night. Faith had joined some of Josie's cousins and sat down with a cup of coffee and a large wedge of red velvet cake. She'd been lucky to snare it. All the pies, especially the rhubarb that Josie flavored with a dash of nutmeg and her brown-sugar caramel, were gone. As were the several kinds of bread pudding, including a banana one, and her apple cobbler, which would be peach in June once the fruit was in season. Josie's was a resounding success, and when the chef made her appearance, everyone stood up and clapped. She sat down next to Faith.

"I think I'll tell the caterer I want red velvet cake as a wedding cake," Faith said. "*This* red velvet cake." She'd practically licked the plate.

"You were wonderful to come—and I don't want to get all sappy, but you know I could never have done this without you. Everything you taught me—and never telling me my dream was foolish, you know the whole 'Do you know the failure rate for restaurants' thang."

"It never occurred to me that Josie's wouldn't be a huge success," Faith said. Maybe they hadn't washed the cobbler pan yet and she could scrape it.

"I just wish Francesca could have been here, too."

Faith had put the girl on a plane for Rome shortly after the trip to New Jersey.

"I think they're probably having, or have already had, a celebration not unlike this one, except a different menu." She wished she could have been a fly on the wall when Francesca showed her grandparents and parents the documents Gus Oliver signed.

"It's an amazing story, all going on right under my nose. I knew she was hiding something. Life! A year ago who would have thought we'd be sitting here at my very own restaurant three weeks before your very own wedding. Where were we anyway? I think it was that big bat mitzvah in Westchester."

Have Faith's jobs were fast receding into the misty past in Faith's mind, occupied as it was focusing on the very near future. She'd made another trip to Aleford, and besides picking out paint colors, presented her plan for remodeling the kitchen. The vestry had given her the go ahead, especially since the church didn't have to spend a penny on the upgrade.

"Well, girlfriend. Time to close up," Josie said. "Remember, we're open for brunch tomorrow, or I should say today, and I'm beat."

Faith took a small box from her pants pocket and handed it to

Josie. She'd had a jeweler make a large silver pin with Josie's logo engraved on it.

"It's your very own Cordon Bleu, and nobody deserves a blue ribbon more than you."

Howard appeared with three flutes of champagne.

"Amen—and cheers."

A week later Faith stood in the middle of her apartment. It was beginning to look rather barren. Her lease would run out at the end of the month, so she'd move home for a week and then head to Long Island with her mother a few days before the wedding. Nana wanted to come, too, and Hope was actually taking that Thursday and Friday off from work to join them. The Fairchilds were arriving on Thursday. Tammy told Faith to invite even more of the wedding guests if she wanted—Poppy and Emma—"I love a house bursting at the seams," she'd said. Faith was sticking to the family, though. Tammy might be able to handle a crowd, but she wasn't sure she could. She wasn't nervous now, but two weeks away made her wedding seem like an event somewhat far in the future. In any case, she knew she'd feel responsible for planning things for people to do and it was enough to think about the Fairchilds, who were, fortunately, easy. They'd be satisfied with the beach and The Cliff's acreage for outdoor games.

All her wedding and honeymoon clothes were at her parents'. She was feeling extremely organized. Tom was borrowing a friend's van and was coming on Tuesday for a quick trip to move most of the rest of her clothing, their wedding presents, her books, a few household items, and the furniture Aunt Chat had given Faith—the Noguchi coffee table and the small chest of drawers—up to the parsonage. The glass-topped table might strike an incongruous note compared with the furniture Faith recalled—some wing chairs, a few spindly Windsors, and an enormous hutch—but she couldn't bear to part with the piece. As soon as she was finished sleeping on her sofa bed, it, the IKEA bookcases, and whatever else was left were going to Housing Works. The profits from their great thrift stores benefited AIDS/HIV individuals who were in need of housing and health care.

With such a small place, she hadn't accumulated much, and in any case, when she'd moved in she'd liked the idea of a stripped-down life. She supposed that would change now, but she was determined not to drown in a sea of possessions—they'd already received two bun warmers and three fondue pots, as well as numerous other nonessentials. She'd thought about adding some of these to her Housing Works donation, but knowing the way New Yorkers were drawn to thrift shops hoping to spot a rare piece of Russel Wright ceramics or an overlooked Eames chair, she didn't want any of her gift givers recognizing a *cadeau* by chance. Better wait until she was in Massachusetts to winnow.

The phone rang. It was her mother.

"Faith dear, we have a minor emergency."

"Minor is good. What is it?"

"The stationer sent the cards for designating table assignments out to Long Island instead of to the calligrapher and she needs them immediately. Apparently, she's leaving for Europe next week and won't be back until after the wedding. And getting another order to her from the stationer will take too long."

"As you know, my schedule is extremely flexible these days. I can run out there this morning and deliver them to her this afternoon."

"I'm afraid your father has the car today and has already gone. You'll have to take the train. If you hurry, you can get the nine forty-five."

"Are we sure they're at The Cliff?"

"Yes, I called the housekeeper and she checked. There have

been several package deliveries. The others must be more wedding gifts sent directly there."

"I'm on my way. I'll call you later."

Faith grabbed her purse and headed for Grand Central.

Knowing her uncle and aunt wouldn't be stirring much, Faith took a cab from the station to the house and went directly to the kitchen. Shirley, the housekeeper, was clearing breakfast dishes from a tray. Someone was up.

"Good morning, Miss Sibley. Your package is right over there."

"Thank you so much, and please call me Faith."

Upon hiring, the new housekeeper had immediately insisted on being called by her first name, eschewing a "Mrs."—honorary or otherwise. But Faith had to keep reminding her to use Faith's first name in return.

"Are my aunt and uncle both awake?"

"Just your aunt, and I'm starting a new pot of her coffee right now. You know she likes it fresh. She should be down soon."

Tammy consumed gallons of the coffee-and-chicory mixture ordered from the Café Du Monde in New Orleans, drinking it *au lait* in oversize cups with large bowls.

"Do you have time to stay and join her? I can make you some breakfast if you like? I'll bet you ran off without eating."

"Just some of the coffee when it's ready would be fine, although those muffins look tempting."

There was a tin of golden brown muffins that must have just come out of the oven sitting on the counter.

"They're morning glories, and I added some sesame seeds to give them even more crunch," Shirley said.

When Faith first heard the recipe for these muffins, she was skeptical. They seemed to have an entire shopping list of ingredients: shredded coconut, raisins, pineapple, grated apple, grated carrots, chopped nuts, cinnamon, and vanilla besides regular muffin ingredients. As soon as she tried one, though, she was a convert. The other glory of the recipe was that it tasted even better the next day, if they lasted that long.

"I know I want one," Tammy said, walking into the room. "And Sky wants a cheese omelet this morning—Havarti."

Faith gave her aunt a hug and told her why she was there. "Good to see you anytime, sugar. And a nice surprise for your uncle. Now, I have to dash out and pick up today's *Times*. Sky says the one they delivered is missing the business section and he doesn't want to wait for a replacement copy."

"Let me go," Faith offered.

"You're an angel," Tammy said. "I really didn't feel like going out just yet. Take my car, and after you get back, when you're ready, I'll drive you to the station."

She left the room and returned with her large pocketbook. Prada. She unearthed her keys—Prada key case—and handed them to her niece.

"Keep my coffee warm. I won't be a minute."

Sky and Tammy were doing so much for her that Faith was happy to do anything, however small, in return.

"Do you have sunglasses? The glare off the water is fierce now that the good weather's here," Tammy said.

"No, but I'll be all right."

She opened her pocketbook again and pulled out a glasses case. Prada again.

"Take mine. They'll fit anyone." She laughed.

They were enormous, Jackie O types. The kind stars wore to avoid the paparazzi. Francesca's description rang in Faith's ears. She could almost hear the subway train again. For a brief moment her whole body felt numb. Don't be ridiculous, she scolded herself. Even if she did want to do away with somebody, Tammy would never go down to the subway.

It was a beautiful day and the bright sunshine chased away any shadows that lurked in her mind. The car, with its tinted windows, was cool and dark. It started right up like the luxury vehicle it was and Faith drove around to the front drive, thinking it was a rare treat—the leather seats, fancy dashboard. *Vroom, vroom,* she thought, and laughed to herself.

But the car was beginning to pick up a little too much speed on the sharp incline and Faith tapped the brake. Nothing happened. The car started to go faster, if anything. She hit the brake again. Still nothing. Panicking, she pressed the pedal all the way to the floor, bracing herself for the sudden stop.

Except there was no stop.

She kept her foot on the pedal and pressed harder. Again, nothing happened. Frantically she tried pumping the brakes, except the pedal stayed down—flat to the floor. She quickly downshifted, wishing it were a standard like her parents' Honda. The gears would act as a brake. For a moment Tammy's big black "whale" lost speed, then the driveway dipped down and the car continued its relentless race toward the cliff—and the sea below.

Keep calm, keep calm, Faith said to herself. There's the parking brake. The Range Rover had one right on the console. She pulled—and pulled again. Useless.

The car was out of control. There was no way to stop it, and if she opened the door and tried to jump out now, it would roll over her. Even if she could get clear, she'd be badly injured.

Tammy? Had she sabotaged her own car, making up the story about Sky and the newspaper, planning that Faith would drive it? Maybe it *was* her aunt on the subway platform. A large woman in a beige Burberry, those sunglasses. But why? Was she totally insane?

Except there was the inescapable fact that she didn't know Faith was coming out this morning. Whoever had tampered with the car had done a thorough job—and done it well before Faith arrived. This wasn't a simple removal of a spark plug. Which further eliminated Tammy. Faith was sure her aunt's automotive knowledge was limited to where to put the key in the ignition, how to work the radio, and how to turn on the heat and air-conditioning.

Her thoughts were racing as the speedometer rose. She had two choices. She could try to make the turn onto the road and hope to come to a stop on the flat stretch. The problem was, if she didn't make it, she'd go over the seawall and straight down to the rocky beach. The other possibility was to steer the car across the lawn into the stone wall at the front of the house and hope the air bag would save her. The fieldstone wall, constructed when the house was built, was higher and sturdier than the wall by the road, put up by the town.

She glanced at the rearview mirror. Someone was coming out the front door and starting to run toward the car. She turned the wheel and bumped across the lawn. The turf slowed the car slightly, but not enough. She kept her eyes wide open and said a prayer. Please, God. Not now. Not here! As she headed for the wall, she took her hands from the wheel and covered her face. She didn't want a broken nose. She didn't want a broken anything, but this was all she could think of to do.

The sound of the impact and the whoosh of the air bag were terrifying, but the car crashed to a stop. She was alive. Very sore, but everything seemed to be intact. Someone was yelling and the door opened. She was being pulled out.

"I think I'm all right," she called. "Something's wrong with Tammy's car. The brakes don't work!"

It was her uncle, and his face was distorted in a twisted mask of rage.

"Damn you! Not again!" He was so angry he was spitting the words out and he wasn't letting go of her arm. His strong grasp was starting to hurt. Her legs were trembling.

"Uncle Sky. What are you talking about? I was almost killed! Tammy's car doesn't have any brakes!"

She tried to free her arm, but he tightened his hold and grabbed her other arm as well.

"Always poking your nose in where you shouldn't! I warned you! But no, you kept going. You've known all along, haven't you!"

She hadn't—but she knew now, Faith realized as she stared into the face of a madman.

"Tammy," she said. "The stone from the chimney. She was supposed to be the one opening the door. You thought I'd gone. And Danny. That was a terrible mistake on your part. She didn't go to her sister's; she decided to come back to play dress up when she found out Tammy was leaving. The blow that killed her was intended for your wife! And today. Just the same. You didn't know I was here. You sent Tammy out for the paper. A tragic accident and you were going to be a happy widower. AGAIN!"

Faith shouted the last word and tried to break away.

Sky looked at her sorrowfully. "You've always been my favorite. I don't *want* to hurt you—and I almost changed my mind on the subway platform. That's how much I care. But you must see I have no choice."

Faith didn't see. Not at all. And the deranged look in his eyes told her it would be useless to argue. He tightened his grip and pulled her close to him.

"The Todds had to go. I knew they'd be after me for money. Danny's wouldn't be enough for them. And Tam. It's her own fault. Stupid prenup. 'Her' money. Supposed to be the husband's. And I need it." He was speaking rapidly and seemed to be thinking aloud.

"Uncle Sky, don't do this! It's me, Faith! Let go! We'll go back to the house and forget this happened!" she shouted, knowing how false her last words were and dimly registering that whatever the Todds had found in Danny's room had been enough to drive her uncle to arson and murder.

"Your own fault, too." She hadn't gotten through to him. "But it will be quick. I don't want to hurt you more than I have to," he said, repeating his earlier sentiment, adding, "I was so looking forward to walking you down the aisle."

Crazy. He was completely crazy, Faith thought, and once more tried to twist away from him. He let go and moved his hands toward her throat. He'd said they were two peas in a pod. Knew what the other was thinking, and she knew what he was thinking now. Those hands were about to choke her to death. He was wearing gloves; she hadn't taken this in before.

She kicked hard, connecting with his kneecap, and he fell, giving her the precious time she needed. She sprinted toward the opening the car had made in the wall.

All those wives. All wealthy. All murdered?

He bellowed, "You're not getting away from me!" and got up, tearing after her. He was so close; she could hear his labored breathing. She looked wildly at what was in front of her and to either side. It was the same vista. She was at the top of the cliff and the only escape was down its face. She kicked off her shoes and gingerly lowered herself over the edge, searching for a foothold and finding it. She could see that Sky was about to do the same. He tore his bespoke loafers off and one went over the side. Faith watched it fall. It was a long way down. She made a mental note to thank her parents for sending her to those wilderness camps with rock climbing, if she made it out alive, and continued to steadily make her descent.

There was no question that Sky was coming after her. He'd been quite the hiker in his youth. She seemed to remember something about the Matterhorn. Still, that was a long time ago. She reached a small outcropping and edged along it so that she wasn't directly below him. For a moment she flashed on Cary Grant and Eva Marie Saint in Hitchcock's *North by Northwest*. At least Sky didn't have a gun.

But he did have rocks and he was throwing them at her with

a surprisingly good aim. One struck her face and she felt the blood trickle down her cheek. She didn't dare take a hand away to check, but kept moving. If she couldn't outrun him on the beach, she'd plunge into the water. The thought of how cold it would be numbed her before the blazing fear she'd been feeling since he'd dragged her from the car returned—a fear so real she could taste it. She kept her eyes on the cliff face, inching straight down, but also trying to move farther to the side, away from his reach. Above her, Uncle Sky's face was deadly still, wiped clean of the emotions that had consumed him moments ago. A cold-blooded, cold-hearted killer. Not just *North by Northwest,* but Hitchcock's *Shadow of a Doubt,* too—her own Uncle Charlie.

Those gloves. If the crash hadn't killed his wife, if she hadn't gone over the cliff, but gone into the wall as Faith had, the gloves were to finish her off and blame the air bag's explosive impact. And now those gloves were providing protection and a better purchase on the rock. Faith's hands were ripped and bleeding. She was afraid she'd slip and wiped them, carefully, one at a time, on her shirt, moving lower and lower down the precipice.

The stairs to the beach were to her right. If she could get close enough, she could reach them, pull herself over, and run up them, crossing the road back to the house. Across the road and away from her uncle. She stretched her right foot toward the outcropping below, letting her left foot drop as she swung out. She had to let go with both hands, and when she did her right foot slipped onto—and off—the rock. For an instant she thought she was falling and then managed to grab frantically with one hand, then the other. She was suspended in the air, unable to find a foothold. Sky was getting closer. His face was still expressionless, but it wouldn't be when he reached her. She knew now that he was beyond sanity, that he would take her over the cliff with him.

She heard voices. Tammy's was the loudest, but Faith couldn't make out her words. People were running down the stairs. She thought her arms would come out of their sockets. Hold on! Hold on! Whose voice was she hearing? It was in her own head, she thought dizzily. It sounded like Tom's.

"Hold on! We've got ropes!" Someone with a bullhorn. The police chief, Matt Johnson.

Sky looked in the direction of the voice, but kept moving. Matt called again, "Stay where you are! Don't budge an inch! We're lowering harnesses. Grab hold of the rope and put your legs through the harness. Can you do that?"

Faith shouted, "Yes!"

"Heard you. It's coming."

Sky didn't say anything.

She watched as a thick rope with a bright red triangular fabric harness swayed in the breeze, coming to rest by her hands. She grasped the rope and was able to loop first one leg and then the other into the seat.

"I'm in."

Her uncle ignored the apparatus, an arm's length away, and as Faith slowly ascended, she called to him, "Uncle Sky, take the rope. Please!" This was one time an insanity defense would work. He wouldn't be giving parties at The Cliff anymore, though.

He smiled at her. The Uncle Schuyler she knew was back for a split second before he gracefully arched his back and pushed off the cliff with both hands and feet. Faith closed her eyes. She didn't see Schuyler Walfort's last wave.

"'Tragic Climbing Accident Claims Life of Old New York Scion,'" Jane Sibley read out loud. The entire family was gathered in the Sibleys' living room, including the soon-to-be newest member, Tom Fairchild. He was sitting on a loveseat in front of the window, holding Faith's hand. He'd arrived yesterday so quickly after Faith called that she was sure he had broken every speed limit in all three states on his way.

"It was Mother's fault," Great-aunt Frances said. "She indulged his every whim. I suppose we all did. He was the most darling little boy. Golden curls, and such fun." She sighed.

As an explanation, Faith thought, it was somewhat lacking, but it *was* typically Great-aunt Frances and she almost smiled.

The previous day she had spent many hours with the local police and Detective Willis. It turned out that Schuyler Walfort had not been as clever as he'd thought and they had been steadily investigating him as their prime suspect in the murder of Mabel Danforth, proceeding on the assumption that he had thought it was his wife, as in "it's *always* the husband." They had sifted through the wood remnants and ashes in the fireplace, finding blood and some hair that matched the housekeeper's. Her assailant was obviously a reader of crime fiction and had gone for the old log trick—burning the rustic weapon up after using it.

Walfort *had* been in Westchester meeting with some potential business partners, but there was plenty of time when they weren't together for him to drive to his home and back. They suspected he'd used his wife's black vanlike car to "break in" to a house he knew was unoccupied in the neighborhood that weekend before staging the break-in at his own.

His grief over Danny's death, however, was very real and pushed him even further over the edge; he began to target Faith, whom he blamed for everything. If she hadn't been the one who'd opened the door—and avoided the falling missile—Tammy would have been crushed, as planned, and then he wouldn't have killed Danny by mistake. Brickwork did occasionally fall from the chimneys at The Cliff and Sky would have been on hand immediately after to remove the telltale rope and filament, while in the depths of sorrow. A grief-stricken widower. A rich widower.

He wanted Faith completely out of the way before his next try, and having learned her work schedule, he stationed himself outside, following her into the crowded subway for a good swift push. Francesca had identified Faith's assailant, just got the gender wrong. Walfort probably removed the coat and put it over his arm, tucking the hat and glasses in a pocket. Francesca had never met him, so would have no idea the elderly gentleman in the subway car was Faith's uncle.

The question was whether Danny had been in on this plot—and others? A kind of Bonnie and Clyde duo that stood the test of time, a lifetime for both? The police in the various parts of the country where Sky had lived when previously married had been informed and a number of natural deaths might be reclassified. Was the piece of paper the Todds had found in the housekeeper's room a confession, or maybe it was a marriage certificate? They loved each other. Had they been lovers, married lovers, all these years?

"But why would he do such terrible things?" Eleanor Lennox asked. "He didn't need money."

"I think he might have—or at least thought he would someday and wanted to have full ownership of Tammy's fortune, which their prenup prevented," Faith said. "The others as well. He was pretty high maintenance. But a bigger reason may be simply that he did it because he thought he could—invulnerable, above the law."

Tom nodded. "Without boring you all with the details, I keep recalling a conversation the two of us had about the Cathari in France with their belief in two Gods—one evil, one good. He may have seen himself that way. It was certainly a concept that fascinated him."

Hope spoke up. "Do you think he put something in your punch at the shower, Fay? Remember, he delivered a big package to Poppy's Garden Room?"

"But how—?" Faith didn't get to finish her sentence before Tom interrupted her.

"I'm extremely ashamed to have discovered from my guilt-stricken sister this week that she's the one who slipped you a mickey—or rather ipecac."

Faith filed the information away. She had a feeling it might come in handy when dealing with dear Betsey in the future.

Schuyler Walfort was buried where he wanted to be, next to Danny, in the cemetery he loved. The funeral was small and private. As for the wedding, the Sibleys had debated moving it to another locale, but after several family meetings had decided that since the invitations had gone out, it would be extremely awkward only two weeks before the event to explain why the nuptials wouldn't be at The Cliff. Excuses such as "Because the bride was almost murdered there" and "Bad karma" were bound to overshadow the couple's exchange of vows.

Tammy had been one of those most vocal about not changing any of the arrangements. She was doing a marvelous job of playing the distraught widow, telling one and all that "Sky would just be torn to pieces if he thought his untimely death had caused his dear niece to be married someplace other than the spot she'd dreamed of since she was a tiny child!" Faith noted Tammy's brutally apt choice of words—"torn to pieces." The rocks at the foot of this part of the cliff were jagged. Her great-aunt was obviously going to be an extremely merry widow, hiding what still had to be terror-stricken anger behind black humor.

And Tammy had no intention of moving, although she was going to be making more frequent visits home now that she was free to do so. Sky had never been a fan of her part of the world, or even her family, which she did not discover until *after* they were married. "He was deep, that one," was all she would say.

She was also planning on having her kin come on up north—if they wanted to. Meanwhile, she was occupied with the wedding and some remodeling—Sky's library and his bedroom would be no more, but she wasn't touching her boudoir. She liked it exactly the way it was. After all, she had planned it, hadn't she?

First Jane Sibley came down the aisle, a long cream carpet extending from the front door across the deep green lawn to a rose-covered trellis erected as an altar, where her husband was waiting to perform the ceremony. She was escorted by Tom's brother Robert. Nana, on Craig Fairchild's arm, came next, followed by his parents. The sun had been shining throughout this perfect June day and the late-afternoon long light made The Cliff look like a dramatic stage set. Hope was resplendent in soft moss-green satin, her dark hair loose—a dryad—and after her, an indulgent chorus of aahs and oohs greeted the little girls in their pretty eyelet dresses, strewing flower petals from small baskets. Intent on this important job, they had serious expressions—until they recognized a parent, and then breaking out in a big smile for the camera.

And then came the bride. The music reached a crescendo. Her grandmother had sewn tiny seed pearls on Faith's lace Juliet cap and the gems sparkled, but not as much as the bride's face as she walked toward her beloved. Her beloved, who stepped away from the altar to meet her halfway down the aisle before turning to take the steps together that would soon make them husband and wife.

"Happy?"

"Ecstatic," Faith Fairchild replied. They were sitting side by side viewing the lively scene in front of them.

"I think everyone's been having a great time," Tom said.

"Your family are definitely party animals. I don't think your parents have sat out a single number, even when Marley's band was playing."

Tom had wanted to meet the young man who had saved the woman now his wife's life and it had been his suggestion that they listen to the band's demo and hire them to supplement the band already engaged for the reception.

Leaning in closer to his bride, Tom said softly, "Faith, my darling, since I met you, it's been quite a ride, a major understatement. But we, or I should say you, made it through safe and sound. Of course, nothing like this will ever occur again. Promise?"

"Oh, Tom, I do. I do," Faith said as she crossed her fingers beneath the folds of her wedding gown.

You could never tell what might happen.

EPILOGUE

Faith raised the window cover a few inches, peeked out at the new day streaking across the clouds, then lowered it. The flight had passed in a kind of half sleep as images from all those years ago filled her mind, starting with one wedding and ending with another—her own.

She could see the portrait of the wedding party posed in front of The Cliff and thought about what the passage of time had brought. Better hairstyles, more comfortable shoes, to start.

Hope was a married lady, too, with an active kindergartner, Quentin Lewis Jr. His father was in the same business as Hope, different firm. Synchronized BlackBerries and a nanny who had been with them since the blessed event governed their lives. Hope had gleefully related a recent rumor to Faith that Phelps Grant had been arrested for an online Ponzi scheme in Canada. Unfortunately, Jennifer, Hope's former assistant, *had* landed her big fish and was currently enjoying five different fabulous addresses spread over three continents, proving that sometimes good things happen to bad people.

Emma Morris had married a poet and promptly produced a set of twin girls, followed several years later by a boy whose birth coincided with the announcement of her husband's Pulitzer, hence his name—Joseph. Poppy was entranced with her son-in-law, having invited him to one of her dinners early on in his career, where he spied Emma. Poppy was taking total credit for the match and subsequent offspring, whom she worked very hard at spoiling. She was a widow now, but had declared that one husband, officially anyway, was sufficient for a lifetime. Faith and Emma thought it more likely that she enjoyed playing the field. Poppy had not gone overboard like her friend Joan Rivers, but Mrs. Morris had had work done and there were days when Faith thought Poppy looked younger than she did.

There were other empty places at the table. Nana and her sister, Great-aunt Frances, were in the family plot at Woodlawn. Faith missed her grandmother terribly and made the trip to the cemetery several times each year to put flowers on the grave—when possible Eleanor's favorite lilies of the valley, and for Frances, violets, the scent of the sachets that had perfumed her clothes.

Tammy was gone, too. Never specific as to age, she moved from thirty-five to forty-nine, where she stayed for some years until she decided to be a grand old lady and jumped to seventy-five. The housekeeper she'd hired, Shirley, stayed with her and was with the family at Tammy's bedside when she died. After her death, The Cliff was sold. No one had the heart—or the money—to keep it.

Happily, Tom's parents and her parents were in good health. Her father had given the church a deadline for his retirement, finally realizing if he didn't they would never look for a replacement.

Josie's in Richmond became a destination in and of itself, and Josie Wells joined the ranks of her beloved mentors with guest appearances on *Top Chef* and the Food Network. She'd actually met the man of her dreams the night Josie's opened—although she didn't know it immediately. He'd returned to the area to follow *his* dream—a self-sustaining farm on the land that had been in his family since after the Civil War. It had gone through several incarnations and was now totally devoted to vegetables—providing the restaurant with greens, beans, and everything in between.

So many changes. Faith was a mother herself. She thought of her son, Ben, very much a teenager filling their days alternately with intense joy and intense aggravation. Everything in his adolescent life was one extreme or the other—no in betweens. And their daughter, Amy, was standing on the threshold, still a little girl in so many ways. She refused to move her stuffed animals from her bed, but she'd added Justin Bieber to Harry Potter posters on her wall. The Millers' anniversary gift had been to move into the parsonage, only steps from their own house, to act *in loco parentis* while Faith and Tom were away.

Faith knew she would miss her kids, but she didn't yet. At the moment she was savoring the idea of no piles of laundry, homework supervision, endless errands, the demands of work, and meals to get on the table. Even though she didn't consider cooking a chore, there were days when she wished she could just give them cereal for dinner.

Their anniversary trip. Which brought her to Francesca. They had kept up all these years and the Fairchilds had gone to Italy, not Spain, for the end of their honeymoon, meeting a very happy, and very beautiful, Luisa Alberti Rossi and her "new" husband.

It was Francesca's invitation that they come and check out the cooking school she had just opened at the family vineyard in Tuscany that had prompted their destination for this trip. Time in Rome and then north. Married, three children, a husband from the same village, Francesca was not hiding anything these days. It would be wonderful, and a real vacation, to be with her. Faith smiled to think how young—and naive—they'd been. She'd been! So very, very young.

She closed her eyes and rested her head on Tom's shoulder. He'd been by her side all these years.

And he'd be there in the morning when she woke up.

HAVE FAITH
IN YOUR
KITCHEN

By Faith Sibley Fairchild
with Katherine Hall Page

Veggie Mac 'n' Cheese

6 ounces sharp cheddar cheese

2 red bell peppers

3 large garlic cloves

1/2 cup water

5 cups cauliflower florets

1 tablespoon unsalted butter

2 tablespoons milk

1/4 teaspoon paprika (preferably
  smoked)

1/2 teaspoon salt

6 ounces penne, ziti, or elbow macaroni

Preheat oven to 350°.

Shred the cheese and set aside. Reserve 1/4 cup to sprinkle on top.

Deseed and dice the peppers, mince the peeled garlic cloves, and place in a saucepan with the 1/2 cup of water. Bring to a boil and lower to simmer until the vegetables are very soft, about 15 minutes.

Start to boil water for the pasta.

Steam the cauliflower and when it is soft, transfer it to a bowl and mash roughly—you want some texture.

Cook the pasta according to the directions on the package and in the meantime place the contents of the saucepan, the butter, and the milk in a food processor or blender. Pulse until smooth. Add the mixture to the cauliflower along with the shredded cheese, paprika, and salt. Drain the pasta and mix into the sauce so all the pasta is coated. Pour it into a casserole and top with the reserved cheese. Bake in preheated oven until nicely browned and bubbling. The red peppers give the sauce a bright color and the smoked paprika, widely used in the Mediterranean cooking, adds a subtle flavor as well as more color.

Serves 6.

You may also serve this sauce over pasta without baking.

You can make a tasty, easy soup with any leftover florets, if the head is a large one, and the stems. Simply chop roughly and put in a saucepan. Add a small sliced yellow onion and cover with chicken broth, your own or store-bought. Bring to a boil and simmer until the vegetables are soft. Puree in a blender or food processor until smooth. Return to the saucepan, add 1 cup half-and-half or milk, and 3/4 cup grated white cheddar cheese. Add a pinch of salt if your broth was no salt. Simmer, stirring occasionally, until the cheese is melted and serve or freeze. A curry spice blend is also nice in this. (Faith, and I, hate to waste food. You can use this recipe for broccoli stems and other vegetables as well.)

Poppy's Popovers

2 large eggs

1 cup milk

1 tablespoon melted unsalted butter

1 cup all-purpose flour

1/4 teaspoon salt

1/2 tablespoon additional melted unsalted butter

Preheat the oven to 450°.

Beat the eggs and add the following four ingredients. Stir, but do not overbeat.

Brush the cups of the popover tin or whatever you are using with the half tablespoon of melted butter.

Bake for 15 minutes. Do not open the oven door. Lower the temperature to 350° and bake for an additional 15 minutes. Ovens vary, so you may have to play around with the timing. James Beard's recipe calls for 30 minutes at 425° in a cold oven—no preheating—and this works nicely. I've found I get a slightly puffier popover with preheating, but the Beard recipe is quick!

Remove popovers and serve immediately with butter or jam. Try flavoring the butter with maple syrup. And an unadorned popover is also delectable.

Makes 6 popovers.

Popovers are impressive and easy. They also lend themselves to all sorts of variations. They can serve as containers for creamed chicken, shrimp, or veggies. Add a teaspoon of fresh herbs to the batter or 1/2 cup of grated cheese. For a nice breakfast treat, add 1/3 cup of finely chopped crisp bacon to the batter. For a sweet popover, add a teaspoon of sugar. Try other flours—buckwheat especially. If you do not have a popover pan, you may use a large muffin pan or individual custard cups. Faith and I recommend a slight splurge on a real popover pan, however. Otherwise you don't make them.

For some reason, popovers have long been associated with brides, appearing prominently in cookbooks for brides. I have two, both titled *The Bride's Cookbook,* one published in 1915, the other in 1954. I picture these brides turning their hands to popovers as a way to impress new in-laws or perhaps hubby's boss—this was another era, remember.

Nowadays two of the best places for popovers, other than a home kitchen, are in Portsmouth, New Hampshire, at Popovers on the Square, and at Maine's Jordan Pond House, a restaurant with its beginnings in the nineteenth century. It is located in Acadia National Park in Bar Harbor. At the Jordan Pond House, besides mouthwatering popovers, you can feast on the view of the Bubble Mountains reflected in the pond's shimmering water.

Southern Fried Chicken

One 3-pound fryer, cut into 8 pieces

Water

1 tablespoon white vinegar

2 teaspoons salt

2 1/2 teaspoons freshly ground pepper

2 large eggs (beaten)

1/2 cup evaporated milk

1/4 cup water

1 teaspoon paprika

2 cups all-purpose flour

Vegetable oil

Place the chicken pieces in a deep bowl and cover with cold water plus a tablespoon of white vinegar. Put in the refrigerator and let soak for 1 hour. Drain and pat completely dry. Season with 1 teaspoon of the salt and 1 teaspoon of the pepper. Whip the eggs, milk, and 1/4 cup of water together in a new bowl. Add the dry chicken a piece at a time and coat thoroughly. As you coat the pieces in batter transfer them to a heavy paper bag containing the remaining salt and pepper, the paprika, and the flour. Shake vigorously and fry in vegetable oil. Faith uses canola oil and a large, deep, iron frying pan. Only put in enough oil to come halfway up the pan, as the level rises when you add the chicken. Also be sure the oil is hot enough by adding a pinch of flour. When it bubbles, it's hot enough.

Good fried chicken takes time. About 15 to 20 minutes, less for the wings. White meat cooks faster than dark meat, so consider this also. Turn the pieces 2 or 3 times with tongs for a crispy, golden brown skin. Serve immediately.

Feeds 4, more if there are children to grab a drumstick or wing.

As with all classic recipes, there are many variations. You can add cayenne pepper, garlic powder, dried spices like thyme to the flour coating. Some cooks add bacon fat to the oil. Others replace the evaporated milk and water in the batter with buttermilk. Buttermilk is also used to soak the chicken instead of the water/vinegar bath.

And don't forget that there is nothing as special as cold fried chicken on a picnic with a good eggy, pickle relish, old-fashioned potato salad and plenty of biscuits and corn sticks.

In addition to the legendary African American cooks, Edna Lewis and Sylvia Woods, mentioned in this book, I'd like to add Leah Chase, known as the "Queen of Creole Cuisine." Now eighty-eight years old, Leah Chase started working at her musician husband's family's restaurant, Dooky Chase, in the Treme section of New Orleans during the 1950s and began to move the menu toward her Creole roots. Her gumbo is world famous, and the restaurant is known for the diversity of its clientele— civil rights activists, artists, musicians, U.S. presidents, and a loyal following among the Big Easy's residents and tourists. After

Hurricane Katrina, Mrs. Chase and her husband lived in a trailer, determined to open again, which they did. Their superb collection of African American art, displayed on the restaurant's walls, was saved from the hurricane by their grandson, who was able to place it in storage in time. In her cookbook *The Dooky Chase Cookbook,* published first in 1990, Leah Chase reminisces about going to Mardi Gras as a child and buying fried chicken from one of the booths selling it fresh from the pan. There were also booths selling fried fish and red beans. She'd watch the parade and eat the chicken out on the street, a rare treat. My copy of her cookbook is inscribed by Leah Chase to my husband, my son, and me: "Life is for living. Enjoy together," which pretty much says it all.

Champagne Punch

1 1/2 cups fresh lemon juice

1 cup sugar

1/2 cup orange liqueur (Grand Marnier or Cointreau)

1 cup fresh orange juice

2 bottles chilled champagne or other dry sparkling wine (You may also use a nonalcoholic wine or club soda.)

Orange and/or lemons, thinly sliced

Mint (optional)

Combine the lemon juice, sugar, orange liqueur, and orange juice, stirring until the sugar dissolves.

Add the champagne and refrigerate, well sealed, for at least 1 hour.

Pour into a glass pitcher and float the fruit slices and sprigs of mint to garnish. Serve in punch cups, champagne flutes, or white wine glasses. If strawberries are in season, these are also a pretty garnish.

This recipe may be doubled or tripled to fill a punch bowl.

Strawberries Romanoff

2 pints fresh strawberries

2 tablespoons sugar

2 tablespoons orange liqueur (Grand
  Marnier or Cointreau)

1/2 cup freshly squeezed orange juice

1 cup crème fraiche

Grated orange zest

Rinse the berries with the stems on and then hull and halve them.

Combine the berries with the sugar, liqueur, and orange juice. You may eliminate the liqueur and use all juice if you wish. Let the berries soak in the refrigerator for an hour. Bring to room temperature and layer the berries and crème fraiche in parfait glasses, clear dessert dishes, or as Faith's caterer did, martini glasses. End with a layer of the crème fraiche and grate orange zest over each portion, topping with a perfect strawberry half.

Serves 4.

This is a versatile, easy, and impressive dessert. You can use whipped cream or vanilla ice cream instead of crème fraiche. When strawberries are in season, another lovely dessert is also a simple one: toss the strawberry halves with a tablespoon of brown sugar and a dash of balsamic or a fruit vinegar. Serve as is or with a dollop of whipped cream or Greek yogurt.

Culinary history agrees that strawberries Romanoff was created by the legendary French pastry chef Marie Antoine Careme (1783–1833) for Russian tsar Nicholas I. In the United States, a version of the dessert was made famous by another legendary figure—Prince Michael Romanoff (not a prince, not Russian, but Lithuanian; his name was, in fact, Hershel Geguzin) at Romanoff's in Beverly Hills, California, his star-studded restaurant in business from 1941 until 1962.

Eve was the first bride and saved a fortune on her dress. The reception—a partially eaten apple—wouldn't have set God the Father back much either, although He might possibly have wished He'd thought to spring for wedding insurance. Since then, through the ages and across the globe, the basic notion of joining two lives through ritual has remained unchanged. The ceremonies and celebratory rites are an entirely different matter.

Our forebears might recognize some of our modern customs. Take rings, for example. The ancient Egyptians believed that a vein ran from the second finger of the left hand directly to the heart, hence the spot for the bride's ring in many countries. World War II servicemen returning to the U.S. brought the European custom of a double-ring ceremony. Today most grooms here opt for a wedding band. Those who don't may have the anonymous canard in mind: "Marriage is a three-ring circus. First comes the engagement ring. Then the wedding ring—and then the suffer-ring." A fact new to me concerned the bride's wedding ring dur-ing Colonial times in this country. An engaged woman was given a wedding thimble. The bottom was cut off for the ring itself (presumably ahead of the ceremony).

"Bridal" comes from Middle English and refers to the wedding feast with its copious amounts of "bridale"—"bride ale." The word "wed" or "wedde," an older term, also derives from Middle English and meant "pledge." A man pledged goods in exchange for the bride. Bride prices, dowries, a father "giving away" his daughter, transferring his power over her to another man, all remind us that marriage across societies and time periods was primarily a financial transaction and the practice of marrying for love is not very old.

Nuptial superstitions know no time limits and we're all familiar with the one about the groom not seeing the bride before the ceremony, common in numerous cultures, as well as the importance of adhering to "something old," linking past and present; "something new," to ensure a bright future; "something borrowed," a token from a happily married friend or relative so her good luck rubs off; "something blue," the color traditionally symbolizes fidelity and purity. In modern weddings the bride usually wears a blue garter. My sister, like Faith's sister, Hope, was my maid of honor and made a lovely garter for me. A friend, Helen Scovel Grey, realized in a panic on her wedding day that she didn't have a blue garter or anything else of that hue. A creative bridesmaid ran to the closest CVS and bought a bottle of blue nail polish. Among Helen's wedding pictures is one in which a single toe is being adorned. She's been married for twenty-three years. Superstitions are best not broken. And she had a sixpence in her shoe, as the last line of the rhyme specifies. Sixpences are often passed down from mother to daughter for even more luck.

The time of year one marries is very important as well. In China couples select an auspicious date, taking into account the animal zodiac symbol of the years of their births. The pragmatism of early New Englanders gave rise to the superstitious belief that it was unlucky to marry in December, October, or May, as they avoided the bad weather during winter months and they needed to devote the others to planting and reaping. "Marry in May and you'll rue the day" also refers to the time period during most of the month following Easter when the Catholic Church prohibited marriages, a prohibition no longer in effect.

A bridal bouquet speaks the language of flowers. Ivy stands for fidelity, and the Greeks believed it symbolized an indissoluble union. Red roses mean love, and when carried with white ones connote unity. White lilacs stand for innocence; lily of the valley, purity; and orange blossoms—especially popular in Victorian times—happiness and fertility. Marigolds, among Queen Victoria's flowers when she married Prince Albert, signify passion, as in sensuality. Considering that theirs was an epitome of marital love and loyalty, producing nine children, the blossoms worked. After the wedding, some of the myrtle from Victoria's bouquet was planted, and royal brides ever since, including Kate Middleton, the most recent, have carried a sprig from the bush for luck. Queen Victoria's 1840 wedding is also generally cited as the start of the widespread adoption of white, as brides copied her satin gown in Europe and North America. In China, India, Vietnam, and some other Asian countries red garments are traditionally worn, although the bride often changes into a white Western dress for the reception. In Japan, a bride may wear as many as three different wedding kimonos as well as a Western gown.

The Greeks and Romans did not carry bouquets but wore wreaths on their heads and garlands around their necks, sometimes carrying them as well. The garlands were composed of herbs, spices, and garlic to ward off evil spirits. Once again that nuptial trendsetter Queen Victoria popularized a custom—that of using fresh flowers in a bride's bouquet. Victorian and Edwardian bouquets on both sides of the ocean were large. Princess Diana carried a replica of an Edwardian one to match the broad width of her dress. The cascading result—gardenias, freesia, stephanotis, ivy, and other flora—was forty-two inches long and fifteen inches wide. The florists, Longmans, assembled three identical bouquets, remembering that in 1947 the orchid one they had made for then Princess Elizabeth went missing following the ceremony and had to be re-created later for the official photographs.

Another wonderful story from my friend Helen's wedding. On the morning of the big day the females in her wedding party gathered around a large table in her home, a parsonage, to make the bouquets and boutonnières. The same group had gathered some weeks earlier at her grandmother Deborah Webster Greeley's house, where she taught them how to make the decorations for Helen's wedding cake. She had the molds and other equipment and they all had a fine time creating white and dark red roses, various sizes of sugar bells, and green leaves (gently assigned to those less adept at roses). Deborah Greeley, president of the Herb Society of New England at the time, made the three-tiered cake itself closer to the big day, adding fresh herbs around the base— ivy for faith and divinity, sage for wisdom, rosemary for remembrance, and thyme for courage. If you ever happen upon the now out-of-print book *A Basket of Herbs: A Book of American Sentiments,* illustrated by wonderful Tasha Tudor, to which Mrs. Greeley contributed, grab it!

Weddings are mnemonics—of ones we've attended, ones we've been in, even ones we've watched on the big screen. Who can forget the wedding scene in *The Graduate*? And Molly Ringwald's sister weaving down the aisle in *Sixteen Candles*? Or Katharine Hepburn and Cary Grant in *The Philadelphia Story*? And then there are *Four Weddings and a Funeral;* the original *Father of the Bride; Fiddler on the Roof;* Fred Astaire dancing on the floor, walls, and ceiling in *Royal Wedding;* and *My Big Fat Greek Wedding* (which must have caused a huge blip in Windex sales). We, especially women, love celebrity weddings—the tasteful and the trashy. We delight in the details and hope for the best. And we read and reread our much-loved books about weddings. Some of my favorites: *Delta Wedding,* Eudora Welty; *The Wedding,* Dorothy West; *The Member of the Wedding,* Carson McCullers; *Weddings Are Murder,* Valerie Wolzien; and a new favorite, *Somebody Is Going to Die if Lilly Beth Doesn't Catch That Bouquet: The Official Southern Ladies' Guide to Hosting the Perfect Wedding,* Gayden Metcalfe and Charlotte Hays. (These are the same very funny, very savvy ladies who wrote a guide to hosting the perfect funeral, *Being Dead Is No Excuse.*) I also like to go back to the books of my childhood for happily-ever-afters—Lucy Maud Montgomery's *Anne's House of Dreams,* where Anne comes down the stairs, "the first bride of Green Gables, slender and shining-eyed, in the mist of her maiden veil, with her arms full of roses," to Gilbert waiting below "with adoring eyes."

And now a word about wedding cakes. These are among the oldest of our nuptial traditions, dating back to Roman times when, after eating a piece of a sweet barley bread loaf, the groom broke it over his bride's head to ensure good luck. Perhaps picking out the crumbs was one of the wedding night's activities! Since then the cake went through numerous configurations, appearing as "Bride's Pie" in the seventeenth century. Some of the cakes were more like what we now call fruitcake. Mrs. Beeton's recipe for "Rich Bride Cake" calls for five pounds of the finest flour, three pounds of fresh butter, five pounds of currants, two pounds of sifted loaf sugar, nutmegs, mace, cloves, sixteen eggs, a pound of sweet almonds, a half pound each of candied citron and candied orange, plus a gill each of wine and brandy. Rich indeed.

Queen Victoria again. Hers weighed in at three hundred pounds, measured three yards wide and fourteen inches tall. It was adorned with roses and topped with an ice sculpture of Britannia surrounded by cupids. Guests were sent home with boxes containing small pieces and more were sent all over the empire in celebration. They turn up every once in a while in drawers and attics. In 1947 the cake Queen Elizabeth cut surpassed that of her ancestress. It weighed five hundred pounds and was nine feet tall. There were twelve cakes in all at her reception. Princess Di had one cake, five feet tall, but there were two copies waiting in the wings lest an accident occur. The cake featured the Windsor coat of arms in marzipan.

It is not known exactly where and when the custom of sending guests home with a small piece of the cake, usually in a little box, originated, but it remains widespread. Put the token under your pillow and you will dream of your future spouse. If already married, the act will lead to good luck in general.

Placing their hands on the knife to cut the first slice of cake is the initial task a married couple performs together and symbolizes their union. Feeding each other from that slice has become common, although when one or both smush the cake into the new spouse's mouth, the act may be a portent of rocky shoals rather than smooth sailing together.

Wrapping the top layer of the tiered cake to freeze until a couple's first wedding anniversary is now customary.

It's supposed to be bad luck for a bride to bake her own cake, but my friend Melissa, who turned out a dozen single-layer dense chocolate ones, her favorite, the day before to accompany the traditional cake, recently celebrated her fortieth anniversary. Thinking of her tale, I had the idea that I would ask a number of friends for the recipes, and stories, of their wedding cakes. Picturing the cake Helen Scovel Grey's grandmother had made, I asked Helen's mother to send me the recipe. Faith Greeley Scovel, like her mother, made wedding cakes for friends and relatives, complete with sugar bells and icing decorations. What she sent is a treat, four pages of instructions for "Silver White Cake," with many notes for multiplying the amounts and obvious signs, even in the ancient xerox, of much use—in places dripped batter has obscured the printing. Faith Scovel noted that the recipe probably origi-

nated from Fannie Farmer or *The Joy of Cooking,* both of which
have excellent, easy-to-duplicate recipes for as impressive a cake as
the $500-plus ones appearing at today's often over-the-top recep-
tions. Faith Scovel also sent me a wedding cake recipe from her
husband's great-grandmother, that appeared in her mother-in-law
Myra Scovel's memoir, *The Happiest Summer.* It seems to be an
American interpretation of Mrs. Beeton's recipe, although it calls
for twenty eggs! It also lists molasses and grape juice as ingredients.

My own wedding cake had three layers, a delicious traditional
white cake concoction decorated with buttercream frosting,
hearts, and the small fruitcake layer on top trimmed with fresh
white French lilacs. When we went to cut it, much as we loved
the trimmings, our favorite one was the finger mark a dear friend's
three-year-old boy had made. He just couldn't wait.

Whatever you choose, whether it be two cupcakes for an elopement, a groom's cake shaped like the helmet of his favorite football
team, a tall cone of profiteroles filled with pastry cream and held
together with caramel and spun sugar—*croquembouche,* the French
wedding gateau—or three tiers with the nuptial couple on top,
may you have your cake and eat it, too.

I love weddings. I love hearing about them, looking at wedding albums, and most of all attending them. And yes, I always
get choked up when the couples exchange their vows. I've been
to weddings in churches, synagogues, chapels, homes, museums,
hotels, restaurants, in city halls, in tents, on beaches, in fields,
in backyards, and I'm sure I'm forgetting some. The brides and
grooms have ranged in age from eighteen to ninety. The music has been as simple as a single guitar to the full New Orleans
Children's Chorus (and after the ceremony a streetcar took guests
to the reception in the Garden District!). The ceremonies have
included several civil ones and most religions. I've learned that
"tying the knot" (a Celtic custom) figures both symbolically and
literally in many cultures. The Hindu wedding ceremony, over

five thousand years old, incorporates ritual tyings of various kinds, binding together not only the bride and groom but also their two families. This joining was joyously acted out during the reception at Lakshmi Reddy and Andrew Kleinberg's wedding as the two families—wearing saris, yarmulkes, and all manner of dress—hoisted the bride and groom on chairs and danced the hora.

The longest wedding I've attended was in Beaujolais, France, the festive nuptials of our baker's daughter. We were living in Lyon at the time and our three-year-old son was one of the *garçons d'honneur,* looking very sweet in pale blue. The wedding began early on Saturday with the civil ceremony at the mayor's office, followed by the church ceremony, and then the entire village was invited to the farm for brioche and wine—with music and dancing. An only slightly smaller number of guests then went to a reception hall for food, more music, and dancing. The celebration lasted well into the following day (and in an earlier time it would have been several days). Onion soup gratinée was served in the wee hours, possibly to keep one's strength up! People came and went, children slept on jacket-cushioned benches. At one point we all took a walk around a nearby pond. It was absolutely wonderful.

However, my own wedding thirty-six years ago was the best of all. We were married in Holmes, New York, at Beulahland, the home of our dear friends Charlotte Brooks and Julie Arden, on the first Saturday in December, holding our collective breaths about the weather. As it happened, it was so warm, guests sat out on the large terraces. A week later the area was hit by a blizzard. I still have my beautiful white dress, and it still fits, although I do have to breathe deeply. My father gave me away, tears in his eyes. Everyone danced. I'm told the food was delicious, but somehow neither my groom nor I sat down long enough to eat—common for wedding couples. One of my parents' oldest friends told my mother, "If they always look at each other the way they're looking at each other today, they'll be a very happy couple." Prescient words. I didn't toss my bouquet, white French lilacs and ivy. Another close family friend, Erik Johns, had made it and I wanted to keep it, later rooting the ivy. It's still thriving.

I had to be back at my teaching job at Burlington High School on Monday, my husband, Alan, to his work at MIT, so only one night for a honeymoon at an inn in Connecticut. Since we hadn't eaten at the reception, we were ravenous and bought submarine sandwiches on the way, consuming them happily with champagne in front of the fireplace in our room. It was a perfect wedding feast, although I'm not sure Faith Fairchild would have approved.

In the end, whoever the couple, what matters most was said in the Old Testament by Ruth to her mother-in-law, Naomi:

"Entreat me not to leave thee, or to return from following after thee: for whither thou goest, I will go; and where thou lodgest, I will lodge: thy people shall be my people, and thy God my God: Where thou diest, will I die, and there will I be buried: the Lord do so to me, and more also, if aught but death part thee and me."

This is what we mean when we turn to our beloveds and say, "I do."